Port Luck
By Timothy King

Savage Rabbit Publishing

Dedication

This book is dedicated to my loving wife, Rhianna. She believes in me when I don't believe in myself.

To my Beta Readers for helping me to complete this book....it only took a year.

And to my Patreon Members:

Shanda

Dan

Trisha

Rob

Liz

Crys

Alexandra

Renee

Kayla

Ali

Sherri

Tammy

Rosina

Desiree

Trigger Warnings

Gruesome Deaths

Homophobia

Racism

PTSD

Other rough shit....

Your mental health matters!

Contents

Chapter 1

Ben Grover groped blindly at his head, trying desperately to pull his orange beanie lower. Despite the gloves, his fingers lost all feeling hours ago. His numb digits danced about unfeeling until they caught the fabric. He tugged hard, stretching it to cover as much of his skin as possible. The strings of his hood blew wildly in the wind. Cursing himself for not checking the weather before their hike, he snatched the drawstrings and yanked on them, pulling the hood as tight as he could. Stealing a glance over his right shoulder, brutal gusts of wind and snow ripped past him. The horrendous storm made it difficult to see his girlfriend about ten feet behind him. Helplessly, he watched as she fought against the wind.

Emily held her arms up to shield her face from the onslaught of snow. Her foot caught on some unseen hazard, and she fell forward, hands outstretched, becoming buried in the ever-growing mounds of snow. The rope tied around each of their waists tightened under the strain, the tension yanking Ben back a step, nearly causing him to lose his balance as well.

From farther behind him, Ben could see the shape of his best friend, Alex, shuffling through the snow. The scrawny hipster staggered up to the fallen Emily. Ben watched him kneel down and say something to her. In his mind, he willed them to stand up and walk. They would freeze to death if they stayed out in the open. He let out a frustrated sigh when he saw Alex motion to him.

Ben turned and trudged through the snow until he reached Emily. She was sitting up and rubbing her knee furiously. He crouched next to her and peeled her hands away from the injured knee. He could barely feel her legs through his dense gloves and her thick pants, especially with his fingers so damn numb, but he continued searching for any signs of trauma.

"Is she okay?" Alex shouted as loudly as he could to be heard above the growing storm. Emily gave Alex a thumbs-up.

Looking around, Ben's heart beat faster. It was a complete whiteout.

The snow hadn't been thick when they began their trek earlier that morning. From their elevation on Kenai Mountain, they could see for miles in every direction.

Great expanses of dead trees cascaded down the side of the mountain in all directions. In the distance, they could make out the navy blue waters of the Alaskan Gulf.

Now, Ben couldn't see more than twenty feet in any direction. The storm had blown in from the north with little warning. Alex had begged to turn back when it first began to snow, but dismissing it as a little snow, Ben insisted they keep going. His entire life he had wanted to reach Truuli Peak, and he would be damned if he came this close just to turn back.

He was kicking himself for that decision.

"We have to get out of the open!" Ben shouted.

Emily peered around searching for some sort of shelter. Squinting her eyes, she tried to make out something fifty yards from them. Barely visible through the blinding snow was a dark spot in the rock face. A smile stretched across her face—it was a cave. She raised her hand and pointed to the spot.

Ben and Alex followed her finger with their eyes. They scanned for a moment before Ben shouted, "I don't see anything!"

A blast of frigid snow blew into his mouth. The blistering cold wind carried shards of ice that pelted the roof of his mouth, and his hands flew to his face as he gasped in pain. Rage ripped through him. How could he have been so stupid? He punched the snow and yelled a barbaric cry.

Emily shielded herself from the snow kicked up by Ben's sudden outburst. She grabbed his arm and pointed again. "I think that's a cave!" Emily hollered

"What?" Ben asked.

Emily pulled him close and yelled directly into his ear. "I think I see a cave."

Following her arm with his eyes, he was able to make out the large opening in the mountain. "Oh, shit." Ben half laughed and half yelled. "I see it."

He pointed at the same darker spot in the wall. Alex nodded, still unable to see what the other two were seeing but trusting their judgment.

"Can you walk?" he asked Emily.

"Yes, help me up."

The two men rose and held out their hands. Emily gripped them firmly and allowed them to raise her. Slowly, she tried to put pressure on her right leg, but a bolt of lightning shot up her leg and radiated throughout her body. She yelped in pain and lost her footing, crashing back into the snow. Frustration and exhaustion overtook her senses, and she punched the ground repeatedly with a furious cry.

Ben and Alex reached down simultaneously and gripped her arms. They raised her back to her feet and forced her arms around their shoulders. Assisting her as she used her one good leg to limp along, the half-frozen trio marched through the snow.

Vicious gusts of wind tore across the mountainside and threatened to send them reeling backward. The ground grew steeper as they approached the entrance of the cave. But with each step toward what would be their salvation, an overwhelming sense of dread came over Ben.

The hole on the side of the wall was massive. It stretched twenty or thirty feet wide and probably twice as tall. Standing at the opening, Ben couldn't fathom how they had been able to barely see it before.

The first ten feet of the cave started wide, then narrowed drastically before making a hard right turn past a jagged rock.

The trio collapsed into a huddled mess just inside the cave's mouth. Trying to force breath into his lungs, Alex let loose a little chuckle. " You still think we'll make the peak?"

Ben leaned his head against the rough ground and smiled. "I probably could, but you're slowing me down, man." He playfully punched Alex in the shoulder. Alex raised his fist to punch back, but Emily threw her hands up to defend her boyfriend.

"Don't do it! You might damage his precious blue jacket!" she playfully shouted.

Alex laughed loudly. "He does love that stupid jacket, doesn't he?"

"Fuck you guys. It's a great jacket." Ben shook his head. He rolled to his stomach and pushed himself to his feet. "Let's get a fire going. It looks like we might be here for a while."

Alex clapped then followed his friend's lead. Pushing himself up, he said, "I'll handle the fire. You get the MREs, and Em?"

"Yes?" Emily smiled with mock sweetness.

"Any chance your crippled ass can dig the waters out of your pack?"

Emily stuck her middle finger up at Alex, then dug in her pack.

Alex smiled and fished out an emergency fire starting kit he packed. Ripping open the package, he placed one of the logs on the floor approximately ten feet inside the cave's entrance. He figured it was far enough away for the cave to shield the fire from the wind yet close enough for the smoke to escape. He lit a match and pressed it against the quick-light log, which erupted into flames. He placed a second miniature log down and allowed it to catch.

"This should burn for about two hours. I have enough of these things to keep the fire burning for about six hours. Hopefully the storm will pass by then."

"Thanks, Alex. Here's an MRE, man," said Ben, and tossed the MRE.

Alex caught it. He tore it open and fished out the contents, laying them on the packaging.

"Em, MRE?" Ben asked as he extended the food package.

Emily didn't answer him. She was staring toward the entrance of the cave.

Ben leaned back to get a view around her. "What are you staring ..." His question trailed off.

At the very edge of the entrance was some sort of construction. It appeared to be a pyramid made out of white sticks that someone had stacked like Jenga blocks.

"What is that?" he muttered to himself. He rose and approached the object. The wind howled louder as he neared the entrance, muffling the nervous questions of his friends. The pyramid was made up of a square base with four sticks rising from each corner before coming to a single point in the middle. He squatted to get a better look. Sliding the glove off his right hand, he stuffed it into his jacket pocket before slowly reaching for the object. His fingers wrapped around it. Its rough texture felt odd against his still-numb skin. Scrutinizing it, he couldn't figure out what material the pyramid was made of. He ran a finger along one of the sticks. His heart beat hard against his chest. No, not a stick, he realized. It was made of bone. He dropped the pyramid. It crashed to the floor and shattered, broken pieces of dried bone fragments exploding and scattering around the cave. He stumbled backward, away from the broken idol.

"What's wrong, man?" Alex asked.

"It's made of fucking bones, man."

"That's creepy," Alex said with a disinterested tone. He turned away from the scene and took a bite from his beef taco MRE.

"There's more," Emily whispered. The others couldn't hear what she said over the howl of the wind outside.

"What, babe?" Ben asked.

"There's more," she said with more force.

Looking around, Ben saw several more objects lining the walls of the cave. Several of them were pyramids similar to the first, although varying in size. One of the objects looked like a box with a single bone running diagonally through the middle. More bones lined the edges of the walls, some broken, some intact.

"Holy shit, they're everywhere," Ben said. Dragging his feet across the cave, he scattered several of the bones. "I'm no doctor, but these look like animal bones." He paused to pick up a small rodent skull. "I wonder what killed all of these animals?"

A guttural growl echoed from deeper in the cave.

Alex dropped his meal. It crashed to the floor, coating the stony earth in ground beef and cheese. "What was that?" Alex asked, his voice trembling.

"I have no clue," Ben answered. He took a tentative step forward, approaching the deeper recesses of the cave.

The growl repeated once, twice more.

"It sounds like snoring," Emily whispered.

Outside, the intensity of the storm increased. The growl permeated from within the cave and mixed with the howling wind outside.

Alex appeared at Ben's side. "Should we check it out?" he asked.

Ben nodded. "We can't sleep here if there's a bear or something back there. We have to check it out."

Alex slipped off one of his gloves and produced a quarter from his pocket.

"Lucky quarter," Ben teased.

"Never go anywhere without it. Call it in the air?" Alex flipped the quarter.

"Tails," Ben called.

Alex turned his hand over and uncoiled his fingers. Tails.

"Guess I'm checking out the creepy noise from the back of the cave." Alex sighed. He crept deeper into the cave. When he reached the rocky outcropping, he looked back at his friends and gave them a thumbs-up before disappearing around the corner.

Ben retreated to where Emily was sitting. He sat beside her and took one of her gloved hands in his. She locked eyes with him. Worry clouded her normally cheerful blue eyes, and Ben gave her a reassuring smile.

"What the—?" Alex's cry erupted from deep within the cave. His sentence was cut off by a blood-curdling scream. A sickening sloshing sound flooded the cave.

Emily gripped Ben's hands even tighter. Her free hand locked onto the arm of his jacket and squeezed. "Wh-what was that?" she stuttered.

"I don't know." Ben peeled her hands off of him and crept toward the back of the cave. "Alex?" he whispered. He took a few shuffling steps forward. "Alex," he whispered a little louder.

The sound of heavy footsteps answered him. Something sharp scraped against the rocky walls around the corner.

The hairs on the back of Ben's neck stood at attention and his blood ran cold.

Something soared through the air from around the corner and crashed into the wall at his side. In the darkness of the cave, he could only make out a round object on the ground near his feet. Hesitantly, he bent over to examine it.

His fingers brushed against hair, and a warm, wet substance clung to his hand. When he rolled it over, Alex's lifeless eyes stared back at him. His face was stretched into a look of terror; his ruined mouth hung agape. Ben gasped but couldn't let go of his best friend's decapitated head. His breath came in frantic gasps, and blood drained from his extremities as adrenaline dumped into his system.

Something smashed into him, throwing him to the floor with tremendous force. His head bashed against the rocky wall as he collapsed to the ground. Warm blood spilled from a massive gash across the back of his head and gushed down his back.

A creature moved past him with incredible speed, appearing to him in flashes. His concussed vision and the engulfing darkness of the cave blurred the beast. His head lolled backward, and darkness crept into the edges of his vision. Forcing himself up, he climbed to his feet, battling the unconsciousness that threatened to overtake him.

Emily's shriek tore through his ears, snapping him back to clarity. He found his footing and rose to his feet, snapping his head in the direction of Emily's cries. A shadowy monstrosity had Emily in its grasp, dragging her out of the cave. She reached out for her boyfriend with sheer terror in her eyes. In an instant, they were swallowed by the raging snowstorm outside.

Ben shouted for Emily. The howl of the wind was his only response.

He repositioned the orange beanie on his head, righted his blue jacket, and charged into the blinding white of the snowstorm after them.

Chapter 2

An abrupt series of bangs snapped Johnny Myers from his sleep. He sat straight up in bed and strained his ears against the silence of the night. There was another rapid series of bangs, and he realized someone was at the front door. Without getting dressed, he launched himself out of bed. His bare feet hit the icy tiles of the floor, the jarring sensation sending a shot of pain up his legs. Pajama pants and a T-shirt did little to shield him from the cold of the house, and the frigid air immediately chilled him to the bone. Goosebumps broke out across his arms.

The house was pitch black except for a few slivers of moonlight piercing through the wooden slat blinds on the window. He navigated the house by memory, slipping out of his bedroom door and walking down the hallway. The banging on his front door continued, echoing through the otherwise quiet house. When he rounded the corner to enter the living room, he paused to fish a nine-millimeter

Glock out of a drawer in an end table. A snapping sound echoed throughout the house when he racked the slide, slipping a round into the chamber.

He positioned himself to the side of the door and gripped the deadbolt with one hand, pistol at the ready with the other. The wooden door shuddered under the heavy rapping. In a series of swift motions, he released the deadbolt, swung the door open, and leveled the pistol.

In front of him, illuminated by the orange glow of the porch light, was Darren Henry, the mayor's pompous and entitled shit of a son. Johnny watched as the man's face transitioned through a series of emotions, first anger, then surprise, and, finally, horror, as he zeroed in on the pistol.

Darren threw his hands up. Eyes wide, he shouted, "What the fuck, sheriff?"

Johnny sighed and lowered the pistol. He pressed his free hand to his eyes and tried to wipe away the sleep built up in the corners. "What do you expect when you beat on a man's door at two a.m.?"

The weasel of a man shrugged. "Maybe you should answer your phone or radio," he said in a condescending tone.

"My radio never went off. I would have heard it."

The angry look on Darren's face returned. "Look, man, my dad sent me down here because you weren't responding. I didn't exactly want to be out at two a.m., either, but here we both are." Darren took a step toward the door. "It's fucking freezing out here. You gonna let me in or what?"

"No," Johnny said resolutely.

Sleep's hold was loosening its grip on him, and the realization that the mayor's son was knocking on his door in the middle of the night hit him. "Cut the shit. What's going on?" Johnny asked.

Darren shrugged again. His nonchalant attitude was grinding on Johnny's already thin patience.

"They said there's a body out by the Graham's place," he said.

Johnny sighed and rubbed the bridge of his nose. "Alright, one minute." He moved to close the door. Darren tried to say something about coming inside, but Johnny slammed the door shut and locked it before he could finish his sentence. "God, I hate that spoiled little shit," he grumbled. He flipped on the living room lights and set the Glock on an end table by the front door, then turned and made his way back down the hallway.

He crept into the bedroom and retrieved his clothes.

"Who's at the door?" Amy asked.

"Darren Henry," Johnny said, pulling on his pants.

"You going somewhere?" she sleepily asked.

"Yes, ma'am. There's a body out by the Graham place."

The mention of a body pulled her out of her drowsy stupor. She sat up in bed, and the covers fell around her waist, exposing the silk nightshirt that covered her torso. He could see a hint of fear in her eyes.

With a smile, he walked over to the bed.

She grabbed the back of his head and pressed her lips to his. "You be careful out there, sheriff."

He slid a hand under her shirt and gripped one of her breasts.

Slapping his hand away, she kissed him once more. "Maybe when you come back to me in one piece."

"I'll hold you to that."

There was another stiff knock at the door.

"Give me a damn minute," he shouted, then whispered, "you little fucking troll," under his breath.

Amy smiled and slumped back into the bed, pulling the covers up to her chin.

Johnny quickly pulled on his clothes. He snatched the forty-five caliber Colt 911 off his dresser and slid it snuggly into the holster on his hip. Grabbing the radio off the nightstand, his fingers reached for the plug only to find it dangling from the wall. He forgot to plug it in. Furious with himself, he clipped the useless radio onto his belt. He would charge it as soon as he got back to the station, he promised himself.

"Play nice," Amy teased when he exited the room.

"I'll try," he called back to her from down the hall.

The pounding of his snow boots echoed off the floor. He slid the deadbolt back and threw the front door open right as Darren was about to knock again. "Let's go," Johnny ordered.

The engines of their snowmobiles roared through the night air as they tore down the road. Johnny waved his left hand, and the two men veered off the road and onto a trail that ran through the forest on the edge of town.

On either side of them, the trees loomed overhead like wooden towers. Barren branches stretched in all directions like curled, arthritic fingers. Above them, the sky was clear, giving them a perfect view of the stars, and the moon's glow reflected off the pure-white snow, creating perfect visibility despite the early hour.

Through the trees, the lights of a cabin came into view. Headlights of several vehicles pierced the trees to the right of the cabin. Slowing their machines, they emerged from the trees to find the normally isolated Graham cabin bustling with life.

Marsha Graham sat on the cabin's front steps, sobbing into her hands, a blanket cloaked over her shoulders. Pale legs stuck out from the bottom of a thin nightgown. The gown was far too thin to be outside in that weather.

Two massive men sat on either side of her with their arms around her. When they got closer, it became evident it was the Harrison twins, Marsha's trouble-making brothers.

A black panel van with chains on the tires sat idling to the cabin's right. The words Medical Examiner were painted in white letters on the side. Dr. Earnest Davies, the town's only physician, also had to pull double duty as their only coroner. The aging man was crouched in front of the van, using the illumination from the headlights to inspect something on the ground.

Deputy Brian Williams, the only other law enforcement officer in their small town, walked around the scene taking photos. His freakishly tall frame was silhouetted against the night sky.

Johnny veered his snowmobile to the right and stopped behind the van. When he shut off the motor, the silence of the night swallowed them. The only sounds besides the distant hoot of an owl were the clicks of a camera and the sobs of an inconsolable woman.

Johnny dismounted his ride. Walking around the van, he immediately came face to face with the grotesque, dismembered body of Eric Graham.

His face and head were unmarked, but those were the only body parts remaining fully intact. The man lay on his back in blood-soaked snow. Arterial bleeding had spread the blood several meters in multiple directions. His right arm was severed at the shoulder, the limb nowhere to be seen. Broken fragments of bone jutted out of the wound, telling Johnny immediately that it wasn't a clean amputation. Large chunks of flesh were missing from his left arm, which lay uselessly to his side. His right femur stabbed through the skin and even managed to cut through his pants. The blood-stained bone stood nearly straight up. Johnny struggled to comprehend what he was seeing when he examined the abdomen. The chest cavity and bones were splayed open to reveal a vacant interior.

For a moment, the frozen tundra around him disappeared. He was back in Iraq, examining the body of another fallen marine. The distant echoes of his men screaming over the sounds of gunshots and explosions rang in his ears. Sucking in a deep breath, he squeezed his eyes shut and counted to ten to fight off a bout of PTSD-induced panic. The sounds of dying marines faded with each passing second. Once he felt steady, he asked, "What do we got, gentlemen?"

Deputy Williams lowered his camera and strutted across the gruesome scene, skillfully avoiding the massacred corpse. The man had worked for Johnny for about four-teen months, and Johnny still couldn't get used to the young man's size. Johnny stood an impressive six foot two, and still, he was dwarfed by his deputy. Brian Williams was also the only black man in Port Luck, a fact that some of the nastier residents on the fringe of town were quick to remind them of when they had to break up the all-too-common domestic disturbance.

A look of dread came over Brian's face. "I'm sorry about calling the mayor, sir. I was trying to raise you and didn't know what else to do." The deputy's face morphed from dread to remorse.

Johnny waved him off. "You did the right thing, kid." He held up his radio. "I think the battery in this thing is no good. I'll have to swap it out at the station."

Deputy Williams cracked a small smile that quickly dis-sipated when he turned back to the scene. "I took a state-ment from Mrs. Graham. She said she woke Eric up when she heard a commotion outside."

"Did she say what kind of commotion?"

"Yes, sir," Brian continued. "She said it sounded like wrestling, and she thought she heard a man scream." Brian allowed the camera to rest against his chest; the straps strained against his neck. He fished a notepad out of his pocket and flipped through a few pages. "She said she thought she heard a man begging for help and then a scream. She woke up Eric, who grabbed his shotgun and came outside."

Johnny held up his hand. "Where's the shotgun?"

Brain rocked his head to his left. "Found it in the tree line. I took photos, then cleared the shotgun. I removed two unfired shells and placed them in an evidence bag. I then combed the scene and located a spent shell in the bushes. I took photos and took it into evidence. They're all in Dr. Davies's van."

"Good man," Johnny said. He couldn't help but be happy with himself. When he hired Brian, the kid was fresh out of the police academy and green as could be. The deputy had come a long way in such a short period of time.

Brian smiled as he continued. "I found some footprints leading in and out of the tree line, along with what look like wolf tracks. Photographed it all."

"Amazing work, Brian. You did an excellent job."

"Well, I learned from the best, sheriff."

Johnny smiled and patted Brian on the shoulder. He moved over to the body and squatted next to Dr. Earnest Davies. "What about you, Earnest?"

"Can't tell you much more than you already know, at least not until I get him back to my office. It looked like an animal attack initially, but there are some oddities."

"Alright, well, let's finish up here and get out of the cold, gentlemen." He stood back up and turned to Brian. "Can you show me those tracks?"

Brian led him toward the tree line behind the house. The snow was thicker there. In some spots, his boots sank completely from view. The deputy stopped about ten feet from the trees. "I found these leading back into the woods, but nothing coming out."

Johnny removed the flashlight from his belt and turned it on. Deep in the snow was what looked to be a wolf's paw print. There were the four distinct toes, deeper holes where the creature's claws dug into the snow, and the clear mark of the wolf's paw pad. Something was off with the print, though. At first, Johnny thought it was just the size—it had to be double the size of his hand. Then he noticed an additional spot about a foot back from the rest of the track. It gave the impression of a heel print, similar to what he would expect to see from a human.

Brian noticed him looking at the spot. "Yeah, I saw that too. Do you have any idea what that is?"

Johnny shook his head. "I haven't the slightest clue." He flicked his light from the footprint up to the tracks leading into the woods. He withdrew his pistol and held it by his hip, barrel pointing down. Taking a few steps forward, he paused and looked back at Brian. The man was standing stalk still in the same place he had been. "You coming, deputy?"

Brian nodded and withdrew his pistol. Removing the flashlight from his belt, he clicked it on.

The men entered the thick patch of trees behind the house. The leafless branches scratched at their arms and faces, snagging their jackets almost as if trying to prevent them from going any deeper. The wind ripped through the trees and shook the branches.

Johnny could make out something orange lying on the ground about a dozen feet ahead of them. He fought through the trees and emerged into a small clearing, nearly tripping over something large lying in the snow. Looking down, he let loose a deep sigh.

Another body lay at his feet.

Brian gasped when he pushed into the clearing behind Johnny.

This body was even more mangled than poor Eric Graham. The tattered remnants of a blue jacket lay spread all around the clearing. Bits of viscera clung to the branches and swayed in the wind. Droplets of blood dripped onto the snow from nearly every tree and shrub. Chunks of what had been a person were scattered about as if the victim had exploded into little pieces. It reminded Johnny of seeing a little boy step on a land mine when he did a tour in Afghanistan.

The legless torso lay in the center of the macabre scene. The orange beanie on its head was like a flare in the middle of a traffic accident, and the two officers couldn't tear their eyes away from it.

Quickly scanning the surrounding area, Johnny holstered his pistol. He pointed at the body. "Take a picture of the head," he ordered.

Brian slowly holstered his pistol. His hands shook as he raised the camera to his face and snapped a picture. The camera's flash momentarily ignited the area in a flash of white light.

Johnny immediately dropped to one knee and set his flashlight down in the snow. Gripping the head on either side, the smashed skull gave way, allowing his gloved fingers to sink into the orange beanie. He attempted to turn the head, but the skull caved in on itself when he tried to move it.

Behind him, Brian scrambled away from the scene. He could hear the young deputy pushing back into the trees before the distinct sound of vomit hitting the ground wretched his stomach.

He tried to tune out the sick deputy and focus on what he found. The face was absolutely unrecognizable. It was completely caved in with no discernible features. Johnny couldn't even be sure the body was a man's. He looked over his shoulder. "Brian, go tell the doc we have a second body."

The deputy wiped his mouth and pointed his flashlight in the direction they came from. He took a few steps in that direction before Johnny stopped him. "Keep it quiet; don't let the Grahams know."

Johnny watched his deputy's tall figure disappear into the darkness of the trees. He turned back to the scene and tried to look for any sort of identification or distinguishing characteristics he could use to identify his John Doe.

A branch cracked to his right. He jerked in that direction, drawing his pistol without being conscious of doing so. Shadows danced between the trees. His vision tunneled on the front sight of his pistol. The neon-coated sight drifted across the impossibly dark section of trees in front of him. A low growl emanated from the darkness. His blood ran cold and his heart thumped against his chest. Gently, he slid his finger onto the trigger.

Behind him, he could hear the murmur of voices growing louder. He turned his head toward the approaching men, then snapped his attention back to the tree line. The abnormally dark area was gone, along with the low growl. Slowly, he lowered his pistol but allowed it to linger near the holster until he heard Brian and Earnest break through the tree line.

"Good god," Earnest gasped.

"Let's get this mess cleaned up and get out of here," Johnny said, keeping his eyes trained on the tree line.

Chapter 3

Johnny rubbed his temples and stared at the ghastly images spread across his desk. His reflection in the black computer monitor looked just as bad as he felt. He managed to squeeze in a few more hours of sleep after cleaning up the scene and helping Earnest load the two bodies into his van.

Staring down at an image of Eric Graham's body, he could tell Earnest took the photo standing by the deceased man's feet. Given Brian's incredible height, all the photos he took were at a much higher angle. The one in front of him was taken much lower and clearly showed the mangled mess that was formerly a torso. Something in the photo wasn't sitting right with him, but he couldn't figure out what it was.

The aroma of coffee filled the room. Johnny snapped out of his trance to see Amy standing at the door to his office.

"I thought you might need this," she said.

A smile stretched across his face and relief flooded his body. Pushing himself away from his desk, he bounded toward her. She held the coffee out before her, but he gently pushed her hand aside. His arm slid around her waist, taking her small frame into his embrace. "No, ma'am, but I did need this." He buried his face into her neck and kissed his way to her mouth.

Giggling, she pushed him away. "Maybe if you had made it home last night," she teased.

He took the coffee from her and inhaled its sweet aroma. "Yeah, I'm sorry about that. By the time we finished up, it was damn near seven. Figured I'd get here and get started." He nodded toward the cot in the corner of his office while walking back to his desk. "I did manage to grab a few hours on the cot, though."

He crumpled back into his chair, and the old seat squeaked in protest. He shuffled the pictures into one enormous pile and dropped a manila envelope over them. Amy knew they had found two bodies at the Graham place, but it was another thing for her to see the pictures.

After his tour in Afghanistan, she had made him a promise. She wouldn't ask for details, but he would talk about it if he needed to. He only had to talk about it once, and they both secretly hoped he would never have to again.

From the front of the station, the desk phone rang. Brian picked it up on the second ring. There was some muffled conversation followed by Brian's boots beating their way across the wood floor. He popped his head around the corner. "Anchorage is on line two for you, boss."

"Thanks, Brian," Johnny said with a sigh.

The deputy disappeared as quickly as he had appeared.

Amy turned to leave. "I have to get going. Class should be getting started any minute." She pecked him on the cheek. "I'll see you tonight. Maybe if you're good, we can finish what you started." With a wink, she turned and wiggled her ass before disappearing down the hallway.

Johnny was still smiling as he picked up the phone. "Sheriff John Myers, how can I help you?"

A gruff voice spoke on the other end of the line. "This is Anchorage Homicide Detective Jameson Winston. I have some bad news for you, sheriff."

Johnny held the phone away from his mouth and let loose a deep sigh. "Let me guess, y'all are snowed in?"

"Unfortunately, all flights are grounded and the roads are iced over."

Johnny leaned forward and dropped his elbows on the desk. "Alright. When can you get here?"

"It's not looking good. Maybe a week at the earliest."

"A week? What am I supposed to do with two dead bodies for a week?" He could hear some movement on the other end of the line before the detective spoke again.

"I just asked my boss; he said if you're sure it was an animal attack to release the bodies to their families."

"Yeah, I suppose you're right," Johnny said reluctantly.

"I am. There's not much use in holding them when we all know it was probably a wolf or bear."

Johnny stood up. "Alright. Well, thank you for your time, detective. I'll call you if anything comes up." He planted the phone down on the receiver a little harder than he meant to. A piece of plastic busted loose from the corner and launched itself onto the floor.

Brian poked his head around the corner. "Bad news?" he asked.

Johnny rubbed the back of his head. There was a patch of hair that was thinning there. "Yeah, Anchorage suggested we release the bodies since this is clearly an animal attack."

Brian walked a little farther into the office, ducking to get through the doorway. The deputy was almost always a perfect vision of professionalism, but today, his khaki pants displayed a yellowish tint around the knee. It looked like a coffee stain, but Johnny couldn't tell for sure.

Johnny had seen lots of violence and death during his time in the marines, but it was all new to Brian. In a small town like Port Luck, they dealt with drunks and the occasional pissed-off moose, but rarely dead bodies. The first and only dead body the deputy had worked was last winter. They had found one of the canners dead in the woods. It was a pretty clean case compared to this. Like this, it was an animal attack, although far less gruesome. Johnny had forced Brian to wait at the station while they gathered up the body. The young deputy only saw photos. Remembering that, Johnny made a note to check in on Brian's mental health when he had a second.

"What do you want to do, boss?" Brian asked.

The sheriff paced behind his desk and rubbed his chin. Stubble was showing on his face. He usually shaved on Monday morning, but given the night's events, he didn't get to it today. Since he didn't have time to shave before rushing out in the middle of the night or after getting back to the station, the facial hair would remain there for a few more days.

"Do you still have the file on that body we found last winter?"

"Yeah, it's in my desk. Want me to grab it?"

Johnny nodded, and Brian crouched under the door frame and walked around the corner to the front of the station. Johnny moved the manila envelope covering the photos. Shuffling through them, he located the photo he was examining before Amy brought him coffee. At the thought of Amy, he grabbed the cup and gulped down more of the steaming liquid. He held the photo at eye level, forcing himself to take in every detail of the massacred body.

Brian returned holding a small manila envelope and dropped it onto the desk.

Johnny set the photo he had aside and flipped open the folder. Overturning it on his desk, he sorted through a few photos until he found the one he was looking for. In the photo, the canner lay dead and half frozen on the side of a mountain. Johnny's eyes stretched wide with realization. The deceased canner found last year also had the torso devoured by wolves, the difference being the hiker's chest cavity was caved in, while Eric Graham's was pulled out.

He picked up his phone, careful not to cause any more damage to the cheap plastic. He punched in a number he had memorized. After a few rings, Earnest answered. "Hello?"

"Earnest, it's Johnny. Can you do me a favor?"

"Absolutely."

"Can you perform an autopsy on those bodies we recovered last night?" There was silence on the other end. Johnny waited a moment longer before saying, "Hello?"

"Ugh, yes, no problem. I'll do it tonight and get you a report in the morning."

"Thanks, doc," Johnny replied, and hung up the phone, then looked up at Brian. "Let's go get some lunch, my treat."

Brian smiled. "Well, if you're buying!"

Walking across the street toward Maddie's Diner, Johnny noticed Jeremiah Jackson standing outside his general store. He waved at the old man. "Jeremiah! How's your grandson?"

Jeremiah looked up and returned the wave. "Justin's doing great!" he called. "He just committed to play quarterback for Georgia!" The old man's face twisted into a look of concern. "I just hope he can stay out of trouble. He's had a few issues lately."

"I'm sure he'll figure it out! Maybe we'll go down to Florida to watch him play before he graduates!"

Jeremiah beamed with pride. "Just tell me when!"

The two officers entered Maddie's, on the other side of the government building. Being one of the only two restaurants in town, Maddie's was always packed. The usual chatter of the diner morphed into excited whispers when they entered. A burly man at the bar area slid his plate one spot over and shimmied to the next stool to make room for the two officers, nodding at them with respect as he did.

Johnny plopped onto one of the stools, but Brian hesitated. Johnny followed his gaze to the back corner of the room, where Frank Mareston sat. Frank's pale skin made it easy to see how hard he was blushing. Brian lingered a moment longer, then sat down next to Johnny.

Maddie approached the two men. "Brian, what can I get you?" she asked, breaking the awkward spell Brian was under.

"Uh, you can take the sheriff's order first," Brian said as he set his hat down on the bar.

Maddie shook her head. "Don't need to. The sheriff here has been ordering the same thing since he was fifteen years old." She turned to look at Johnny. "A half-pounder burger, American cheese and ketchup, fries, Coke."

Johnny smiled at the older woman. "Don't tell Amy. She's been getting on to me about something called cholesterol."

The burly man seated next to them snorted a laugh.

"Your secret's safe with me," Maddie said with a wink.

"I'll have the same, please," Brian said.

Maddie set two bottles of Coke in front of them and disappeared through the saloon-style doors into the kitchen.

From the back of the dinner, a series of excited voices grew louder. Without looking up, Johnny shook his head. "Here we go," he said.

One voice rose above the rest. "So, are you planning on telling us what happened at the Graham place, sheriff?"

The entire diner fell silent.

Brian strained to see around Johnny. He couldn't get a good view of the speaker.

Johnny never looked up from his Coke. He smacked his lips and flatly said, "As soon as I got something to tell you, Eddie."

Eddie Hall stood up and strutted to the edge of the bar. He leaned one arm onto the bar, doing his best to look tough. The man wore a long-sleeved shirt with several holes in it. His tattered shirt matched his gap-toothed smile and scab-infested cheek. "I'm just saying we have a right to know if there is a," he paused for dramatic effect, "murderer in our midst." Eddie swung around to face the rest of the diner.

Brian leaned back to get a view of the man. "Why don't you head back to your seat, Eddie? We're not discussing it right now."

Eddie stood straight up. "I wasn't talking to you, faggot."

Johnny pushed himself up from his stool and jabbed a finger into Eddie's face. "You cut that shit out right now, Eddie."

"Or what?" Eddie said as he took a step closer. "It's not my fault your deputy hit the Uncle Tom Trifecta!" His voice raised a few octaves so the whole bar could hear. "A pig, fag, and a jig. Goddamn, you sure know how to pick 'em, sheriff!" Eddie turned his head to shout over his shoulder toward the rest of the patrons. "That's right! We all saw him making fuck-me eyes at ole' Fruity Frank over there!" Eddie waved his arm in Frank's direction.

Poor Frank's mouth fell open in shock. He pulled up his coat to hide his face and sank lower in the seat.

The other men Eddie was eating with snickered and whispered a series of unintelligible slurs.

Brian leaped to his feet, but Johnny put a hand on his chest to stop him. "I got it, Brian," he whispered through gritted teeth. He leaned in close enough to Eddie to smell the stench of his chewing tobacco. "You listen here, you strung-out piece of shit. I better never hear you talk like that again, or I'll lock your ass up for a couple of weeks." Johnny nodded as he spoke, his cheeks flushing red. "You'll miss your shifts at the cannery. What do you think will happen?" He pointed at the window in the front of the diner, where they could see the mayor's office. "You know he'll fire your ass. You can't support a meth habit with no money, you disgusting junkie."

Eddie took a step back, recoiling at the venomous threat, then put his hands up in surrender. "Alright, sheriff! I was just playing. Ain't that right, boys?" He pointed to a table full of rough-looking men, who all murmured half-hearted responses.

Johnny pushed past Eddie, making sure to bump shoulders with him as he did. "Alright, I'm not fielding questions on it, but yes, Eric Graham was found dead last night."

A few women at a table to his right gasped.

"As far as we can tell, it appears to be a wolf attack and is most likely an isolated incident." With that, he turned back to the bar and took his seat.

The diner erupted into a flurry of questions. Several of the patrons even left their seats and approached the sheriff.

Maddie rushed through the double doors and threw her arms up. She clapped several times and shouted, "Now that is enough! The sheriff and the deputy work very hard and deserve to have their meal in peace." Eddie began to protest, but Maddie clapped her hand again. "No. The next person to bother the sheriff is gettin' charged double."

The patrons reluctantly shuffled to their seats.

Johnny couldn't help but smile at the old woman. She disappeared through the door to the kitchen and returned a moment later, setting their food down in front of them. "Damn vultures, I swear," she said with disgust before disappearing into the kitchen.

The two men finished their meals in silence. Johnny dropped forty dollars on the counter and took a final swig of his Coke. He spun on his stool and moved toward the door.

Blake Sholes pushed himself up from his chair at that moment and quickly walked across the diner to cut Johnny and Brian off at the door. "Sheriff, if you need help catching that wolf, I just bought a new Remington a week ago. I can help you out," he said excitedly. "Or I can shoot something else for you," he said with a smile. He motioned his head toward Eddie's table.

The stench of cheap whiskey hit Johnny's nostrils and caused him to physically withdraw from the man. Then he leaned forward. "I appreciate that, Blake." The sheriff pushed open the door before pausing. "Oh, and Blake? I better not see you out here driving." Johnny flashed a smile and exited the building.

Brian patted Johnny on the shoulder. "Canners, huh?"

Johnny nodded. Brian was referring to the cannery workers who lived out by the docks. They lived in a bunkhouse owned by the cannery, which happened to be owned by the mayor. The employees were made up primarily of single men who worked six days a week. On the seventh day, unlike God, they did not rest. Instead, they liked to make trouble for the town. Johnny mostly looked the other way at the harmless stuff. Public intoxication, pissing in public, fights, and hunting out of season were the favorite pastimes of those men. He could bust them all, but then his jail cells would burst at the seams and the town's primary source of income would be dried up.

The two men walked in silence for a minute before Johnny worked up the courage to ask. "Is it true?"

Brian's face dropped. "Would it matter if it was?"

Johnny shook his head. "No, but Amy has been trying to set you up with Susan for a year now."

Brian bursted out laughing. "Is that why she keeps inviting us to your cookouts?"

Johnny laughed. "Sure is. She said you two would be great together. I'm just saying, if you'd have told me, I could have been inviting Frank this whole time and saved myself a lot of headaches."

Brian shook his head. "I thought you liked Susan."

"Hell, no. I hate that bitch. I'd rather hang out with Frank. At least he won't talk my damn ear off about who some famous person is dating this week."

Brian shrugged. "We're, uh ..." He trailed off.

Johnny patted him on the shoulder. "It's ok, man. It's your business. Tell me, don't tell me. Just know I'm cool with whatever."

Brian nodded. "We've been seeing each other for a few months, but we're not open about it." He glanced back at the diner. "Or at least we weren't. It's hard to be the only gay guys in a town this small."

Johnny shook his head. "Well, it has to help that you get to carry a gun."

Brian snorted a laugh. The two men completed the short walk from the diner back to the station and were preparing to enter the building when someone yelled, "Sheriff, just a minute."

Johnny turned and gave a half-hearted wave to Mayor Victor Henry. "I'm so sick of talking about this," Johnny mumbled.

Brian opened the door. "I'll be inside if you need me. Good luck."

Johnny spun on his heel and walked down the sidewalk. He met the mayor and the two men shook hands. The mayor's portly belly shook as he spoke. Victor immediately mimicked the concerns the townsfolk had about the body. "The people are concerned, Johnny. Finding a body ..."

Johnny stopped him. "Between us, mayor, there were two bodies."

"Dear god," Victor Henry proclaimed.

"Don't worry. Earnest is writing up an autopsy, and I'll get you the report the next day or two." Johnny pivoted away from his boss, desperate to end the conversation. "All signs point to an animal attack," he lied.

He pulled open the door to the station and walked across the room to where Brian sat, filling out a report. "Tell me when he's gone," Johnny instructed.

Brian glanced up and after a few moments said, "He's walking away."

"I really can't stand the asshole," Johnny said, closing the door to his office.

Chapter 4

Eddie pushed himself up from the table. He took another long draw from his flask, draining it of the cheap whiskey he picked up at Jackson's General Store.

"Come on, boys," Eddie slurred. "Gotta get back to the bunkhouse so I can top off." He shook the empty flask. Despite Maddie's not serving alcohol, it was always full of drunks. Eddie stumbled toward the exit, kicking over a chair in the process. The bang it made when it hit the floor seemed even louder in the nearly empty diner.

From behind the counter, Maddie rolled her eyes. She watched as Eddie drunkenly tried to pick up the chair only to nearly fall flat on his face. "Just leave it," she ordered. "I'll grab it when I mop up."

Eddie sprang to his feet and tossed her a sarcastic salute. "Yes, ma'am!" he shouted. Behind him, his three cronies giggled. Eddie smiled a snaggle-toothed grin at Maddie and pushed through the diner door into the snowy street.

The sun was setting over the water of the inlet, bathing the snow in a golden hue. Eddie remembered a time when he would have appreciated the beautiful view. He couldn't remember exactly how long it had been since Tiffany had run off with the kids, but that was probably the last sunset he ever enjoyed.

"Let's cut through the woods, boys," Eddie said. "If we take the long way, I'll lose my buzz."

"Do we have to? It's fucking creepy at night, man," Hank said. Despite being the largest man in the group, he was generally considered to be the softest. He didn't drink like the others. He didn't fight like the others. And he damn sure didn't use narcotics like the others.

Kevin smacked him on the arm. "Don't be such a pussy. Let's go before I sober up and blame you for it."

Sighing, Hank stepped onto the road and followed the others between two buildings that led into the woods. The path through the woods would only shave about twenty minutes off their walk, but that would get them to their stash of booze that much faster.

The low-hanging sun was almost fully blocked out by the trees. It created an eerie atmosphere of partial darkness and deep shadows between the trees that seemed to move as the gang walked.

Vladamir stepped up beside Hank. "If you get scared, Eddie might hold your hand," he mocked in his thick Russian accent. "But only if you ask nice."

"Or trade him an eight ball," Kevin added snidely.

Eddie whipped around to face the man, his face flushed red. "What was that?" he demanded.

Kevin held his hands up in surrender. "I was just kidding, man." He looked at the others for backup. "Just making a joke about what the sheriff said."

Eddie shook his head. "Fuck that guy. He thinks he's hot shit. Let me catch that little bitch without his badge on. I'll beat the fuck out of him."

Hank nodded. "Fuck the deputy too. He threatened to write me a ticket for taking a piss!" he exclaimed.

Vladamir laughed. "That's because you were pissing on the side of the church, you heathen."

Hank shrugged. "I had to go," he replied nonchalantly.

That forced Eddie's aggressive demeanor to falter slightly. The hint of a smile played at the corner of his lips. "Yeah. Fuck the deputy too." Eddie scratched one of the scabs on his cheeks with his gloved hands. "I can't fucking stand that guy." He turned away from the group and trudged through the snow toward the bunkhouse. "You know what?" Eddie continued. "Times have changed. We used to beat the shit out of queers like him in high school."

"You went to high school?" Kevin asked incredulously.

Eddie shrugged. "I hung out near it." He chuckled.

"Too bad we can't go kick his ass now," Vladamir said.

Eddie stopped. "Why can't we?" he said, turning to face the group again.

"Uh, because he's a fucking cop?" Hank asked.

"Fuck that noise. I'm sick of those two acting like they run shit around here," Eddie said as he veered off to the right.

"Where you going, man?" Kevin called after him.

"Going to pay our deputy a visit. You pussies coming?"

Kevin quickly fell in line and rushed after his friend. Hank looked to Vladamir, who simply shrugged and walked after his friends. Hank lingered for a moment, eyeing the path that led to the bunkhouse. With his shoulders sagging, he jogged after the group, calling for them to wait up.

The walk to Deputy Williams's house didn't take very long, but the sun was completely gone by time they got there. The trees blocked out most of the moonlight, causing the men to stumble blindly up to the edge of the tree line. With a few falls and several curses, they made it. The four men knelt in the shadows, eyeing the deputy's small cabin. Its wooden roof was coated with snow, and a single yellow light bulb illuminated the front steps.

"What's the plan here, Eddie?" Vladamir whispered.

"Alright," Eddie said. He pointed to Hank. "You're going to knock on the door. When he answers, tell him someone got hurt down the road. We'll all hide over there." He motioned toward some bushes. "And then we'll jump his faggot ass."

"I'm not sure this is a good ..." Hank said, but something moving in the woods behind him caught his attention. He allowed his thoughts to trail off as he stared into the darkness behind him.

"Yo, pay attention," Eddie said, snapping his fingers in front of Hank's face.

"Sorry. I thought I heard something." Hank allowed his eyes to drift away from the shadows in the forest. "I don't think this is a good idea."

"I don't give a fuck," Eddie said a little too loudly.

Kevin pressed a finger to his lips and made a *shh* sound, but waved him off. "You're going too ..."

A deep growl emanated from behind them. In unison, the four men jerked their heads toward the darkness. They silently stared into the forest, each straining their eyes.

"What was that?" Vladamir whispered.

The sound came again from their right. Its low rumble sent shivers down Hank's spine, and goosebumps broke out along his arms. Slowly, he stood up and took a step away from the sound.

"Where the fuck do you think you're going?" Eddie snarled. He jumped to his feet and turned his back to the noise. He pointed toward the cabin. "Get out there and do your—" Eddie's sentence was cut off by a deep gasp. His eyes stretched wide.

With the few slivers of moonlight, Hank watched the man's snaggle-toothed mouth turn to a grimace. The man levitated momentarily before collapsing to the ground in a blood-soaked heap.

Something moved quickly from where Eddie had been standing moments before. It rushed forward and pounced on Vladamir before Hank could even react. A creature plunged its hand deep into Vladamir's chest and ripped out a handful of organs. Dark liquid spurted from the gaping wound, hosing the beast like a blood-filled sprinkler.

Kevin shrieked a high-pitched wail. He turned to run into the woods, but a single swipe of the creature's enormous paw decapitated the man. His headless body crumpled to the ground, blood spurting from the stump of his neck.

Hank stood glued to his spot, his frozen extremities refusing to move. The beast disappeared into the shadows. It took a few more seconds for Hank to realize that someone else was talking. He forced himself to ignore the warm sensation of his own urine flooding his pants as he turned his head to see Brian standing on his porch, pistol drawn. Relief flooded his body, and he turned to wave at the deputy. He tried to scream, but no words came out. He made another raspy attempt to call out when another warm sensation came over him. Hot liquid poured down his chest and shoulders and searing hot pain tore through his neck. Instinctively, his hands flew to his neck to discover a massive wound. Blood seeped through his fingers as he desperately tried to call for help, but no words came.

Hank's knees buckled under his weight, sending him crashing into the snow. He reached toward Deputy Williams, begging the universe to get the deputy's attention.

Another man, wearing a long white bathrobe, appeared at the door of the deputy's cabin. Hank recognized him from the diner. The robed man squeezed Brian's shoulder. Slowly, Brian turned away from the forest. The deputy took one last look around before disappearing into his cabin, pulling the door closed as he went.

Darkness crept into the edges of Hank's vision. He gasped for air but only managed to choke on his own blood. Tears rolled from his eyes. The warm breath of some unseen beast beat down on the back of his head. Something sharp dug its way into his back, pushing him deeper into the snow. What little air he had left in his lungs was forcefully exhaled, causing specks of blood to coat the snow around him. The pressure on his back continued increasing. The agony of his bones cracking and shattering under the monster's weight was unbearable, and he mercifully slipped into unconsciousness.

Brian slid the deadbolt into place and returned his service pistol to its place in the duty belt that hung next to the door. Johnny had encouraged him to keep a gun nearby when he moved out there, something about not knowing what you could come across in the wilderness.

Frank's hand slid from Brian's shoulder to his chest and down to his abs. "Come back to bed," he whispered.

Brian stole another glance through the window but saw nothing except trees and snow. Shaking his head, he turned back toward Frank. "I swear I heard something," he insisted.

Frank took Brian's large hands in his and pulled him toward the bedroom. "It's probably just an animal." He let go of Brian's hand and disappeared through the bedroom door.

Brian relented and followed Frank into the room, having to duck through the doorway. He paused at the foot of the bed, watching Frank get cozy under the covers. Smiling, Brian walked around to his side and dropped into his spot. His long legs protruded from the end of the bed. He kicked at the covers a few times in an attempt to cover them before relenting and tucking his knees up.

"You ok?" Frank asked.

"Yeah, just in my own head tonight."

Frank squeezed Brian's arm. "It's those bigots at the diner, isn't it?"

Brian rolled onto his back and stared into the darkness of his ceiling. The springs in the cheap mattress squealed in protest. "Not really," he whispered. "They just reminded me of my dad."

Frank pushed himself up to his elbow. "Want to talk about it?"

"Yes and no," Brian admitted. "Talking about it won't really solve anything."

Frank made a smacking noise with his lips. "No, but it might make you feel a little better."

Brian allowed his head to loll to the side. In the sliver of moonlight that slipped between the curtains, he could see half of Frank's face. He wore a half-smile that matched the concerned look in his eye.

"I don't think he'll ever come around. I really thought he would have broken down and called me by now."

Frank's fingers danced across Brian's chest. "He might not be ready yet."

"He never will be." Plastering a forced smile across his face, he looked into Frank's eyes. "You know I'm jealous of you, right?"

Frank scoffed. "And why is that?"

"Because you're from California!" Brian blurted out. "That's like homo HQ!" He chuckled

Frank barked out a laugh and playfully smacked Brian's chest. "I'm from Northern Cali! Trust me, the HQ is further south."

"Maybe you can show me one day?" Brian asked, the humor in his voice gone.

Frank fell back onto the bed. "You won't even acknowledge me as your boyfriend in public, and you want me to take you to meet my parents?"

A pang of guilt stabbed Brian in the chest. He knew it hurt Frank that he wasn't fully out. It was easier for Frank, though; he was an architect. People didn't care if their architect was gay. His eyes drifted to his police jacket, draped over the chair in the corner. He shook his head. "It's not like that," he whispered, a tear forming in the corner of his eye. "Nobody's going to respect a gay cop."

Frank rolled over and put his head on Brian's chest. "I was just teasing you."

Brian kissed the top of Frank's head. "I know, but the truth hurts sometimes." He glanced back at the jacket in the corner of the room. "I bet they have gay cops in California."

Frank laughed again. "And you would look amazing in those short-sleeved uniforms."

Brian slid his hand under Frank's chin and tilted his head up so he could look into his eyes. "I'm not ready yet," he said. "But I will be soon."

Frank held Brian's gaze for a moment longer before leaning in for a kiss. "And I'll be right here waiting when you are."

Chapter 5

Dr. Earnest Davies held the front door to his office open for his last patient of the day. The tough-looking man thanked him as he limped past, and Earnest put on his best fake smile, dreading what was to come next.

"Now, you try to stay off that leg," he ordered.

The man mumbled a disgruntled reply and exited the building.

Earnest pulled the door shut and slammed the deadbolt into place with a loud click. Through the window, he watched the sun as it retreated behind the trees in the distance. He allowed himself a moment to admire the beauty of the orange and yellow rays streaking across the horizon, trying to freeze the beautiful snapshot in his mind.

Sucking in a deep breath and exhaling slowly, Earnest braced himself for the more morbid part of his job. He pulled the Open for Business sign off the window before yanking down the roll-up curtains. They blocked out what little light was available from outside, casting the room that doubled as a waiting room and living room into an eerie dusk.

Earnest walked down the hall to the staircase leading into his basement, which doubled as the town's morgue. As soon as he opened the door, he flipped the switch to the side of the staircase. The weak overhead bulb illuminated the stairs but failed to reach farther into his basement's dark abyss. The stairs were old and squealed in protest under his weight. Whether it was the journey down the dark steps itself or knowing what awaited him at the bottom, Earnest couldn't be sure, but a sense of dread washed over him. He avoided the basement morgue as much as possible. It had seemed less perilous when the sheriff and deputy had helped him carry the bodies down and place them onto gurneys.

He reached the bottom step and peered into the darkness. The air conditioner in the corner of the room blasted frigid air despite the already frozen weather outside. Careful not to trip, he took short, shuffling steps into the darkness. Having lived in that house for so many years, he had the entire floor plan memorized. He counted off his half steps until he got to ten. Then he turned to the right and extended his hand. His fingers quickly found their target and flicked another switch.

The large bulbs that ran the length of the ceiling buzzed with electricity. They grew an orange hue, flickered, then washed the room in a sterile-white light.

Earnest sighed in relief. He had put in several requests to the mayor to have a new switch installed at the base of the stairs. It was technically his house, but the town paid a fee to use the basement and he couldn't make changes without the mayor's permission.

Mayor Henry only ever responded with a spew of bureaucratic bullshit, droning on about budget cuts and prioritizing projects that do the most good for the most people. Everyone knew the mayor only invested in infrastructure to assist the cannery—the cannery that the mayor owned.

Earnest was old enough to know better, and eventually, he stopped pressing the issue.

Shaking his head, Earnest expelled the mayor from his mind. He retrieved two gloves from a box on a table next to the cooler, then threw open the large metal door. He grabbed the first gurney and wheeled it to the center of the room. The wheels dropped into perfectly made grooves in the floor, positioned directly below one of the long bulbs overhead. He locked the wheels, then retreated into the cooler and withdrew the second gurney, more carefully that time as the tattered remains of their John Doe in the blue jacket and orange beanie threatened to spill onto the floor. He positioned the bodies a few feet from each other, under their own lights.

Earnest dressed himself in a black apron, elbow-length black gloves, and a face shield. In his typical obsessive-compulsive manner, he placed the necessary instruments onto a tray in the order they would be used and slid the tray into place between the two gurneys. He retrieved a tape recorder from his desk, inserted a new tape, and pressed the record button. Once the red record light blinked to life, he deposited it into his breast pocket.

"This is Dr. Earnest Davies, coroner for the town of Port Luck. Today is January twenty-third, twenty-twenty-four." He glanced at a clock above the cooler. "And the time is approximately six forty-three p.m. I am performing the autopsy of Eric Graham and what appears to be a John Doe, both found deceased outside the Graham residence at..." he turned to consult his notes. "Which is located at 210 Winding Tree Lane."

The doctor moved around the table to Eric Graham's head. Using his pointer finger, he pushed on the chin, tilting the head slightly to the left. The subtle movement exposed the deep lacerations in the cadaver's neck. Strands of sinew clung to the open maw like spider webs.

"I'm beginning with the body of Eric Graham. The first thing of note is a large chunk of flesh missing from his neck. The hole measures," he grabbed a ruler and held it to the wound, "approximately seven inches wide and penetrated the esophagus. I judge the shape of the wound to be consistent with a bite. Judging by the pattern and length, it appears to be from a wolf or large canine."

The doctor moved to the man's side and buried his hands into Eric's chest. "Additionally, the ribs and sternum are cracked open. This appears consistent with an animal attack as the bones are splayed out." He paused to consider his assessment. Running his fingers along the cracked ribs, a shudder ran through him. "On second thought, this seems to indicate a pulling motion, which is unlikely to come from a wolf or canine. As for the internal organs," he paused and pushed his hands deeper into the abdomen, "they are missing." His voice quivered as he spoke. "The chest cavity and abdomen are completely empty." He dug deeper into the body, searching for any sign of the cadaver's organs. With a shaky voice, he continued. "And as far as I know, the police did not recover any organs from the scene."

He withdrew his hands and gazed at them with amazement. Pink specks of blood coated the gloves, but the abdominal cavity was completely cleared out. In all his years as a doctor and coroner in Alaska, he had never seen an animal eat body organs and not the muscle and flesh. The hair on the back of his neck stood on end and his heart beat rapidly against his chest. Slowly taking in breaths, he fought to calm himself. He had a job to do, and Johnny was counting on him.

"Continuing on," he tried to stifle the quiver in his voice, "the final obvious trauma appears to be five massive lacerations to the inside of Eric Graham's right thigh." Earnest held his gloved hand up to the wound. The pattern of the lacerations didn't resemble any animal attacks he had seen in the past. He traced his fingertips along the grooves of the shortest laceration. Spreading out his fingers, he mimicked scratching the skin. He knew at that moment a wolf wasn't responsible for the attack. Additionally, the cuts were far too deep. Burying his fingers inside one of the wounds, he could feel the rough texture of bone. There was a grooved, jagged edge on the femur which he recognized right away. The creature's claw had cut straight through several inches of fat, muscle, and tendons, shredding a path all the way to the bone, then shredding the bone as well. Skeptically, he dictated his findings into his recorder, sure that whoever listened to the recording would demand his retirement immediately.

"After careful consideration, it appears the cause of death was the lacerations to the thigh. There appears to be evidence of arterial spray in some of the photos taken at the scene. This coincides with the femoral artery being severed in several places."

The doctor stepped away from the body and swapped out his gloves, allowing the used, bloody ones to fall into the waste disposal bin, and turned toward the second body.

"Continuing with our second autopsy. The subject has yet to be identified, so I will refer to him as John Doe." He took a deep breath and set a pair of scissors onto the gurney. "I will begin by removing the jacket from his torso. I would like to note for the record the deceased is wearing a blue jacket and orange beanie. The pants," he paused again, eyeing the mutilated remains of the man's legs, "are unidentifiable in color or make."

Earnest took the cold steel of the scissors in his hand. Starting from the base of the jacket, he cut a few inches before coming to a massive gash of missing fabric. Skipping over it, he repositioned the scissors farther up the jacket and continued to cut the fabric away. His sharp, surgical-grade scissors sliced their way through the jacket and shirt with ease. "Unlike the late Eric Graham, this cadaver's chest cavity has not been torn open, but the abdomen does appear to be slashed open." Earnest buried his arm into the unknown-man's stomach. He had to reach in about elbow deep before he reached any organs. Feeling around, his hand rubbed around the distinct feeling of a lung. "Similar to Mr. Graham, some of the abdominal organs have been removed. In fact, it appears everything below the lungs is missing." He withdrew his arm, bits of human viscera coming away from it. The chunks of gooey body parts fell from his glove and splattered against the metal gurney. Earnest ignored the disgusting sound, switched his gloves, and moved to the corpse's head.

Earnest gripped the edges of the beanie and slid it away from the man's forehead. It came away with a sloshing sound, accompanied by a few strings of bodily fluids. The contents of the man's head spewed from the open wound. Gray chunks of brain matter intermixed with blood and spinal fluid formed a gnarly soup on the gurney. Earnest stifled a gag.

"The, uh, the brain is completely destroyed. The deceased's face is caved in, making it impossible to identify any distinguishable facial features. In my professional opinion, it appears as if he was struck many times with something hard." He balled his fist and held it next to the collapsed face. "The wounds are roughly double the size of my fisted hand. Judging by the erratic nature of the strikes, it would be my opinion that the attacker stood over the deceased when striking the victim."

Earnest finished removing the cadaver's clothes. Once the corpse was fully nude, Earnest removed his gloves and tossed them into the waste bin, then washed his hands. He retrieved a camera from a nearby table. "The only distinguishing characteristic of our John Doe is a tattoo on the inside of his left arm." He snapped a photo with the digital camera. "There is some damage to the tattoo," he continued, "but I believe it is the outline of Alaska. There appears to be a solid black cross in the middle and a star approximately where Port Luck would be on a map."

Earnest proceeded to snap more pictures before placing the camera on a desk in the back of the room. Above him, the lights flickered then cut out, leaving him swallowed in darkness.

Earnest held his breath with anticipation. After a moment, the lights flashed back on. He recoiled from the light, blinking hard. He must have been staring at the lights when they flicked on because stars danced in his vision. That would be the part in every horror movie he ever saw where the deceased bodies in front of him came to life. He half expected them to sit up on their metallic slabs, gore dripping onto the floor, but nothing happened. The two bodies lay motionless on their gurneys.

"Quit being a damned fool," he muttered to himself.

Stepping forward, he gripped the handle on the first gurney. Using his foot to release the wheel locks, he guided Eric Graham's body across the room. He slid the gurney back into the cooler and moved it to the side. As he emerged from the cooler, a deep growl reverberated off the walls.

"Doc," he called, hoping his German Shepherd would appear at the top of the stairs. The dog always refused to go into the basement. Earnest lingered at the edge of the cooler and waited for another growl.

When none came, he grabbed the second gurney and pushed it toward the cooler. The gurney had just dropped into place when the aggressive bark of his German Shepherd ripped through the otherwise silent house. Panic rose in Earnest's chest. As quickly as he could, he sprinted from the cooler, slamming the door shut behind him.

His feet hit the wooden stairs, bounding up them as rapidly as his aging knees would allow. The thumping of his feet bounced off the walls and mixed with the panicked barks of his dog. He burst through the doorway at the top of the stairs.

"Doc?" The sharp report of another bark sent a wave of pain through his ears. He sprinted down the hallway and into the kitchen, where the moon's glow through the open kitchen window illuminated the silhouette of his dog. He fumbled for the light switch, his fingers dancing frantically against the wall. They found the switch and flicked it, washing the room in light.

Before him, his usually calm dog was growling at the window. Teeth gnashed at an unseen threat, and its hackles stood on end.

Earnest's heart lurched in his chest. Doc had been his companion for eight years, and he had never once shown any sign of aggression. "Doc," he yelled. The dog showed no sign of stopping. Doc leaped forward and placed his front paws on the kitchen counter, all the time brandishing his teeth and growling.

Earnest took a step forward and grabbed the dog by the collar. Doc spun in a blur of motion and buried his teeth into Earnest's arm. Earnest yelped in pain and fell backward, landing hard on the ground. The momentary jolt of pain in his buttocks and back vanished as his eyes settled on the blood gushing down his arm.

Doc released his owner and let loose a whimper. Clarity returned to his previously feral eyes, and the fur on his back smoothed out.

Earnest slid on his butt away from the dog and gripped his bleeding arm. Blood seeped from his shredded flesh, fighting its way between his fingers.

The dog dropped to its stomach with his head cocked. A look of concern and confusion came over the Shepard's face.

Slowly, Earnest staggered to his feet. Pain radiated up his arm and supplanted itself firmly in his shoulder. Tentatively, he tiptoed around Doc and made his way to the sink. He used his elbow to turn on the faucet and plunged his injured arm into the icy water. Relief flooded through him as the water numbed the pain and washed away the blood. Examining the damage, it was obvious he would need stitches, but it didn't appear any permanent damage had been done.

He rested the hand of his good arm on the window. Through the pane of glass, the moon illuminated the thirty or so feet of his yard, which backed up to a wooded area. White snow covered the expanse, pristine and undisturbed.

Shaking his head, he moved to turn back toward his dog, but something in the trees caught his eye. A space just above a tree limb appeared darker than the rest. It was like the area was devoid of light. He stared intently at it, desperate to find a reason for the darkness.

Two yellow balls appeared in that dark abyss, glinting in the moon's light.

Earnest squinted against the darkness, trying to make out what they could be. Ice flooded his veins and he sucked in a sharp breath.

They were eyes.

Behind him, the German Shepherd howled.

Chapter 6

Johnny opened the door to the police station and walked inside. The station's fluorescent lights stood in stark contrast to the darkness outside.

Brian looked up from the computer on his desk and checked his watch. He rubbed his eyes and said, "Good Morning, boss. Thought you weren't coming in until ten today?"

Johnny grabbed the pot of coffee and poured himself a cup. He took a swig of the burning liquid and waited a moment for the warmth to spread across his chest before responding. "Couldn't sleep," he said flatly.

Brian nodded. "I couldn't sleep either." He pushed his chair back and stretched his arms. "Haven't gotten a full night's sleep since we found those bodies." Brian pressed his own coffee mug to his lips and took a swig. "Doesn't help that there was an animal or something outside my house. I heard it growling all damn night."

Brian's words reminded Johnny of his mental note to keep an eye on his deputy's well-being. Quickly, he decided he would get settled in and drink his coffee, then he would have a conversation with Brian to make sure he was properly handling everything.

Johnny moved past Brian's desk and into the hallway leading to his office. He paused. "Have we heard anything from Dr. Davies? I need that autopsy report."

Brian pressed a hand to his forehead. "Shit, sorry, sheriff. He called around six and asked you to call when you get into the station."

Johnny peeked at his watch. It was only six thirty in the morning; Earnest must have found something interesting to get back to him so quickly. He dipped into his office and shut the door. Collapsing into his leather office chair, he took another sip from his coffee before picking up the phone. He typed in Earnest's number with the same hand that held the receiver then pressed it to his ear.

Earnest answered on the second ring. The doctor sounded wide awake despite the early hour. Johnny could hear the man moving around on the other end, and it sounded like coffee was brewing in the background.

The doctor immediately began telling Johnny about his findings. He went into great detail regarding the injuries, using medical terms like evisceration, slipping into his role as a doctor and approaching the deceased from a scientific perspective.

Johnny scribbled furiously on a notepad. He tried to keep up, but several times, he had to pause and try to sound out some of the terminology. After a few minutes, he gave up on taking notes and interrupted the doctor. "Earnest," he interjected. The doctor continued rambling, completely oblivious to Johnny's interruption. "Earnest," he said more forcefully.

"Yes, sheriff?"

Johnny rubbed his forehead. "Can you type it up and email all this to me? It's too early and I can't keep up."

"I did that around three this morning."

Johnny hadn't even fired up his computer yet, let alone checked his emails. With a frustrated sigh, he asked, "Did wild animals kill them?"

There was a prolonged pause on the other end of the phone. Deeper in the station, the front desk phone rang, and he could hear Brian talking to someone. Johnny closed his eyes. "Earnest, are you there?" he said in an exasperated tone.

"No, Johnny, I don't believe wild animals killed them."

Johnny's blood ran cold. He quit rocking in his chair and sat straight. The implications of Earnest's statement hung between them like a noose around his neck, tightening with every passing second. The silence on the other end of the phone throbbed in his ear.

Finally, Earnest broke the standoff. "I can't say who or what, but it wasn't a wolf or bear." Johnny could hear the doctor sipping what he presumed was coffee. "That much I *am* confident in."

There was a flurry of movement on the doctor's end of the phone. After a moment, the doctor continued. "As for our John Doe, the only identifying mark I could find was a tattoo on his arm. I sent a photo of it to you."

Johnny pressed the power button on the computer. The fans whirred to life, and his computer monitor lit up. While he waited for it to boot up, he thanked Earnest. He could hear Brian's footsteps coming down the hallway. "Listen, Earnest, I really appreciate you getting this done so quickly."

"It's no problem, Johnny."

There was a gentle knock on his office door. It cracked open slightly, and Brian poked his head in. Johnny waved for him to enter. "I got to run," Johnny said. He eyed Brian; the young deputy fidgeted nervously in front of his desk. He dropped the phone back onto the receiver without waiting for Earnest's reply.

"You look like you're bringing me bad news," Johnny said. He opened the email icon on his computer and scrolled through several emails, most from the mayor, until he found the one containing Earnest's report and opened it.

Brian rubbed the back of his neck. "Just got a call from old man Petrov. He said a bear attacked his dog." Brian shrugged. "Said he shot it and it ran off." Brian paused, then slowly asked, "Want me to go out there and check it out?"

Johnny shook his head. He tapped a finger to his lips and examined the photo on his computer monitor, then looked up at Brian. "You ever heard of anyone around here having a tattoo of Alaska with a cross and a star in it?"

Brian's gaze twisted into a confused look, but Johnny could tell the man was trying to recall any tattoo like that. Brian wagged his finger. "Ben Grover might have a tattoo like that. He was in the diner a few months ago, before going back to the university. He said he got a tattoo. I never saw it, but I heard someone tease him about getting a tattoo of the state. Something about using it as a map if he gets lost."

"Do you know if there was a cross in it?" Johnny asked.

"No, sir. I never actually saw it. Grabbed my lunch and came back here."

Johnny nodded. "I'll handle Petrov. That old Russian can be a real pain in the ass." Johnny stood up from his chair and downed the remainder of his coffee. He retrieved the keys to the snowmobile from his desk drawer. "I'm actually surprised he called. The old Russians don't really care too much for law enforcement."

Brian nodded his understanding but didn't move from his spot by the door. "Can I ask why you wanted to know about that tattoo?" Brian asked.

Johnny turned to face his young deputy. "I think Ben Grover might be our John Doe."

Brian's face morphed into a sad look. "You want me to call his mom?"

Johnny shook his head. "Not yet. I want to be sure first. Let me handle Petrov, and then I'll head over to the mayor's office."

Without another word, Brian left his boss's office and returned to his desk at the front of the station.

Johnny grabbed a fresh radio from the charging station in his office and clipped it to his belt. He pulled on his heavy coat and hat. Passing by Brian's desk, he paused. "This probably goes without saying, but you need to keep this info to yourself for now."

Johnny locked eyes with Brian; he didn't blink. The young deputy nodded confidently. Johnny exited the building and climbed onto his snowmobile.

It was nearly ten a.m., and the sun was just beginning to crest the mountains to the east. On this side of town, the trees were an assorted bunch. Some stood dead with their gnarled branches extending in every direction. Others still held on to their leaves and collected piles of snow.

Between the trees, Johnny could see the Petrov cabin. He hated going out there and dealing with the Petrov family. They were old blood in Port Luck. Their ancestors settled the land when Alaska was still a Russian territory. The Petrov's loved their Russian heritage a bit too much, even going as far as teaching their kids Russian as a primary language. They were an isolated bunch, living off the land and avoiding other people as much as possible. They rarely interacted with the town, and for them to call the sheriff, it would have to be something big and it must have scared old man Petrov. The thought of something frightening the grizzled outdoorsman gave Johnny a renewed sense of dread.

Sergei Petrov, the patriarch of their clan, was sitting in a rocking chair on the front porch when Johnny pulled up. A double-barrel shotgun rested across his lap. Disdain painted the man's face when he made eye contact with the town sheriff.

"You called about an animal attack?" Johnny shouted.

Sergei leaned his shotgun against the chair and stood up. "That's right," he said with a thick Russian accent. "It attacked my dogs." The old man pointed a finger to the tree line on the left side of the house. "I shot it, and it ran off." The old man held out his hand in a stop motion. "Now, you know I wouldn't have called you, but we heard about those bodies you found. Figured the right thing to do was to give you a call."

"I appreciate that, Mr. Petrov. Do you mind if I look around?"

The old man's lip twitched, but he reluctantly grunted his approval. He returned to his seat and picked up his shotgun. Resting it across his lap, he resumed slowly rocking.

Johnny turned and trudged through the snow to the area Sergei had pointed to. A large patch of snow had been disturbed, showing obvious signs of a struggle, and there were droplets of blood scattered about. He located a spent shell casing, confirming Sergei's story. He continued walking toward the tree line when something caught his eye.

A few feet in front of him, a black liquid tainted the pure snow. Approaching the spot with caution, he knelt down and examined his surroundings before giving the liquid his full attention. He pressed two fingers to the goo and held them up. It came away like black tar, strands stretching from his fingers to the snow.

"You know what that is?" Sergei's voice asked from behind him.

Johnny had been so focused on the liquid he hadn't heard the old man approach. His heart gave a little hop, and he took a moment to collect himself before responding. "Not sure," he answered truthfully.

Sergei seemed to appreciate the honesty. "Me either," the old Russian said. "But whatever I shot last night was no animal I've ever seen."

Johnny wiped the sticky substance on his pants, knowing full well Amy was going to throw a fit about the stains. He scanned the trees around them. Nothing seemed out of place, yet nothing seemed quite right, either.

"Sergei," Johnny said, "I think you should keep your family close for the next couple days."

Chapter 7

Just as she did every weekday morning, Amy Myers stood in front of her class. She called out the names of her students in alphabetical order, checking them off as they responded with the customary "Here."

Education wasn't the priority for most families in a small fishing town like Port Luck. Many of her students would miss school to assist the family in daily tasks. It wasn't uncommon to see young children fishing with their fathers, cutting firewood, or stocking the family-owned store. With that in mind, she had come to expect a few absences each day, but never ten. Hell, the class only had eighteen students in it.

She gazed over the rows of mostly empty chairs. Those who showed weren't even her best- or most-dedicated eight, but at least they were there. Amy inhaled deeply. The day wouldn't be a total waste, and if she was lucky, maybe she could end class early.

"So, class, has anyone heard from any of their friends? We have a lot of absences today," she asked as gently as she could, trying her best to paint on a reassuring smile.

"Monster probably got them," Timmy Johnston said from his spot in the back of the class.

Amy bit her bottom lip hard enough to send a ripple of pain through her mouth. Timmy was a little shit. No matter how many times Amy reprimanded him for it, the asshole constantly picked on the other kids in class. Once, Amy tried to address it with Timmy's father. Mr. Johnston came into the parent-teacher conference reeking of whiskey so bad it stung Amy's eyes. She tried to explain the situation as gently as she could. Using every ounce of her patience and experience as an educator, she provided examples of Timmy's poor behavior. She offered some potential solutions they could implement to get him on a better path. Mr. Johnston wobbled in his chair, his head dipping several times. After a few minutes of Amy's lecturing, Timmy's father called her a cunt, knocked over a few desks, and left. It was pretty clear to her where Timmy learned the flowery language he used every recess.

Amy contemplated telling her husband, but she knew Johnny would take his badge off for the night and beat the drunken shit stain half to death and decided it wasn't worth it. They couldn't afford for him to lose his job.

"There's no monster, Timmy." Amy struggled to hide her exasperation. She didn't have the patience for Timmy's antics. Pinching the bridge of her nose and clenching her eyes, she tried again. "Anyone else?"

Veronica raised her hand, speaking before Amy called on her. Amy pressed her fingers to her eyes and rubbed furiously. She wanted to scream about waiting to be called on, but it wouldn't do any good. The children were working themselves into a frenzy.

"My grandmother said it's a Winniego." The little girl's eyes went wide. "I don't know what that is, but my grandmother seemed really scared."

"No, that's—" Amy started before being cut off.

"You mean a wendigo, dumbass!" Timmy shouted.

"Timmy! That is enough!" Amy scolded. She lowered her class roster and marched to the back of the room, stopping right in front of his desk. "Do I need to call your father?"

Timmy grinned. "You and I both know you don't want to do that."

Amy squeezed her clipboard. "Last chance," she warned. As soon as she turned her back to return to the front of the class, Timmy spoke again.

"I bet it's a werewolf," Timmy said.

"There are no—" Amy tried to say, but she was cut off again.

"Maybe it's a vampire," one of the other children offered.

"Class!" She projected her voice to be heard above the murmurs of her eight frightened students. "There is no monster." She stormed to the front of her class and tossed the clipboard onto her desk. Without facing the class, she said, "My husband is the sheriff, and he thinks it was a wolf or bear." She pushed herself away from her desk. "And whatever it was is long gone! Now, let's move on to our lesson for the day."

Amy turned to the whiteboard and uncapped a black marker. She furiously wrote Founder's Day in big letters and underlined it twice for emphasis. Facing the class again, she threw on her biggest smile. "Today, we're going to learn more about the history of our little town! Now, who can tell me what our town used to be called?"

In the far corner of the class, Yura raised his hand.

Amy smiled, genuinely pleased to see him. He lived on the outskirts of town, and his family was very proud of their Native heritage. They rarely interacted with the town, and he only attended class a few times a month.

"Yes, Yura?"

"Portlock?" he answered sheepishly.

Amy clapped her hands. "That's absolutely correct! Excellent job." She wrote Portlock on the board, then put a hyphen and wrote 1786. With the marker still uncapped, she picked up a stack of papers she had printed out with a picture of the town founders on it. She handed them to Victoria. "Can you please pass these out?"

Victoria nodded and took the papers, proceeding to pass them out.

Amy continued her lesson. "Our town was originally named Portlock after a ship captain, Nathaniel Portlock. He discovered this area in 1786 and thought it would make an excellent port." She held up a finger. "But it wasn't until 1921 that an official town was set up." She then wrote 1944 on the board. "Does anyone know what is important about this year?"

Yura slowly raised his hand again.

Amy smiled and pointed to him. "Yes, Yura?"

"That was when the town was abandoned the first time?"

"That is absolutely correct," Amy said. "The people of the town abandoned it in 1943, except for the postal officer." She underlined 1944. "He stayed for one full year, finally leaving in?" She looked back at the class expectantly.

In near unison, they read off the year.

Yura raised his hand again.

"Yes, Yura?"

"I heard my grandfather talking." The boy looked down at his lap, unwilling to meet his teacher's eyes.

Amy knew of Yura's grandfather but never met the man. He was an Inuit elder who sometimes traveled to the Metlakatla Indian Community to lead various religious practices.

"He said he could feel it in the air."

Amy eyed the boy with suspicion. Something told her to put an end to it, but the faraway look in his eyes forced her curiosity to get the better of her. "What can he feel in the air?"

"He said the town was abandoned all those years ago because a beast attacked the settlement." The boy locked eyes with Amy. "He said our people have been battling the evil spirits that live across these lands for thousands of years."

Goosebumps prickled her arms. She knew about the legend of Portlock. There were rumors of monsters and ghosts but no evidence of anything supernatural. The accepted reason the original settlers left was a financial one. A new highway opened around the time the original villagers left. The story was that it became economically impossible to keep the town alive. Fishing in the bay took a bad turn, and the small settlement was no longer viable. Supposedly, several people came forward years later and claimed to have lived in the town when it was abandoned. They all alleged some sort of monster was stalking the town and that was why they left.

Amy sucked in a deep breath to regain her composure. "I respect your grandfather's opinion." Her voice felt weaker. "But again, this was nothing but a very unfortunate animal attack."

"He said that's how it started last time."

The class was uncomfortably silent. Even Timmy was transfixed by his classmate's words. The other seven students stared at their teacher, their little eyes searching her for a response.

"Everything is fine," she finally said. Her voice betrayed her. When Timmy brought up werewolves, it was easy for her to dismiss him. He came from a rough family and was a regular problem in Amy's life. Yura's grandfather was a different story. Rumor had it the old man was here the first time the village was abandoned.

"He said it was an Amarok," Yura insisted. "It's a wolf-like creature that hunts people." Yura's words hung in the air like a toxic fume, suffocating the people around him. Out of nowhere, Yura shrugged. "But grandfather said the beast doesn't hurt Yupik people, so I'm safe."

"I knew it!" Timmy exclaimed, slamming his hand down on his desk. "It's a werewolf!" Several of the students burst out laughing, and for the first time in her teaching career, she was grateful for Timmy's smartass remarks and the humor they brought.

A pit formed in Amy's stomach, and for some inexplicable reason, she believed Yura's grandfather. "One moment, class," she said, raising one finger. Amy quickly returned to the seat behind her large wooden desk. As inconspicuously as she could, she pulled out her phone and sent a text to her husband, summarizing what Yura relayed from his grandfather. She knew it was silly to be so afraid of an urban legend, but she couldn't shake the feeling that something was wrong. The air in the town felt heavier. She could feel the fear when she walked down the street. Something had been off ever since those bodies were found.

She looked back up at her class, who were all staring, anticipation in their eyes. "Change of plans," Amy said sharply. "Please open your books to chapter ten." She waited for the sound of shuffling paper to stop. "We're working on multiplication today." Her declaration was met by a series of groans.

"Way to go, Yura!" Timmy said. "You scared the teacher so bad she's making us do math."

"Enough, Timothy!"

Timmy recoiled in his seat, crossing his arms over his chest.

The rumble of a motor shook the thin wooden walls of the school building. Through the window, she could see her husband speed past on a snowmobile. She only glimpsed him for a moment but could see a look of concern wrinkled across his forehead. Judging by the direction he was traveling, he was probably heading in the direction of the government building.

He's going to meet the mayor, she thought. Amy knew her husband avoided the mayor at all costs. Every time the two met, Johnny would spend the remainder of the night complaining about the mayor being a pompous asshole and a "fake-ass marine."

She glanced back at Yura. Her own fear was reflected in the young boy's eyes. Something was definitely wrong.

Chapter 8

Johnny followed the secretary as she opened the large oak doors to the mayor's office. He couldn't recall her name and, after meeting her countless times, was too embarrassed to ask. Confident Amy would remember the woman's name from her work with the school, he made a mental note to ask her that night.

The secretary announced his entry to the room like she was presenting a member of the British royal family. He choked back a chuckle because when Johnny walked past her, the overwhelming aroma of her fruity perfume smacked him in the face. It reminded him of his grandmother. The cranky old broad would have said the young secretary smelled like a whore.

Victor Henry reclined in an oversized leather chair. Ornate bronze decorations stretched out above his head, giving the mayor the appearance of a much taller man. Johnny took in the sight of his gaudy desk with its gold inlay around the trim. The chubby mayor was even overdressed, wearing a ridiculous outfit that looked like a cheap tuxedo.

Darren, the little shit that had woken him up a few nights ago, leaned against a windowsill behind his father. The punk's stance gave off an aura of arrogance, which was impressive for someone who had never done anything besides be born to the right family.

"Take a seat, sheriff," Victor said, motioning to a gray chair facing the desk.

Johnny couldn't help but shake his head. It was the only spartan piece of furniture in the room, likely brought in for their meeting. For a moment, Johnny considered declining but decided it would be easier to do as instructed. He plopped down in the seat, smacking his knees as he did. The grip of his pistol pressed against his arm, which, in turn, caused the pistol to press into his hip. Johnny wiggled around, attempting to dislodge the weapon from its uncomfortable spot.

"So, what's going on around here?" Victor asked.

Johnny leaned deeper into his seat, finally finding relief from his pistol. "We got two bodies; that's all we know for sure."

Darren stood up and walked behind his father's desk, stopping directly behind his father. He leaned against a bookshelf and crossed his arms. The kid looked like Johnny just spit in his Cheerios. "Come on, man. Quit wasting our fucking time," Darren spat, disdain dripping from his words.

The mayor turned to address his son, but Johnny spoke first.

"First off, I don't answer to you." He shifted forward in his seat, locking his eyes on Darren. "Second, if anyone is wasting anyone's time, it's you guys." He threw up in his hands in a sign of frustration. "I could be out there hunting this guy down. Instead, I'm in here talking to your spoiled ass." He reclined into his seat again, anger bubbling inside. He knew he crossed the line, making the situation much worse with his outburst, but it felt amazing.

Victor threw a hand up. "Now hold on."

Darren left his spot against the bookshelf. Uncrossing his arms, he balled his hands into fists and approached Johnny. "You can't talk to me that way." There was a hint of whininess in his voice. He glanced at his father for support.

Johnny jabbed a finger in Darren's direction. "I can talk to you any way I like." Shifting his finger to point at the mayor, he continued, "Victor, can the grown-ups talk without this kid in the room?"

"He's my son," Victor said, rubbing his forehead. "He's going to be taking over my businesses for me one day. He'll probably get elected as mayor whenever I'm done with this place. That's why I have him sit in all meetings." After a brief pause, he looked up. "Johnny, you know we don't have to fight every time we meet, right?" Victor turned to his son. "And you. Your job is to shut up and listen."

Darren slumped against the bookshelf, his head hanging in quiet resignation.

Slowly, Victor turned his attention back to Johnny. "You said hunting this guy down?"

Johnny nodded.

"So you think these are murders?"

Johnny relaxed his posture. It took everything in him not to strangle that spoiled little fucker, but now that Victor had put Darren in his place, maybe they could have a serious conversation.

"I don't know," Johnny relented. "I had Earnest do autopsies, and he says the injuries aren't consistent with a standard animal attack. But I don't see how a man could have done this."

A grim expression washed over the mayor's face as he pushed his chair back. Meandering to the window, he stared out for a few minutes before saying, "He's wrong." He spun back around to face the confused sheriff. "Listen,

Johnny, I haven't told anyone this yet, but I'm running for a seat in congress next year."

"Dad!" Darren exclaimed.

Victor's face turned a deep shade of red. "Quiet!" he spat at his son, spittle flying from his mouth. Sucking in a deep breath, he continued. "Darren is going to take over running the canneries and some of our other businesses." The mayor stood up straight and tugged at the bottom of his coat, fixing his stately appearance. "So, no, sheriff, we don't have a murder in my town. Much less two."

Johnny shook his head in disgust. "What're you asking me to do, mayor?"

"He's asking you to do your job." Darren snickered.

For a moment, Johnny considered punching the kid in the face.

Victor shot his son a death glare. "I want you to get a hunting party together, find the wolf or bear or whatever it was that killed those men. Then everyone can get back to work."

"I just told you—" Johnny started, but Victor immediately cut him off.

Victor shook his head. "No." He charged at Johnny and jammed a finger into his chest. "I just told you. You're not fucking up my plans with your fantasy of catching a murderer. You're just a small-town cop. Start acting like it." He poked Johnny a second time, his finger digging into Johnny's chest. "I don't intend to waste my entire life in this podunk-ass town. I'm worth millions." His eyes grew wide. "Unlike you and these people, I want more for my family."

Johnny nodded. He pushed himself out of the chair, coming to his full height and looking down on the smug little man. A smirk crept across Johnny's face. He pushed past the mayor and walked toward the door.

"I didn't dismiss you yet!" Victor shouted. "I'm ordering you to put together a hunting party. Offer a $5000 reward for the capture of the wolf that killed those men."

"And how are we paying for that reward?" Johnny asked with disdain in his voice.

"You know how," Darren snapped back.

The mayor held up his hand again to silence his son. "I'll pay for it myself. Just see that it's done."

Johnny gripped the handle of the door, ready to leave. He paused. "You know you're only mayor because you own the cannery, right?" He asked it without looking back. "Nobody in this town actually respects you."

"I don't need their respect. I own them. There would be no Port Luck without me! My businesses are the only reason you're here." Victor waved his hand. "You're dismissed now."

Johnny jerked the door open, stepped through it, and slammed it shut.

The secretary, in an all-pink dress suit, sat at her desk with a startled look on her face.

He decided at that moment that he wouldn't ask Amy for the secretary's name. He knew all he needed to know about the people in that building.

"Your boss is an asshole," he said as he stormed out of the building.

Johnny descended the icy steps of the government building, the town laid out before him. Victor had called it a podunk-ass town and insulted everyone in it. From where he was standing, Johnny had an excellent view. Despite the decreased activity since they found the bodies, the town was still beautiful. Ice caught the sun at the right angle and glinted off old roofs. Smoke bellowed from chimneys. Massive trees hugged the town from all directions. To the west, he could see the mountain peaks. To the east, he could see the Pacific Ocean. He glanced back at the window to the mayor's office.

Darren was staring down at him, a stupid grin stretched across his worthless face.

No matter what that little shit and his father thought, his town was beautiful, and Johnny was going to protect it.

Chapter 9

"Sheriff, crazy lady Grover called while you were with the mayor. She said something ate her cats," Brian said as soon as Johnny entered the station.

Looking his deputy up and down, for a second, Johnny felt guilty for running the man ragged. He could see deep bags had formed under Brian's eyes. Johnny tried to remember when the man said he got into the station. It was before the sun was up, that much he knew for sure.

Then he remembered he had requested the funds to hire a second deputy and the mayor rejected the proposal.

Johnny wondered if he looked just as tired as he rubbed the bags under his own eyes. "Jesus Christ." He sighed. "Did she say anything else?"

"Just that whatever attacked them was massive and ran away really fast." Brian mirrored Johnny's actions and rubbed at his eyes.

"Alright," Johnny said, retrieving a cup of coffee from the nearly empty pot. "Voldemort wants me to put together a hunting party."

Brian bursted out laughing. It was a nickname Brian had used to describe the mayor several times, but he had never heard Johnny use it. He watched Johnny take a sip of the steaming coffee and gave him a knowing smirk. "You're going to see Hanta, aren't you?"

Johnny sighed, took another swig of the coffee, and set his mug down. He grabbed a fresh radio from the table and replaced it with his old one, waiting for the red light to flash to be sure it was charging.

"Unfortunately." He hiked up the belt on his pants a bit. "Brian, what did I tell you about leaving burnt-ass coffee in the pot?"

"That you would arrest me for assaulting the sheriff?" Brian answered sarcastically.

"Last warning," Johnny said dryly. Moving to the front door of the station, he paused. "Oh, and Brian?" He looked over his shoulder at the deputy. Brian stopped typing and looked up at his boss. "I want you to go home and get some rest. Forward the station's calls to my cell."

"But, sheriff, I'm—" Brian tried to protest, rising to his feet.

"Brian," Johnny snapped.

"Yes, sir?" Brian responded with a dejected tone.

"Go home. Sleep. That's an order."

"Yes, sir."

Johnny exited the building. As the door swung shut behind him, he reminded Brian to lock up. He knew he didn't need to remind the deputy, but he said it out of habit. The man was a true professional. Eventually, he would move to Seattle or Portland or maybe work for the state. Whichever agency got him when he was done with Port Luck would be lucky to have him.

Johnny mounted his snowmobile and flipped the key. The engine roared to life between his legs, vibrating throughout his whole body. In the mirror above the handle, he watched Brian turn off the station's lights and flip a sign around that had Johnny's cell phone number written on it. The sign wasn't really needed, everyone in town already had his number, but it was a precaution he insisted on.

The young man locked the door and gave his boss a half-hearted salute before walking down the road.

Johnny gassed the snowmobile. It lurched forward and sped down the winding trails that led to the town's farthest reaches. He knew the way by heart despite rarely going out that far. There were only a few lonely hermits who lived that far outside of town, and they weren't exactly supporters of law enforcement.

The area where Hanta lived was known to the locals as either Dead Man's Ridge or Rib Cage Valley, depending on whom you asked. The terrain was notoriously treacherous. It wasn't uncommon for hikers to get lost, fall off a cliff, or get eaten by a bear. Several out-of-towners had hiked out to the valley never to be seen again. They did find the skeleton of one man who had gone missing more than forty years ago. His rib cage was sticking up through the snow, thus the valley's new nickname.

Hanta Kovloz lived right in the middle of the valley. He was an older man, although Johnny didn't know how old he was. He wasn't in any of the police databases. Johnny wasn't sure if his last name was really Kovloz or even if the man had a social security number. He was another descendant of the original Russian settlers who mixed in with local Native tribes, and Johnny doubted he was born in a hospital. He made himself a mental note to look Hanta up in his systems when he made it back to the police station.

Over the ridge, a thick cloud of black smoke bellowed from a chimney. Johnny depressed the throttle a little more, causing the nose of the snowmobile to pitch upward. The wind ripped past him as he sped toward the cabin. A growing sense of anxiety built up inside him with every yard traveled.

He stopped about twenty yards from Hanta's hut. The single-room, wooden building rose up from the snow like a ghostly apparition. It blended into the wooded area surrounding it, camouflaging it from anyone who didn't know where to look. To the left of the hut sat a small stone building used for smoking meats. A subtle gray smoke rose from an opening at the top of the building. Bones adorned ropes that hung over the door of the small patio like wind chimes. A dwindling supply of firewood lay to the side.

Johnny shut off the snowmobile. It gave one last rumble then went silent. Inhaling a sharp breath, he dismounted his ride. He only made it about five feet through the deep snow before hearing Hanta's deep voice from behind him.

"What're you doing out here, sheriff?" Hanta said in his thick Russian accent.

Johnny whirled around to see Hanta emerging from the trees, weapon in hand. It was a compound bow with a quiver of arrows attached to the side. Hanta was clad in furs from head to toe, two freshly killed rabbits dangling from his belt.

"Need your help," Johnny replied.

"Must be something big for you to come all this way, city boy."

Johnny shook his head. Never in all of his years had he been referred to as a city boy.

Hanta approached Johnny, who instinctively reached out to shake Hanta's hand. The older man eyed it suspiciously before walking right past Johnny, bumping his shoulder on his way toward the house.

Johnny looked down at his outstretched hand with an embarrassed look across his face. Hanta had never shaken his hand before; why did Johnny expect he would do it every time?

"Yeah, two of the townsfolk got killed out at the Graham place a couple of nights ago. Whatever it is has been lurking on the edge of town, killing cats and dogs."

Hanta stomped his boots off on the wooden front porch. He leaned his bow against the wall of the hut and slid a second quiver of arrows from around his shoulder. "What is it?" Hanta asked, sounding disinterested.

Johnny shook his head. "I'm not really sure."

Hanta eyed him, his face painted with distrust. Johnny tried not to take it personally; Hanta distrusted everyone. Still, as the town sheriff, he was used to being at least respected by the townspeople.

"I'm going to skin these hares," Hanta said as he unwrapped them from his belt. "Why don't you come in from the cold and tell me all about what you don't know?"

Johnny shook his head and reluctantly followed Hanta into the hut. The air inside was heavy with smoke. The hut had a chimney for the wood fire stove, but the ventilation was terrible. Johnny couldn't tell if it was a poor design or a lack of cleaning, but the smell was atrocious. The smoky air permeated his nostrils and snaked its way into his lungs, sending him into a coughing fit.

Hanta smiled and motioned for Johnny to sit on the only chair in the room, an old wooden rocker.

Johnny covered his mouth as he hacked into his arm. Slowly, he slid into the rocker and awkwardly positioned himself with his feet spread apart to keep it from moving.

Hanta slapped the rabbits down with a sickening squelch on what Johnny assumed was a makeshift table. The older man pulled an enormous knife from a hidden sheath at his side. He must have caught Johnny staring at the shiny steel because he smiled. "You like that, do ya?" he asked.

Johnny nodded. "It's a nice knife," he acknowledged.

Hanta grunted. "So, tell me about these bodies." He buried the knife into the first rabbit and dragged the blade down its abdomen. The creature's guts spilled onto the table. Using his knife to fish out the remaining innards, he slid them off the table. They fell into a bucket on the floor.

Johnny stifled retching at the ripping sound created by Hanta's knife tearing through the rabbit's carcass. He watched Hanta toss the first rabbit aside and grab the second, lining up the knife with the top of the animal's chest.

"The bodies?" Hanta asked.

"Right." Johnny nodded. "They were, uh, massacred, for lack of a better word. Ripped apart."

Hanta nodded. "Must be a bear then. It has been a harsh winter." He sank his blade into the second rabbit. "Normally they load up and hibernate, but it wouldn't be the first time one got hungry." The blade caught on some bones, forcing Hanta to saw back and forth aggressively.

Johnny shook his head. "That's the thing. I'm not even sure it was an animal. The attacks didn't really seem consistent with a wolf or bear." Johnny fished a photo from his pocket and tossed it onto the table, careful to avoid the pooling blood.

Hanta leaned forward and eyed the photo. "Continue." With a massive yank, the bones in the dead rabbit's chest cracked.

"Witnesses around town don't think it is a bear, and the couple of prints I found definitely weren't from a bear."

Hanta's cutting came to an abrupt halt. His eyes filled with curiosity at this statement. "What did they look like?"

Johnny rubbed his chin as he contemplated how honest he wanted to be with this hermit. After a moment, he decided Hanta needed to know everything if he was going to hunt the creature, if the creature even existed at all.

"The tracks looked like a wolf's print but longer. That's the only way I could explain it. Oh, and the pattern seemed like whatever this thing is, it walked on two legs."

A devilish smile stretched across Hanta's face. His yellow teeth made the look appear sinister. "Sounds like you have Amarok," Hanta said in a matter-of-fact tone.

Johnny perked up. The thought that Hanta might know what was stalking his town had never crossed his mind. "What's that?"

Hanta buried the knife into the rabbit and began cutting again. "It's from Inuit legend. It's said to be a giant wolf that stalks people who hunt alone."

Johnny tapped his chin and pondered this. "Then why hasn't it stalked you?" he asked.

Hanta laughed. It was an obnoxious sound that filled the cabin and hurt Johnny's ears. "Because it's not real." Hanta shook his head and began cutting again. "Didn't take you for the superstitious type, sheriff."

"Look, real or not, the mayor is offering up a reward. You interested in hunting this thing for me?"

"Depends on what you're offering."

Johnny sighed. He stood up from the rocking chair and approached the table. Setting his palms firmly on the wood, he leaned forward. The rickety old table creaked under his weight. "Five grand, cash."

Hanta shook his head. "What do I need with five grand?" He brandished the knife and used it to make a broad sweeping motion around the cabin. Blood dripped from the blade and stained the wooden floor red.

"What do you want then?"

Hanta stabbed the knife down into the table, causing Johnny to leap backward. His heart rate accelerated at the sudden outburst.

"I'll take the five grand, but I want something else."

Johnny folded his arms across his chest and did his best to appear disinterested. "Quit with the theatrics and spit it out."

"When I kill it, I get to keep it."

Johnny wasn't the least bit surprised by the request. A few antlers adorned the walls of the cabin. Johnny assumed the next time he was out, whatever creature was stalking his town would be mounted on those walls.

"Fine by me. If this is really a beast, just kill it and do it quickly. The mayor's riding my ass." Johnny pushed open the door and stepped out into the frigid Alaskan air. He inhaled deeply, trying to rid his lungs of the smoky air in

Hanta's cabin. He allowed the door to slam shut behind him, then marched down the porch steps and across the frozen expanse to his snowmobile.

"No problem, sheriff!" Hanta called after him. "I'll kill you an Amarok."

Johnny shook his head. Not wanting to give Hanta a chance to get another word in, he fired up his snowmobile and gassed it. Leaving the abrasive hermit behind, he sped down the trail toward Mrs. Grover's place.

Chapter 10

Kendra Grover's house was nearer to town than the previous attacks but still not within the city limits. From the patio, Johnny could see the vague outlines of the houses below. The sky was awash in streaks of orange and red. Shadows blanketed Port Luck. The light from fireplaces flickered through the windows of the buildings. In the dying light of the day, they almost looked like red eyes blinking at him.

The door to her house creaked open when he knocked, his fist inadvertently pushing it inward. No light came through the opening. The hair on the back of Johnny's neck stood on end. His hand flew to his waist and gripped his pistol. Sliding it from its holster, he raised it to ready position. "Mrs. Grover? It's Sheriff Myers," he called into the darkness.

A slight rustling arose from within the cabin. He raised his pistol slightly and pushed the door open the rest of the way with his left hand. Johnny stared into the complete darkness. When a pale, skeletal face emerged from the darkness, Johnny's muscles tightened. If his finger had been on the trigger, he would have pulled it. Luckily, the marines were very strict about trigger discipline.

"Mrs. Grover?" he asked. "Are you ok?" He lowered the pistol to his side but didn't holster it.

Kendra Grover stepped into the light, her emaciated frame barely held up by her trembling knees. "Johnny?" she asked in a meager voice.

"Yes, ma'am. You called the station and said something ate your cats?"

Recognition dawned on her face as she took another small step forward. Tears welled in her eyes, threatening to burst the dam and send her into a crying fit.

Johnny slipped the pistol back into its holster.

She reached up and gripped his face, shaking violently against his skin. Her icy fingers stung his face. "Bless you!" she cried. "Thank you so much for coming." She pulled his head down and pressed her cold lips against his cheeks; her tears left a wet residue on his skin.

"Of course, Mrs. Grover. What's going on?"

The tears poured down her cheeks. She wobbled and nearly fell. Johnny grabbed her by the elbows to support her. "Why don't we get you back inside?" Johnny suggested. He guided her inside the dimly lit home, his hands fumbling against the wall. He found the switch and illuminated the room.

The state of the house shocked him. There was a solid layer of trash covering the entire floor. Dirt and mold caked the walls and clung to the ceilings. The couches were stained yellow, presumably from cat urine. The stench of it punched Johnny in the face. Burying his nose into his coat, he decided it was definitely cat urine.

Mrs. Grover took a seat on the couch and shoved a pile of trash off the seat next to her.

Johnny held up his hands. "No, thank you. I've been sitting all day," he lied. "So, what's going on?"

She nodded and trembled as she spoke. "There's a monster out there."

Johnny eyed her. "A monster?" If it was any other time, he would have considered this the ramblings of a crazy old woman, but given everything that happened over the last few days, he was inclined to believe her. Trying to appear unalarmed, he strutted around the room. He studied the rows of pictures decorating the mantle of the fireplace.

"Yes, a monster," she blurted. "It was running around in the woods. As soon as I could see it, it disappeared again."

"So you didn't get a good look at it?"

She shook her head. "No, but I heard it. It sounded heavy."

"Heavy?"

"Yes, heavy. Its steps were loud. I could hear branches and tree limbs snapping."

Johnny rubbed his chin. "And then it killed your cats?"

The woman's eyes drifted off toward the kitchen. "My cats?" she muttered softly.

Johnny patiently waited for the woman to return to the present, making a mental note to discuss her current condition with Dr. Davies.

"Oh, my poor kitties." She sobbed, burying her face into her hands.

"What happened to them?"

She pointed one shaky finger toward the back door. "They're out there. I ... I must have forgotten to bring them in. Oh, god. I was so scared."

"It's ok. We all would have been." He tried to put on his most empathetic voice. "I'm going to take a look. You stay here, OK?" Not wanting to give her a chance to object, he turned and crept across the room to the back door. His fingers wrapped around the icy handle. Slowly, he pulled the door open, revealing a dark expanse of densely packed snow behind the house. He strained his eyes to see, but the setting sun was already blocked out by the trees. Retrieving his flashlight from his belt, he clicked it on and scanned the area from within the house. The yellow-tinted beam darted across the snow and reflected off ice dangling from tree branches.

Once satisfied nothing was in the immediate area, he stepped outside. The snow crunched under the weight of his boots. Moving cautiously, he constantly scanned the area with his flashlight, the beam reflecting off the pristine snow. It ran across something red, but he moved the flashlight before his brain could register the image. Snapping the flashlight back to the disturbed spot, the light washed over a patch of blood that had already congealed in a pool. His eyes snapped to blood droplets that created a trail leading into the woods.

Johnny drew his pistol again and took another cautious step. He set his pistol hand at the ready on top of the hand holding the flashlight. Prepared to fire at a moment's notice, he approached the trees. Slowly, he continued to sweep the flashlight back and forth. He strained his eyes against the blackening sky, desperate to find her damn cats so he could get the hell out of there. Besides his time in the marines, he had been here his entire life, and never once did the snowy terrain make him uneasy. But he was feeling uneasy now. Despite the rapidly falling temperature, sweat built up under his jacket.

He forced himself to go slower with the flashlight. He managed to stop the light while passing over a clump of hair on the ground. He sucked in a deep breath and approached it. Each crunch of the snow beneath his boots echoed through the trees. His heart beat faster with each step. It had to be Mrs. Grover's dead cat; he knew that. But for some reason, that feeling of uneasiness turned to fear.

Standing over the deceased cat, Johnny couldn't seem to wrap his mind around what he was seeing. It was a black and white cat, but everything was wrong. It lay flat against the snow, unmoving legs sprawled out to each side. He searched his brain for a word to describe the cat, and the only thing he could think of was... flat.

He glanced around the woods, aware of the utter silence enveloping him. He listened for any of the regular sounds he was accustomed to hearing. No bugs, no owls, no animals scurried about. It was as if everything in the woods had died with the cat.

Cautiously, he bent down and grasped the cat's deflated paws. When he lifted it, he understood why it looked the way it did. Whatever killed the cat had skinned it. There was a perfect dissection from under the chin to the tail. He held it in front of his eyes and examined the ghastly scene.

Each incision seemed to be done with surgical precision. The flesh wasn't simply torn away like a wild animal would do. Those were clean lines. Whatever killed the feline must have held it down and stripped it with intent. Johnny's stomach did somersaults.

A branch cracked to his left. For the second time in as many days, he found himself scanning the darkened forest with his gun drawn. He expected something to lunge out of the darkness, but nothing came. He wasn't sure how long he stood like that, but it was long enough for his gun hand to become shaky under the pistol's weight.

Slowly backtracking out of the forest, another branch snapped. Then another. They came from different directions. He spun from his left to his right and back again. Something was out there with him. He could feel the oppressive gaze of the unseen entity. His breath quickened with his heart rate. Sweeping his gun from side to side, he searched for the source of the noises, his fingers trembling.

Once again, everything fell silent. He lowered his pistol slightly to give his aching arm a reprieve but continued scanning the trees with his eyes.

When another branch cracked, he ran. The direction of the Grover's house wasn't a clear path, so he ran blindly through the woods. Branches licked at his cheeks. A stinging sensation radiated across his face as superficial cuts opened up. The muscles of his legs cramped. The cold air stung his lungs. Right as he thought he might collapse, he exploded through the trees and made it a few more feet before his foot caught a stone. During his fall, he must have turned because his shoulder blades smashed into the ground. The impact expelled the air from his lungs. He lay there dazed for a moment before a sound snapped him back to focus.

It sounded like a laugh, but not a human's. It reminded Johnny of a hyena on the Discovery channel. It was the awful cackle of a predator enjoying the hunt.

He scrambled back to his feet. No monster exploded through the trees. Nothing jumped down and devoured him. Walking backward, he slowly retreated to Mrs. Grover's back door. He stuck his left hand out behind him, terrified to take his eyes off the forest. His numb fingers found purchase on the metal door handle and fumbled at it clumsily before he managed to push it open.

He stepped through the threshold and pushed the door closed behind him. Pressing his back against the wall, his chest heaved up and down in a non-rhythmic plea for air. Clenching his eyes shut, he tried to focus on slowing his breathing. A memory from his time in the Middle East flashed in his mind. He sucked in a breath and held it for ten seconds. He repeated the process, and within a few minutes, his breathing stabilized.

When he opened his eyes, he was surprised to see Mrs. Grover standing in front of him. Her skeletal features appeared haunting in the minimal light of her house. She took one step forward. "You saw it, didn't you?" Her voice was full of fear and angst.

"I, uh ..." He searched for a way to explain what just happened. "I didn't see anything," he lied.

Mrs. Grover gave him a dejected look, recoiling into herself and crossing her frail arms.

"But I would feel better if you came back to town with me. We could put you up at the Jacksons for a night or two. Just until we know it's safe."

She smiled at him. "Thank you," she whispered.

The two of them walked through the house toward the front door. Johnny stopped as they passed the mantle of the fireplace. There was a picture he hadn't noticed earlier. It was a photo of Ben Grover. The young man was smiling triumphantly atop the peak of some mountain. He was wearing a blue jacket and orange hat, just like the one found on their John Doe a few nights ago. He held the photo up for Mrs. Grover to see. "Is this Ben?"

The old woman nodded. "That's my Ben." She said it with such pride.

Johnny's heart shattered for the woman. She was about to find out the last remaining member of her family was dead.

"He should be home any day now." She touched the picture. "He loves that silly jacket. It was his father's, ya know? It means the world to him."

And now it's shredded up, along with his body, in the basement of Dr. Davies's house, he thought. His eyes drifted across the old woman as he examined her. He was afraid if he told her about Ben she might die on the spot. He decided at that moment that it wasn't the time. It could wait until he got her safely back to town and for Earnest to examine her.

"He's a fine boy. Let's get going now," Johnny said, taking Mrs. Grover by the arm.

Sliding the deadbolt back, Johnny cracked the door and looked around in front of the house. He felt silly running from a monster. Still, he couldn't deny what happened to him in the woods. With all the strangeness going on, maybe his reactions weren't unreasonable after all. It was only a few feet of open terrain from the front door to the snowmobile, yet Johnny was terrified to walk it. It reminded him of his first firefight in Afghanistan. He had to run across an open street while under fire and had actually pissed his pants when a bullet ricocheted off a car in front of him and glanced off his helmet. His squad never let him live that down. They called him Waterfall for weeks after. A small smile cracked his bruised and battered face. He hoped he didn't piss himself again.

The two made it to the snowmobile without further incident. In fact, they made it all the way to town with no other issues. He dropped Mrs. Grover at the Jacksons. Jeremiah Jackson ran the town's general store, and he was known for putting people up in his spare room. Once Johnny made sure she was safely inside, he drove straight home.

He crept into his bedroom, where Amy lay in their bed. He listened to her steady breathing to be sure she was asleep. Tiptoeing through their room and into the bathroom, he quietly pulled the door shut behind him before dipping into the closet. Opening his gun safe as quietly as possible, he retrieved his twelve gauge and a box of shells. Muscle memory kicked in, and he locked the action open. One after another, he slid shells into the tube. Once the shotgun was fully loaded, he racked a round into the chamber, wincing at the loud noise. He turned the light off and quietly opened the door to their bedroom.

Amy was sitting up in bed. Her face morphed from one of anger to one of concern when Johnny stepped into the room with the shotgun.

He walked across the room and wedged the shotgun between the bed and nightstand before collapsing into their bed. He rolled to face his wife.

"There's something in the woods."

Chapter 11

Dr. Davies closed and locked the front door to his practice. He reached up and pulled the sign off his window that declared his business Open. It was a routine he completed every night, but with all of the strangeness happening in the town, he was thinking more and more about never doing it again.

His eyes drifted to a photo of his late wife hanging on the wall. Her beautiful smile and bright eyes stared back at him. Before she died, Earnest had promised her they would retire and move to Florida. More than once, they joked about getting a tan and wrestling an alligator. That promise died with his wife.

He shuffled to the kitchen to retrieve a bottle of Tylenol. Every winter, the cold caused more and more stiffness in his joints. A sigh escaped him as he poured himself a glass of water to chase the pills down with. The thoughts of the Florida sun faded from his mind. He knew he would die in this town. These were his people, and he would treat them until he couldn't.

He drained the rest of the water and set the empty glass back on the table. Turning to his left, he grabbed the bag of dog food off the counter. Shaking it, he said, "Come on, boy, it's dinner time." He listened for the sound of his old canine's nails scraping across the wood floor. Nothing. He shook the bag again. A pang of panic struck Earnest's heart when Doc didn't come running. The dog never missed a meal. The old boy was getting chunky in his age and was quick to scarf down his food. Earnest listened intently for any sign of his dog.

From outside his house, he heard the muffled sound of a dog bark. The bag of dog food fell, bits of brown kibble scattering across the kitchen floor. They crunched under his feet as he scrambled over them. Earnest rushed down the hall to the back door only to see it standing ajar. Frigid air blasted through the opening, pushing snow deeper into the house. A shiver tore through his body as the icy wind hit his exposed skin.

"Motherfucker," he said under his breath. The back door had been messed up for at least a year. The dog jumping against it or a strong draft through the house would be enough to throw it open. That was the first time Doc had run off since he was a puppy, though. Earnest knew he had trained the dog better; something must have drawn him out. Cursing to himself, he pulled on his coat and rushed outside, being sure to slam the door closed behind him. The door clicked into place and didn't re-open.

Frozen air ripped across his face, its icy sting turning his cheeks red within seconds. The faint rumble of a snowmobile in the distance whirled through the air. The vehicle was probably miles away, and the sound was carried by the aggressive winds only to be washed away in its howl.

Doc barked again. Earnest shielded his eyes from the flurries of snow beginning to kick up at an accelerated pace. He could make out the silhouette of his dog frantically running back and forth in front of the trees. The incoming snow storm amplified and muffled the dog's barks and whimpers to create a distorted mockery of his wailing.

"Doc!" He took a few steps forward, his tennis shoes sinking into the snow. Water permeated the thin material. Earnest winced from the icy pinpricks stabbing the bottoms of his feet. His foot smacked into some unseen obstacle buried in the snow, and cried out as he fought to right himself. Pain burned its way up from his toes. Doc stopped pacing and jerked his head in Earnest's direction. Fighting through the pain, Earnest patted his hands on his thighs. "Come here, boy."

The dog stood completely still, his hackles raised. Something rustled in the trees. Doc turned away from his owner and released a loud growl.

"Doc!" Earnest called again.

Doc ignored the call and sprinted into the woods after some unseen creature.

"No! Come here, Doc!" Earnest pleaded. Going after the dog, he ran toward the trees as fast as his old, stiff legs would take him. "Doc! Doc!" He held up his arms to shield his face as he sprinted into the forest. He chased the echoes of his dog's barking deeper and deeper into the abyss-like darkness of the forest. The only light came when momentary slivers of moonlight broke through the thick branches overhead. He continued calling his dog, but Doc seemed only to run farther.

He reached desperately for a nearby tree, nearly falling in the process. His bare hand found the rough texture of the tree's bark. He leaned against it, allowing it to support his full body weight. Helplessly, he listened as the sound of his dog's barks grew fainter. The dog was too fast; he would never catch him. His head rested against the tree, his chest heaving up and down as he fought to suck in enough air, which dried out his mouth and burned the back of his throat. He considered turning back, but when he turned around, he couldn't make out the trail behind him.

He looked in every direction. The trail he had blazed through the trees had disappeared. The forest had swallowed him. He tried to look at the moon to get a sense of direction, but between the trees and the clouds, he couldn't tell where it was. Pain ripped through his chest as the panicked beats of his heart increased. There was no way he would survive in the woods overnight. He had only grabbed a light coat; hell, he didn't even have gloves on. Forgetting about his beloved dog, he attempted to backtrack to the house. He scrambled blindly in the dark, feeling for anything recognizable. Every step felt wrong and unfamiliar.

After a few steps, the sound of Doc's whine froze him in place. The cry was high-pitched and full of anguish. Earnest's heart sank as the whimper cut short. "Doc! Doc!"

Earnest sprinted in the direction he thought the whining had come from. He slipped on a patch of ice and landed face first on the ground. Blood erupted from his nose and gushed like a geyser. Dragging his sleeve across his face to wipe the blood away, he turned to see what he had slipped on but couldn't make it out. The viscous fluid shimmered in a beam of moonlight that wrestled through a crack in the canopy overhead. He submerged his hand into the warm, sticky liquid and knew it immediately for what it was—blood. Yanking his hand away, strands of it clung to his fingers and dripped down his sleeves.

He stood as quickly as his old joints would allow. "Come on, Doc." His calls were growing weaker. "Please, boy," he said, almost to himself.

The hair on his arms stood up as the feeling of being watched came over him. He looked around for any sign of his dog or anything else that might be out there. A lump formed in his throat.

To his left, obscured in the darkness, was something massive. He couldn't see it—it was more akin to sensing it. An overwhelming sense of dread flooded his body. The darkness seemed darker there, somehow more devoid of light than the surrounding forest. He stared at it and begged his eyes to form an image his mind could process.

Two yellow eyes appeared in the blackness.

Earnest's body reacted before his mind did. He sprinted in the opposite direction before he was even entirely sure what he saw. Somewhere in the primal subconscious of his mind, he knew it was a predator. The thunderous sound of feet smashing into the earth behind him confirmed it. Turning right and left, he sprinted in different directions in a panicked attempt to lose his pursuer. Out of the corner of his eye, he caught a glimpse of a clearing and his back door. The view was fleeting, but he turned and ran for it with every bit of strength he could summon.

He sensed the beast gaining on him. Its enormous presence loomed right behind him. Monstrous paws nipped at his heels. The end was coming. Earnest clenched his eyes and braced for the impact.

Then it sprinted past him. He could feel a rush of wind as it passed just to his left. The small view of his back door disappeared behind a hairy mass now standing mere feet in front of him.

He attempted to stop himself but lost his footing. He collapsed to the ground at the creature's feet. Quickly, he scrambled to his hands and knees. Crawling through the snow, he attempted to gain purchase. The beast approached from behind, standing above him; its shadow taunted Earnest. A fleeting thought ran through Earnest's mind. *It's tormenting me.*

He managed to get his feet underneath him and resumed his sprint back into the forest, away from his house and the monster. His feet sank into the snow, the cold biting into his skin. Having to work harder to get through the deep snow, his legs fatigued quickly. He ran until he was once again on the verge of collapse. His vision darkened around the edges. Finding a large tree, he propelled himself around it, doing his best to appear small behind it.

Heavy footsteps fell all around him. They swirled in with the howling wind, echoing everywhere.

He squeezed his eyes shut. The sound of growling screamed in his ears.

It fell silent.

He opened one eye, then the other. There were no heavy footsteps. No growls erupted from the darkness. He listened intently but heard no sign of the creature that chased him. Even the screams of the wind seemed to die down. It was as if it had all been his imagination.

A sigh of relief slipped through his lips. He steeled his nerves and was preparing to move from his hiding place when something wet hit the bridge of his nose. He wiped at the substance. It smudged across his face, mixing with the dried blood from his broken nose. Glancing up, his heart dropped.

High in the tree was an enormous black figure.

He spun away from the tree and backpedaled as the beast watched him. Its massive arms raised above its head. It gripped something in its hands. There was a brief moment when time seemed to stop. The beast shattered the illusion when it launched the object at Earnest.

It smashed into his chest, expelling the air from his lungs. The weight knocked him off his feet, planting Earnest hard onto the ground. He had only a second to examine the massive heap pinning him down. Despite the darkness, he could make out Doc's snout. The poor dog's tongue flopped lifelessly from his mouth. His lifeless eyes glared into his owner's.

A single sob escaped Earnest before the creature leaped upon him.

Chapter 12

Without getting dressed, Hanta exited his small hut. The frigid, pre-dawn air enveloped his nude body. The soles of his bare feet burned against the ice that formed overnight on his deck. Stretched out before him was the expanse of the Alaskan wilderness, still shrouded in darkness.

Hanta knew the people in Port Luck considered him an outsider. To him, it was a compliment. The hard life of an outdoorsman was all he knew. Even the people who were hard enough to live in a rural town like Port Luck considered him too hard for their society.

He forced himself to stand there, breathing in the frozen air. The shivering started in his fingers, slowly spreading outward until he was convulsing uncontrollably. Hanta bit his lip, fighting to linger a few minutes longer. The crest of the morning sun broke the tree line. Smiling at the warm rays licking his face, he finally relented to Alaska's power.

Inhaling a final blast of icy air, he turned and entered his hut.

Fully awake, he crowded the fireplace to wait for the warmth to return to his body. The pain from his defrosting digits felt exhilarating. The warmth crawled across his skin like a wave washing over sand. Once he was sufficiently heated, he tossed clothes out of a hamper and onto the nearest chair. Throwing them about, he searched until he settled on his uniform for the day. He quickly dressed and laced up his boots.

On the small table in the corner of the room rested a large Bowie knife, a smaller straight blade, and a re-volver. He tucked the Bowie knife into a sheath on his left hip and the smaller knife into his right boot. Lifting up the revolver, he pressed the cylinder release. The cylin-der popped open, exposing the empty chambers. Hanta opened the drawer of a nearby nightstand. Shells rolled around, clanging loudly against one another. He method-ically loaded the pistol with six rounds, then spun the cylinder before snapping it back into place and tucking the piece into the waistband at his back. He knew spinning it did nothing, but it had become a habit at that point. One time in town, he had shown the revolver to a man at the bar. The man saw him spin the cylinder and called it "guy code," whatever that meant.

His long gun stood on its stock in the opposite corner of the room. He picked up the rifle and slid the bolt part way back to confirm there was a round in the chamber. The weight of it felt heavy in his hands. His finger slid into the grooves his father had whittled into the wood to give him a better grip while shooting. It was questionable if that actually worked, but it was all Hanta had ever known.

He retrieved a few more rounds and dropped them into his pocket, then tucked the revolver into his belt before slinging the rifle over his shoulder and stepping back into the cold.

He trudged through the knee-deep snow to the side of the house, where a blue tarp, weighed down by heavy snow, covered his snowmobile. Grabbing the edge of the tarp, he yanked as hard as he could. It came away, sending the snow flying.

Hanta flipped the key, causing the engine to roar to life. Standing next to it, he revved the motor a few times to warm it up. Simultaneously, he climbed onto the snowmobile and pushed it into gear. The machine rumbled beneath his legs until he released the brake, speeding off into the woods.

The blistering cold slapped at his cheeks and chapped his lips. He embraced the stinging sensation for a few more minutes before it became too much and he was forced to pull his mask over his face. Most people would complain about the cold, but he loved it. He loved the Alaskan outdoors and everything that came with it. It reminded him of his late mother. She was Inuit and proud of it, even though she married a white man. His father's family had lived in Alaska for generations. His family was one of the original Russian families that settled on the frontier back when Russia still owned the Alaskan territory.

He turned onto a well-used trail and proceeded up the incline leading to the Graham's place. He wasn't exactly sure what he would find there, but he assumed it would be the best place to start. He brought the snowmobile to a stop a few yards from their cabin.

Three dogs were in a pen on the side of the house. They brandished their teeth and barked, the hair on their hackles rising.

As he dismounted his ride, the front door flew open and Mrs. Graham emerged, waving a double-barrel shotgun. "Who the fuck are you?" she demanded.

He raised his hands and casually walked toward her.

"My name is Hanta. The sheriff hired me to hunt whatever attacked your family."

She lowered the rifle. "You're here to kill that fucking monster?"

"I'm going to try to ma'am." He lowered his hands and continued his approach.

The woman screamed at the dogs, and they fell silent, one of them whimpering in the corner.

Hanta rested one of his boots on the edge of the porch and leaned against his knee. "I'm sorry for your loss, ma'am," he said, trying his best to look remorseful.

"I'm sure you are. Just kill that damn thing." She retreated back into the house, slamming the door behind her.

Hanta kicked off the porch and trudged through the snow toward the back of the house. As he passed the dogs' cage, he paused. He squatted and pulled a few pieces of jerky from his bagsliding one to each of the dogs. "Good boys." He stood up and brushed his hands off.

When he rounded the side of the house, the area of the attack became apparent. Despite the heavy snowfall, blood still stained the trees and the snow surrounding them, the heavy branches protecting the area. He was grateful for that but disappointed in the lack of tracks. The snow outside of the cover of the trees seemed to have erased them from existence.

He unslung the rifle from his shoulder and gripped it with both hands, holding it in the ready position as he crept into the forest. He followed the trail of blood smeared on the trees until he came to a clearing. The area was much the same as the other; there was blood on the trees but not on the snow and no tracks showed. He lowered the rifle and prepared to exit the woods when something caught his eye.

To his right was what looked to be a yellow powder. He approached it, squatting down to get a better look. Removing his glove, he ran his fingers through the powder. It was fertilizer. Hanta smiled. There was only one place around there where you could find that powdery substance.

Hanta knew about the old fertilizer facility up in the hills, a few miles past the Graham place. His father told him it had once been a good source of income for the community, before the town was abandoned for the first time. It was never reopened.

Hanta slung his rifle over his back and continued his trek through the woods. At that pace, he could reach the old buildings before sundown. Since the animal only attacked at night, he wanted to find a good hiding place before sunset.

He emerged from the trees to see another clearing. In the distance, he could make out the dome-shaped buildings of the fertilizer processing plant poking above the trees. He paused to take in his surroundings. The clearing was packed with pristine snow except for a trail leading toward the plant. Trail was the wrong word for it; it was more like displaced snow—freshly disturbed.

Recognizing this as his opportunity, he doubled back to the Graham's house and retrieved his snowmobile. Parking it at the edge of the tree line, he approached the trail.

Hanta weighed his options before deciding to take the more cautious approach. He took a few steps back into the trees and began creeping along the edge of the clearing. He gently unslung the rifle and pressed it to his shoulder.

He planned to walk completely around the clearing and then find high ground to scout the facility, but after only a few feet, a horrific smell hit his nose. He recognized it immediately as rotting flesh. As a hunter, he had encountered many dead animals in the woods throughout his years and knew that smell well.

A tree on the edge of the clearing showed signs of trauma. Deep claw marks were buried in the trunk, disfiguring the bark. He approached it cautiously, looking in all directions for any potential traps. When he reached the tree, he rubbed the claw marks with his hand, and his blood ran cold. The claw marks were each as wide as three of his fingers and dug impossibly deep into the wood. Blood stains ran down the bark, forcing his head up to get a better view of where the blood was coming from.

Above him, the desecrated carcass of a deer stood pinned to the tree with branches. The carcass was split down the middle, the chest and stomach cavities devoid of organs. The front legs were snapped and posed in unnatural angles. Large branches appeared to have been broken off nearby trees and jammed into the poor creature, impaling it to the tree.

Hanta's first instinct was to run. This wasn't a regular bear or wolf. It was something much worse. Images of sitting in his grandfather's lap listening to stories about the monster that destroyed the town flashed before his eyes. A wave of nervous heat washed over him despite the frigid cold.

He slowly inhaled a deep breath before releasing it through his nose. The wave of heat subsided, and he regained his senses. He looked out over the field. The trudged-up white snow marking the path the monster would take sat about two hundred yards away, clearly visible.

He glanced back at the dead animal hanging in the trees, an idea formulating in his mind.

There were two sturdy-looking tree branches on either side of the deer. The one closest to the clearing sat slightly higher than the other. He realized he could sit on one of the branches and use the other to steady his rifle. The stench of the decaying animal would mask his scent.

A smile crept across his face. He would kill the thing tonight.

Chapter 13

In his sleepy haze, Johnny couldn't tell if the phone was actually ringing or if it was in his dreams. He smacked his hand around clumsily against the bedside table. It sifted through the various items he kept there, sending several things crashing to the floor. After a few attempts, his groggy fingers found the phone.

"Hello?" His voice came out hoarse. He coughed to clear his throat, then immediately tried to swallow. The back of his throat felt like sandpaper. Ever since his time in the marines, he had developed a pretty intense snoring condition that had caused, on more than one occasion, Amy to joke about filing for divorce.

"Good morning, sleepy head," Amy replied. Johnny glanced at the LED clock in the corner of the room. It was already eleven a.m. He rubbed his eyes and rolled onto his back.

"It's the only day I've had off in weeks." Johnny stretched his free arm above his head, causing the joints to pop in protest. He pulled the cell phone away from his ear and switched it to speaker phone.

"I know. I'm sorry I woke you up, but I'm worried."

Johnny sat straight up. Adrenaline dumped into his veins, forcing the drowsiness to vanish instantly. "Why? What happened?"

"Well, nothing really. A couple of the parents mentioned Dr. Davies didn't open the office today."

Johnny allowed his posture to relax slightly. "Good. That old man hasn't taken a day off in forty years." He chuckled.

"It's just not like him, ya know? Mrs. Morris said she even knocked on the door."

"And he didn't answer?"

"Nope. She said the house was completely silent."

Johnny tossed the covers aside, the chill immediately assaulting his bare legs. He pushed himself up from the bed and walked into the closet. "Alright, babe. I'm getting dressed now. I'll head over there and check on him."

Amy's normally cheerful tone returned to what he called her teacher's voice. "Thanks, babe! I love you."

Johnny grunted out an affirmation before replying, "Love you more." He tossed the phone onto the bed and retrieved the remainder of his clothes from the closet. Sighing at the thought of another long day, He clipped on his gun and badge before spinning on his heels and exiting the house.

His first thought was to call the station to see if his deputy might have heard anything. Ultimately, Johnny decided against it. He would have to pass by the station on the way to Earnest's house and could just stop in to get some coffee and ask Brian if he had heard anything.

He arrived at the station a few minutes later. Before going inside, he looked around at the town. Despite the town being lightly populated, there were usually tons of people going about their day. On a weekday morning, he expected to see people packing the diner, coming out of the general store, or entering town hall. None of that was happening. The town was eerily quiet. Subtly, Johnny let his hand drift toward his gun while he scanned his surroundings. Behind him, the door to the station flew open.

"You know it's your day off, right?" Brian teased.

Johnny slid his hand off the grip of his pistol. "Hell, I'm the sheriff. I never get days off."

He followed Brian into the station.

"I sure hope I never find out," Brian replied.

"I believe you will," Johnny said. "And I think you'll hate it even more than me." He made his way across the lobby to a little end table with a half-full pot of coffee resting on the coffeemaker. "Hey, any chance you've heard from Earnest?" His hand trembled slightly as he poured coffee into a small styrofoam cup. He clenched his eyes and forced himself to draw in a long, slow breath. Amy's words danced in his mind, chiding him for relying so heavily on caffeine. Sighing, he filled his cup to the brim and decided he would try to cut back on the coffee... some day.

Brian gave him a quizzical look. "Dr. Davies?"

Johnny nodded and pulled the cup to his nose, taking in its rich aroma.

Brian shook his head, "No, sir. Should I have?"

He took a sip from his coffee. Involuntarily wincing from the heat, he forced down a large gulp and exhaled harshly. "My wife called this morning, said he never opened his office."

Brian threw his arms up at his side. "I haven't heard anything, sir, and as you can tell, it's been pretty quiet around here."

Johnny looked back over his shoulder. "Careful what you ask for, kid. A cop who says it's too quiet is a cop who's asking for a bad day. Has it been like this all morning?"

"Yes, sir. There were some people coming and going first thing, mostly parents dropping their kids off at school. I haven't seen many people since."

Johnny took another large sip of his coffee, then tossed the half-full cup into the trash. He turned around and opened the station door. "Alright." Motioning toward the open door with his head, he said, "Come on, let's go check on ole Earnest."

The two men fired up their snowmobiles and drove toward the doctor's office. Johnny took his time scanning the windows as they sped past the shops. Jackson's General Store was open, but it didn't appear anyone was inside. Even the diner looked deserted. He slowed his snowmobile to take in his surroundings properly. Port Luck looked like a ghost town.

"Everything good, boss?" Brian asked.

Johnny shook his head. "No," he said flatly, then gassed his snowmobile.

They ran the machines as fast as they would go until they came to a stop in front of the doctor's house. Almost in unison, they dismounted and approached the front door. Johnny knocked several times while calling the doctor's name. After a few tries, he turned to Brian and said, "Stay here. I'm going to go around to the back door."

"He might not be home," Brian protested.

"It's not looking like it, but I've lived here my entire life, and he's never closed up shop."

Johnny walked around the side of the house, trudging toward the back door through the thick snow. He stopped dead in his tracks. The snow behind the house was disturbed, and a set of footprints led into the woods. He cautiously approached them, bending down to examine them more closely.

"Brian!"

Brian leaped off the porch, landing hard in the snow. He sprinted around the side of the building. "Everything alright, sheriff?" he called as Johnny came into view.

"It looks like he went into the woods," Johnny said. He raised his hand and pointed at the set of tracks.

Brian looked around. "I don't see any tracks leading out."

Johnny stood back up and shook his head. "Me either." He scanned the tree line for a moment longer before slowly unclipping his holster. Sliding his pistol out, he raised it to the low ready position. Brian nervously mirrored the sheriff's motions. "Stay close," Johnny ordered.

Johnny crept toward the tree line. The leafless trees in front of him felt menacing in a way that was becoming all too familiar to the sheriff. He continued walking along the lone set of tracks, his eyes bouncing from tree to tree. Brian kept pace, walking a few feet behind. Johnny could hear his deputy's breathing as it sped up. He felt his own heart rate increase with each step.

Johnny froze, and an icy shot ripped through him. There was something in the snow. He crouched and examined a new footprint. The monstrosity was unlike anything he had ever seen. Motioning for Brian to join him, he returned his gaze to the tree line.

Brian rushed up and came to a knee beside him.

"You ever seen anything like that?" Johnny asked.

Brian shook his head. "No, sir."

The footprint was nearly twice as long as a man's. The front resembled a wolf's paw, with four long finger-like marks protruding from a mostly oval center. A long, skinny line protruded from the rear, ending in a sharp point.

"It could be a hoax," Brian offered.

Johnny shook his head. "A week ago, I'd have written it off, but something strange is going on around here." Johnny withdrew his phone from his pocket. "Watch the treeline for a sec." Brian crept a few steps forward and angled his pistol toward the trees, while Johnny positioned his phone so he could get the entire footprint on the screen and snapped a picture. "Let's keep moving." He returned the phone to his pocket and stood up.

The two of them continued their trek deeper into the woods. Frigid air nipped at the exposed skin on their faces. They rounded a tree to see a streak of red-stained snow stretching out before them. Johnny's heart slammed against his chest. He continued creeping forward, careful to avoid the blood-soaked snow. His eyes flicked quickly from tree to tree, scanning for danger, when they landed on something. Sticking out from behind a tree was a pair of legs. Shoeless, frost-covered toes pointed toward the sky. Johnny stopped and dropped to a knee.

He pointed it out to Brian and waited to see the realization on the young officer's face. He watched as Brian's face shifted from concentration to realization and, finally, to horror. Once he was confident his deputy grasped the severity of the situation, Johnny stood then rounded the tree first and released a pained gasp.

The scene before him was ripped right from a nightmare. His friend's lower half rested against the base of the tree. The body had been torn completely in half at the waistline. Coagulated pools of blood covered the ground and filled every crevice of the tree. Organs spilled out in every direction, decorating the scene with entrails.

Johnny involuntarily stumbled backward, losing his balance and crashing to the ground. From his new vantage point, he could see a trail of blood running up the tree. His eyes traced the path up about twenty feet, where the top half of the good doctor came into view. Earnest's torso hung high in the tree, a pair of broken deer antlers protruding from his chest. Even from that distance, Johnny could tell the deer antlers were embedded into the tree, pinning his friend's corpse in place. A look of sheer terror consumed the dead man's face.

Johnny had seen awful things as a marine. The deserts of Afghanistan were filled with corpses. He had seen more terrible things as sheriff, but nothing had prepared him for this. He screamed. From somewhere deep inside, he released the pain and fear he felt. For a split second, the scream filled the air.

Then Brian appeared at his side and covered his mouth. His large hands wrapped firmly around Johnny's face, pinning him against the ground. "Sheriff, calm down." Brian's voice was calm and reassuring.

Johnny sucked in a deep breath through his nose. He nodded for Brian to release his grip.

Slowly, Brian let Johnny go. "Are you ok, boss?"

Johnny rocked up to a knee. Lowering his head, he sucked in a few more calming breaths, then stood back up and dusted the snow from his pants. "No, Brian," he said as his eyes drifted back up the tree. "I don't think any of us are ok." The two men stared at the massacre in front of them, neither entirely sure what to do next.

"Ok," Johnny said, "we gotta be professional about this. It's a crime scene. What do we do first?"

Brian pulled his cell phone from his pocket. "Photograph the scene," he answered. He unlocked his phone and opened the camera app. The young deputy proceeded to take pictures from multiple angles.

Johnny stood with his back to his deputy and scanned the woods for any sign of disturbance.

Brian tapped Johnny on the shoulder. "All done, sheriff."

Johnny sighed. "Alright, let's get his body down and get him inside. We'll store his body in the morgue until we can get in touch with the state."

"You think we need the troopers out here?" Brian asked incredulously. He had worked with the sheriff long enough to know the man hated working with the state or the feds. Johnny was always droning on about bureaucracy and the slow-moving wheels of justice. The sheriff constantly reminded Brian that they handled their own business out there. Once, Johnny had told Brian about the one time he called out the state troopers. Hunters found two bodies shredded by nine-millimeter rounds a few miles outside of town. Despite everyone knowing it was a meth-related shooting, the case was ruled a hunting accident by the troopers, and they never charged anyone with the shooting. Johnny had promised himself he wouldn't call the troopers ever again if he could help it.

Johnny shook his head. "Might need more than that." He stepped forward and grabbed what was left of Earnest's waist. "Grab the legs; let's get this over with." Brian joined him, holding Earnest's stiffened legs by the ankles. Together, the men lifted the half of the carcass and carried it through the woods. They made it inside, carried it down the stairs, and set it on an empty gurney in the center of the morgue.

Breathless, Brian hunched over and said through gasps, "The other half is going to be a whole lot harder."

"Yeah, I know. Let's just do it." Johnny started up the stairs but stopped when his phone rang. "Sheriff Myers," he said into the receiver.

"Johnny, it's Mayor Henry. We have a problem."

Johnny stifled a groan and mouthed the word mayor to Brian. The deputy rolled his eyes and whispered, "Speaker?"

Johnny clicked the speakerphone button before replying. "Mayor, I'm kind of in the middle of something right now." Johnny couldn't hide the annoyance in his voice.

Ignoring Johnny's tone, the mayor continued. "Well, you need to stop. We have an emergency!" He shouted the last word into the phone.

Usually, when the mayor had an emergency, it was more like a minor inconvenience to him or his family. "Ok, ok." Johnny soothed the excited mayor like a child. "What happened?"

"None of the cannery workers showed up for their shift today. None! Not a single one!" The mayor's voice went wild with panic again.

"Did anyone go down to the village and see if they were there? Maybe they're striking or something?" Johnny offered.

"No! Goddamn it, that's your fucking job, Johnny! Get your ass over there and check it out," he ordered.

Johnny sighed. "Ok, I'll finish up here and head right over."

"Now, you fucking buffoon!" the mayor screamed.

Johnny's muscles clenched. "Mayor, Earnest Davies is dead. I'm going to sort this out and then look into your missing cannery workers. I need you to contact the state troopers and get me some extra officers down here."

There was silence on the other end of the line.

After a moment, Johnny spoke. "Mayor, you still there?"

The mayor replied, but in a much more subdued tone. "What's going on, Johnny?"

Johnny relaxed a little. "Nothing good." He paused to steady his tone. "Get me those troopers. I'll call you once I get to the bunkhouse." Johnny ended the call and looked at Brian. "Let's hurry up and get Earnest in here," he said.

Chapter 14

It took nearly an hour to dislodge the top half of Earnest's body from the tree. The two men couldn't reach it, and Earnest didn't have a ladder in his house. They resorted to pulling up one of the snowmobiles, Brian standing on the seat and hoisting Johnny up.

Johnny managed to fight through the gut-wrenching sight of his friend's mangled corpse. Knowing the ghastly job would burn itself into his mind forever, he tried his best to let his mind wander. He thought back to all of the talks and wisdom the old doctor had shared over the years. At that moment, a realization struck him. Earnest wasn't a friend; he was a father figure. Earnest had been there for all of Johnny's life achievements, even seeing him off to the Marine Corps when his own father quit talking to him. The care packages Earnest sent to him were some of the only things that kept him going while he was overseas. The man even looked in on Amy while he was deployed.

Sighing, Johnny gave Earnest's torso a final tug, and the body came free from the deer antlers holding it in place. The blood-coated body slipped from his grasp. It free fell to the ground, smacking the snow with a squelch and sending bits of gore raining down around them. Johnny managed to squeeze his eyes shut at the last second—the last thing he needed was for the traumatic memory to get worse.

The two men quickly jumped off the snowmobile and moved to pick up the half corpse. They elected to stand on either side of it, grabbing it under the arms. Johnny shook his head. He hated thinking of Earnest's body as it rather than he, but it was a trick he learned in Afghanistan. It allowed him to dehumanize his fallen friends. He could stuff its death way down inside and deal with it later, allowing him to push on through his mission. The catch was he never really dealt with any of it. He just kept it compartmentalized in his mind.

They carried it inside, taking it down the stairs and into the morgue. The two men gasped for breath after carrying the body so far.

"You know," Brian said between pants, "I hate coming down here."

Johnny gave him a knowing smile. "Me too, buddy. It's always a bad day when I have to come down here."

Brian smiled. "That's not what I meant."

Johnny gave him a curious look.

"I watched a zombie movie where the dead people crawled out of the morgue. Scared the fuck out of me, boss." He waved his hand toward the cooler in the back of the room. "They came bursting right out of a cooler like that." Brian shook his whole body, exaggerating a shiver.

Johnny couldn't help himself. He chuckled at the ridiculous thought of his nearly seven-foot-tall deputy wetting his pants during a zombie movie. "Come on, we have more work to do," he said as he led the way back up the stairs. He made it about halfway up before stopping.

"What's wrong?" Brian asked.

Johnny looked around. "Earnest has a dog."

A look of realization came over Brian. "Shit. I haven't seen any sign of his dog."

Shaking his head. "Me either. Let's finish this. Hopefully Doc will turn up." He shrugged and trudged up the stairs.

They finished bringing in the rest of Earnest's remains. They found a large storage container in the shed and used it to scoop up the frozen organs lying on the ground. Johnny knew there wasn't much of a point and it might be a waste of time, but he couldn't stand the thought of animals getting hold of any more of Earnest. They continued the grizzly task until every speck of blood was cleaned up and deposited in the basement. When they were done, they locked up the doctor's house and mounted their snowmobiles.

"You good?" Brian asked in a solemn tone.

Johnny nodded. "No choice but to be." He revved the motor and nodded for Brian to do the same.

They gassed it toward the docks. The stillness of the afternoon caused Johnny's heart to skip a beat. There should have been people traveling to and from the docks with supplies, but they were alone. He looked over to Brain and could tell by the nervous movement of his eyes as he looked around that he shared the same concerns.

The inlet the town was founded on came into view ahead of them. Johnny knew the full story because Amy wouldn't stop talking about it when it was time to teach the town's history to a new class. When British Captain Nathaniel Portlock first founded the town, he had done so because of how easy it was to navigate the waters. It was later turned into a cannery and fishing town and even had a productive fertilizer plant before being abandoned in the forties.

A huge brown building that resembled a warehouse more than a bunkhouse sat across from the docks. The mayor's company built it when they realized they lacked enough locals to fully staff the cannery. They resorted to bringing in seasonal workers, who stayed in the bunkhouse "free of charge." That was what the workers were told, anyway.

Johnny knew better. The company would charge them for supplies, food, and water. It created a dangerous situation where the workers were making less than minimum wage, and it wasn't uncommon for many of them to actually owe the company money when they left for the season. As far as he was concerned, it was little better than slave labor.

They reached the side of the building and brought their snowmobiles to a stop. Johnny was about to dismount when deep gouges in the side of the wooden building caught his eye. His blood ran cold, a dagger of fear stabbing him in the heart.

He slid from his seat and approached the gouges. His fingers drifted over the indents as he took in the impressive size.

"What is it, sheriff?" Brian asked.

Johnny carefully stuck his fingers into the grooves. They disappeared entirely into the holes. Whatever animal made those marks had claws bigger than his whole hand. "I think ..." He trailed off, noticing there were more claw marks near the roof. "I think they're claw marks," he said. The realization that no sounds were coming from inside the building sent another chill down his spine. Motioning toward the front of the building with his head, he said, "Come on."

The two men trekked cautiously around the side, seeing more, albeit less aggressive, claw marks along the way. They turned the corner only to be greeted with a massive puddle of blood. Red liquid coated every part of the front porch like a poorly performed paint job. It dripped from the porch light, splashing into coagulating pools of gore. Streaks of blood coated the windows. It ran down the glass to the floor, seeping between the wooden planks. The door was pocked full of deep holes and slashes, and its metal exterior was peeled back like an aluminum can someone jabbed a knife into.

Johnny reached for his holster and drew his pistol. He waited a moment for the distinct click of Brian's holster releasing his pistol then moved across the porch. He did his best to avoid stepping on the chunks of skin intermixed with the blood. Maintaining trigger discipline, he reached in through the open door and patted around, searching for the light switch. When his fingers brushed against it, he hesitated there a moment, not sure if he was ready to see what was to come. Taking a deep breath, he flipped the switch.

Fluorescent lighting filled the room. It took a second for Johnny's eyes to adjust, but when they did, he had to fight the urge to puke.

The scene before him was something straight from a horror movie. In the many years he had spent fighting terrorists and the Taliban, he had never seen anything like it. Blood coated every surface. A ceiling fan in the center of the room spun, dark-red entrails dangling from the blades. The ruined intestines rained blood in all directions as it rotated. Dismembered and disemboweled corpses lay scattered around the room, bodily fluids draining from open chest cavities. The coppery stench of blood intertwined with the smell of decaying corpses to create a horrific malodor.

Standing right behind him, Johnny could feel Brian shudder at the gruesome sight. The young officer took several steps backward, losing his footing and tumbling off the deck into the snow.

Johnny quickly scanned the room again to be sure there were no signs of life before turning toward his deputy. Just as Brian had done for him back at Earnest's house, he hoisted the younger man back to his feet.

Brian's dark skin paled. He smacked his lips, and Johnny could see how much he was salivating. Fighting the urge to puke, Brian wiped his mouth. He left his sleeve resting over his face, covering his nose. "How many do you think are in there?" he asked.

Johnny turned his attention back to the door of the bunkhouse. "I don't know," he whispered. "But we have to check it out." Johnny pushed the door open a little wider and stepped inside. His police training told him to avoid stepping in blood as it would contaminate the crime scene, but the sea of it coating the entire floor told him that wasn't going to happen. He stepped as gingerly as he could manage. Blood and stringy bodily fluid clung to the bottoms of his boots as he walked farther into the bunkhouse. Each step created sickly sloshing and slurping sounds like he was wading through water, causing Brian to gag a few times.

Johnny kept his pistol at the ready as he approached the first body, which was the least mangled of them as far as he could see. It was a white man with a large, bushy beard. The cannery worker probably would have had a beer belly if it weren't for the open gashes running across it. Johnny knelt, careful not to dip his knee into the blood, and pressed his fingers against the man's neck. It felt like a pointless exercise, but he had to be sure.

He looked back at Brian and shook his head. They continued moving forward, bypassing the completely mangled corpses. Slowly, they cleared each room in the building. There was no animal or killer hiding in any of them. Each room was essentially the same. Disfigured body parts were tossed around haphazardly as if something had been playing with them.

When Johnny was satisfied that whatever had done this was no longer in the building, he holstered his pistol.

Brian stood next to the sheriff, shaking. His eyes were stretched wide, still taking in the grotesque display.

"Holster your weapon, Brian," Johnny ordered. Brian didn't respond. He continued shaking, his finger hovering dangerously close to the trigger. Johnny had seen that response too many times before. The human mind could only take so much before it shut down.

"Brian!" Johnny said much louder.

That snapped the deputy from his daze. He blinked a few times, forcing the bewildered look from his face. "Huh? What?" he stammered.

Johnny slowly extended a hand and placed it on the slide of Brian's pistol, forcing the weapon down. "Holster," Johnny pushed the weapon down a little more, "your weapon," he finished.

The deputy looked down at the pistol like he was surprised to see it. He had only pulled his weapon once before in the line of duty. One of the fishermen found a deer stuck in a fence, and the town veterinarian was confident the creature would die either way. Brian put it out of its misery. Now he had drawn it twice in one day. Brian slid the pistol into his holster and buttoned the strap.

"You good?" Johnny asked.

Brian opened his mouth to speak before gagging. He turned away from his boss and sprinted out of the building, not even attempting to avoid the enormous chunks of flesh strewn about the room.

Johnny sighed and followed his deputy.

Brian was on his hands and knees, vomiting into the snow. He heaved until nothing came out, then heaved a few more times. When he was done, he wiped his mouth on his sleeve and stood up.

"Are you good now?" Johnny asked, pulling the tattered remnants of the bunkhouse door closed behind him.

Brian shook his head. "Think I busted a blood vessel in my eye or something." He cracked a sad excuse for a smile. "What do we do now?"

Johnny looked around. The area around the bunkhouse was pristine. The snow was undisturbed, the building down by the docks seemed intact, and fishing boats floated gently in the waves. "We need to get back to town," he said over his shoulder as he walked back to his snowmobile. "We're not equipped to deal with whatever's happening around here."

"State police?" Brian asked.

Johnny nodded and fired up his snowmobile. Brian mounted his own and matched the sheriff's actions. "Hopefully the mayor got through to someone."

"And if he didn't?" Brian asked.

Johnny found himself growing frustrated with his young deputy. "I don't fucking know, Brian. We'll figure it out."

Brian looked like a kicked puppy, and Johnny immediately regretted his words. "Yes, sir," Brian said.

Just before he revved his snowmobile, Johnny heard someone calling him.

"Sheriff! Sheriff!"

He looked back to see two fishermen running toward them from the docks. They were panting heavily by the time they reached the two officers. Johnny recognized them from around town, but they weren't locals and he couldn't recall their names. He was pretty sure they had come in on a crabbing boat a week prior.

"What's going on, guys?" he asked.

"There are," one of the men tried to say between pants, "bodies in the water!"

Johnny looked down at the inlet but couldn't see anyone in the water. He rubbed his fingers against his eyes, feeling a headache forming in the center of his forehead.

"What should we do?" Brian asked in a low voice. The young man's eyes reflected Johnny's own feeling of defeat.

Johnny patted him on the shoulder. "You go to town. Stop at the church and tell the pastor he might have a bunch of house guests soon."

Brian looked at him, clearly not understanding.

"I'm going with these men to fish those bodies out of the water. When I'm done, I'm gathering everyone who isn't in town and bringing them to the church." Johnny glanced back at the two men, who looked terrified. "Don't worry, guys," he said, patting the handle of his pistol. "Brian, when you finish that, get your ass over to the mayor's office and get help. Bring the staties, the National Guard, the fucking governor if you can get him here. Just bring help."

"You can count on me, sir," Brian said with a grin.

"I know I can. Get on it."

Brian gassed his snowmobile and headed toward town.

Johnny watched him for a minute before turning to the two fishermen. "Show me where the bodies are."

Chapter 15

Hanta glanced down at his watch. Catching the moon-light just right, he could see it was just after ten. He allowed his head to rest against the trunk of the tree. The hunting trip was getting him nowhere. He had been positive the beast would take that trail either into or out of town, but the sheriff's elusive monster didn't seem to want to make an appearance.

A rifle rested across his lap, rounds loaded and safety off. Allowing his mind to wander, he thought of his grandfa-ther. The old man was obsessed with old Inuit lore. The whole family would gather around the fire and listen to him retell ancient legends.

His eyelids grew heavy. Every few minutes, his stomach rumbled. He wasn't sure how long it had been since he had eaten. Patience was the essential virtue for every hunter, and his were running out.

Sighing, he clicked on the safety of his rifle. He lifted his arms above his head to stretch, several of his stiff joints cracking and popping in the process. The tree limb in front of him looked pretty sturdy, so he slung the rifle over his shoulder and leaned against it. Just as he was about to swing down and drop the ten or so feet to the ground, the sharp crack of a breaking branch echoed across the field.

Hanta's breath seized in his chest. With his hands still on the limb in front of him, his eyes drifted back to the opposite tree line. Despite the late hour, the moon's reflection off the snow allowed him to see clearly.

Across the clearing, approximately one hundred yards away, something stepped out of the trees and onto the trail Hanta scouted earlier. Hanta's blood ran cold. The creature was unlike anything he had ever seen. Thick black fur covered rippling muscles. Its enormous size reminded him of a bear, but it was far too lean. It walked on all fours at a leisurely pace, its wolf-like head held high, nose sniffing the air.

Hanta's senses slowly returned to him as he watched the creature pick up speed, effortlessly moving through the snow with the grace of a ballerina. He unslung his rifle, careful to make as little noise as possible. He judged the distance and speed of the beast. Luckily, there was little wind. Pressing the stock of the rifle into his shoulder, he took a few shallow breaths before exhaling all of the air from his lungs. His finger drifted to the safety and flicked the switch. The sound of the safety disengaging seemed incredibly loud in the stillness of the night, but the creature didn't seem to notice. That same finger moved to the trigger. He pulled it back slightly, removing the slack until he felt resistance. He took one more short breath, exhaled, and pressed his cheek to the side of the gun.

Despite being in an awkward firing position, he quickly got the beast in his sights. He set the front sight just below the beast's shoulder. Pivoting slightly so as to lead the creature, he squeezed the trigger.

The report bellowed across the quiet night. The sudden burst of the rifle disturbed the snow above him, covering his face with a thick layer of snow. The impact shifted his weight, nearly sending him tumbling to the ground. Flailing his hands, Hanta managed to steady himself against the tree trunk. Once he was sure he wasn't about to fall, his eyes shot back to where the beast had been.

There was nothing there. No body. No blood. No disturbance in the snow. It was as if there had never been any creature at all. His heart rate picked up as he scanned the surrounding area for any sign of the thing.

An eerie noise rang out from the trees to his right. It sounded like a deep cackle but lacked any semblance of humanity, causing the hair on Hanta's neck to stand and goosebumps to break out across his arms.

Acting quickly, he tossed the rifle over his shoulder. He gripped the tree limb in front of him and swung down. His feet crunched on the snow when he landed. Flipping the rifle around, Hanta dropped to a knee and pulled it against his shoulder. The iron sights of the gun tracked across the trees around him. He searched the shadows for any sign of movement.

An overwhelming stench of rotting meat permeated the air. It assaulted Hanta's senses, causing his eyes to water. A snapping twig to his left drew his attention. He swung the rifle in that direction and pulled the trigger. An explosive bang reverberated off the trees around him. In the split second of light from the shot, Hanta saw the creature's face poking out between two trees, its yellow eyes transfixed on him. When they locked eyes, its snout-like mouth turned up in a wicked grin.

The monster slowly stepped back into the shadows. Moonlight glinted off its massive fangs before it disappeared from view.

Hanta slowly stood up, keeping his gun pointed in that direction. His snowmobile was parked behind some trees about fifty yards away. Every fiber of his being told him to make a run for it, but he knew the monster was toying with him. He had seen it in those haunting yellow eyes. He glanced in the direction of the snowmobile before taking a couple reluctant steps.

There was a flash of movement from left to right. Hanta jerked the rifle up and attempted to track the creature with muzzle, but the beast was gone. He heard a rustling in front of him and slowly positioned the rifle in that direction. Trying to calm his nerves, Hanta exhaled slowly. He strained his ears, searching for any indication of the beast. The rustling seemed to be moving toward his left. He leveled his rifle at a gap in the trees. His finger tightened around the trigger, ready to pull. As if reading his mind, the beast hesitated. Without warning, it sprinted back to the right. Hanta jerked his rifle over, firing at a glimpse of the beast. The round caused a tree branch to explode in a shower of splinters. Farther to his right, another tree branch snapped under the impossible weight of the monster.

Breathing heavily and shaking, he swung the rifle in that direction. His eyes strained to see into the darkness of the surrounding trees. The rifle's weight bore down on his arms, causing his muscles to scream in protest. The gun shook as his eyes darted back and forth, sweeping the area for the beast.

Another branch cracked in the darkness, and Hanta made up his mind. He turned and sprinted toward his snowmobile. The rifle swung wildly in his right hand.

There was another flash of movement to his right. A few seconds later, a massive crash echoed through the trees. Hanta froze. He drew the rifle back to his shoulder and continued walking around the wall of trees that obscured his snowmobile from view.

After a few steps, he glimpsed his snowmobile through the last few trees. The machine was flipped over, and massive dents covered every inch of metal. It looked as if a hail storm had come through, totaling the machine. Both tracks were broken in half, and a tear ran down the center of the seat.

Whatever the thing was, it was fast enough and strong enough to trash his snowmobile. He shuddered at the realization that he couldn't outrun it on foot. Taking a few more cautious steps, he left the cover of the tree line. He approached the dismantled snowmobile and dropped to a knee in front of it.

Hanta glanced around for any sign of the creature. When there was none, he slammed the butt of the rifle into the snow and laid it against the torn track. Being an experienced outdoorsman, he always carried an emergency walkie-talkie that should be attached to the other side of the machine. He used his shoulder to rock the machine off the ground, straining against its overturned weight. Reaching underneath, he felt around for the radio.

His gloved hand found nothing but debris from the snow machine. Sighing, he lowered the machine and grabbed his rifle. Leaning against the tattered seat, he pushed himself up.

Hanta moved around the side of the machine and continued walking toward town. It would be a several-mile walk, and it would likely take him the rest of the night in this deep snow. But he knew two things. He couldn't stay there with the monster, and he needed to warn the sheriff.

He got about two steps when a crunching noise erupted from behind him. Hanta froze in place. There was another crunching noise, followed by the soft patter of debris falling onto the snow.

A soft rumbling noise drifted through the air behind him. It was so close he felt the vibrations more than he heard the growl. Hot wind tickled the back of his neck. The creature's foul breath reeked of sour meat, mixing with the coppery hint of blood permeating from its fur.

His knuckles turned white against the wooden grip of the rifle. Adrenaline coursed through his body. He squeezed his eyes shut and took a deep breath.

His eyes shot open as he turned. The barrel of the rifle led his movement. He spun as fast as possible to point his weapon at the thing behind him, coming face to face with the creature.

It towered over him, at least double his height. A dog-like snout snarled at him, revealing massive fangs, each longer and thicker than his fingers. Yellow eyes stared down at him with a look of unadulterated hatred.

Hanta's eyes went wide and he pulled the trigger. The creature smacked the barrel with a massive paw, shifting the gun as it went off, sending the round flying off into the night sky. Hanta stumbled back a few steps.

The creature wrapped its enormous fingers around the barrel and yanked it from his hands. It gripped the barrel with one hand and the stock with the other, and its muscles flexed slightly as it snapped the rifle in half like a twig. The monster loosed an eerily human cackle. It tossed the broken rifle into the snow and swiped its massive clawed hand at Hanta.

Pain tore through Hanta's chest as the monster's claws dug deep into his skin. He collapsed backward into the snow. Hot blood gushed from his open wounds. His breathing quickened with the pain and panic setting in. Acting on years of training and instinct, he drew his revolver from the holster at his hip. Without aiming, he fired. He pulled the trigger again and again. Each time, the revolver answered with a jerk and a loud bang. He watched through the muzzle flashes as the beast continued forward, unfazed by the bullets.

The gun clicked. He pulled the trigger again. The cylinder turned and clicked again. In one last desperate act, he threw the weapon at the monster. It effortlessly swatted the gun to the ground and leaped on him.

One of its massive hands came down on Hanta's left arm. The crack of his bones echoed in his ears as loudly as the gunshots. His mouth stretched wide in an attempt to scream, but only a muffled cry escaped his lips. He squirmed with all his might, his feet digging uselessly into the snow.

The monster slowly pulled on the broken arm, and Hanta's eyes grew even wider. A burning sensation tore through him as ligaments and muscles popped and separated from his shattered bones. His skin stretched to the ripping point. Hanta shook his head. "No, don't!" he begged. A smile crept across the beast's face, and with a sickening pop, his arm came free. The white, powdery snow absorbed his blood, staining it red. Streams of blood spurted from the torn arteries. Hanta released a subdued gasp. His body turned cold as shock immediately set in.

He made a few more incoherent pleas before the creature rested its hand across his mouth, silencing him.

It pressed down. Slowly, it applied more and more pressure, savoring the kill. Hanta punched at the beast's arm with one remaining hand, but it had no effect. The cartilage in his nose separated, followed by the shattering of his front teeth. They splintered into little pieces, filling his mouth with painful shards as the pressure increased. The creature exhaled its hot breath into Hanta's face. Hanta tried to scream, but his shouts were stifled by his ruined mouth and the monster's massive hand.

It loosened its grip momentarily before bringing its hand down harder. Hanta's head exploded from the pressure, spilling his brains across the snow. One of his eyeballs erupted from its socket, momentarily dangling from a strand of muscle and nerves before snapping off and sinking into the snow.

The beast roared. Its cries filled the still night air. It dug its claws into Hanta's abdomen, ripping the skin apart. It buried its hand into the open cavity and ripped out a handful of organs, the entrails dangling limply from its hands as it shoveled them into its mouth. The beast roared again then buried its face into the dead man's body, consuming the remaining internal organs. Blood dripped from the monster's chin when it finished, and it disappeared into the trees, leaving Hanta's ruined corpse in the snow.

Chapter 16

Mayor Victor Henry ran his hands through his thinning hair. Many years of running businesses and political life had aged him prematurely, but the events of the last week had worsened the years of stress lines. He felt his heart thundering against his chest. Racking his brain, he tried to remember if he had taken his blood pressure medication.

"What do you want to do, Pops?" Darren asked. He reclined against the wall behind his father with his legs crossed. It was becoming an all-too-familiar position.

Victor continued rubbing his hands through his hair as he contemplated his options. Admitting the town was in a crisis would be terrible for both his political and business aspirations, but if what the deputy was saying was true, they needed help.

His eyes drifted up to the portrait of his father that hung prominently in the corner of the room. It sat in a gaudy picture frame with gold inlay at the edges. He wondered if his dad had ever faced any challenges like this during his career.

"Dad?" Darren asked again.

Victor slammed his fist down on the desk, spilling his cup of coffee. The blistering liquid splashed across the desk and dripped off the side, staining his pristine carpet. "Goddamn it!" he yelled, then swiveled his chair to face his son. "I'm the fucking mayor. Give me a goddamn second to think!" He swiveled back to face Brian, jabbing a shaky finger at him. "And you, Walters, right?"

Brian glanced down at the name tag over the left breast pocket of his uniform. "Williams," Brian corrected. He stifled his urge to make a sarcastic comment.

"Williams, Walters, I don't give a rat's ass." He slammed his hand on the desk again. "Why the fuck are you here and not the sheriff?"

"He's coming, Mr. Mayor. He had to help a couple of fishermen pull bodies out of the inlet," Brian said as he held the mayor's gaze, refusing to be intimidated.

"There were more bodies?" the mayor asked.

Brian thought the mayor meant for it to come out as a shout, but it sounded more like a whine.

"Why didn't you tell me that part?"

Brian shook his head. "My apologies, sir. You instructed me to stop talking." The corner of Brian's mouth twitched.

A look of exhaustion came over Victor. Using the sleeve of his shirt, he dabbed at the sweat on his forehead. He dismissed Brian's insolence with a wave of his hand. "Don't be a smart ass." He rubbed his eyes. "OK. OK. Let me get this straight." He slid his chair back and stood up. Victor picked up the spilled mug and held it out for his son. "Would you get Andrea to fill that up and then have her clean up this mess?" He motioned with his finger to the coffee coating his desk.

A look of dejection came over Darren's face. Without a word, he took the mug and exited the room, lightly bumping against Brian's arm with his shoulder on the way out. Brian didn't budge, causing Darren to stutter-step and nearly drop the mug. Brian lost his battle with the urge to smirk as Darren went through the office door.

"Is your dick-measuring contest with my son over now?" the mayor asked with a furious expression.

Brian toyed with the idea of making a smart-ass remark but elected to ignore the comment.

"So we have at least twenty dead?"

Brian nodded, every sense of humor drained from his face. "At least, sir. Earnest, Ben Grover, Eric Graham."

Brian counted the names off on his fingers. "Twenty or so in the bunkhouse and the ones down in the water." Brian held the mayor's angered gaze with his own stoic expression. The sheriff had told him many times the mayor was a bully, and as a black man of his sexuality, Brian had experience in dealing with people like Mayor Victor Henry.

"That's so many people," a woman's voice interrupted them. Andrea entered the room right after Brian finished rattling off the fatalities. The typically attractive and bubbly young woman looked disheveled. Her makeup wasn't done and her hair was thrown up in a messy bun on the top of her head.

The mayor gave her a furious glare, and she quickly lowered her head as she crossed the room with his coffee.

Darren entered the room behind her and returned to his usual position against the wall.

Once the young woman handed the mayor his coffee, she moved to his desk with a roll of paper towels to clean up the mess.

Brian started to speak again, but the mayor held up a hand to silence him. Victor waited impatiently for his assistant to finish cleaning the spilled coffee and exit the room.

"Alright. I guess we do need to—" A knock at the door interrupted him. "Jesus Christ! Now what?" he bellowed.

Andrea cracked the door and poked her head in. "I'm so sorry, sir," she said, sounding like she was on the verge of tears. "Sheriff Myers is here for you."

Victor nodded and motioned with two fingers for him to enter. The secretary threw open the door and stepped aside for the sheriff.

Johnny strutted into the room. He moved right past Brian and to a table in the corner of the room. Opening a glass decanter, he took a sniff. The whiskey gave off the pungent aroma of hickory. Knowing the mayor, it was likely high-end. He poured a few fingers into a glass and lifted it to eye level, swirling it around.

"Sure, Johnny. Help yourself to my five-hundred-dollar bottle of whiskey," Victor said sarcastically.

Johnny ignored him. Pressing the cold glass to his lips, he paused to clear his mind. He took a slow sip of the whiskey and leaned against the wall. Leaning his head back, he smacked his lips. "Damn, that's good stuff." He quickly drained the rest of the glass and set it down on the table.

"What took you so long?" Darren asked. His high-pitched voice startled Brian. The mayor's son had been silent for so long Brian forgot he was in the corner.

"Shut up, Darren," Johnny snapped. "The grownups are talking."

Darren stopped leaning against the wall and took a step forward.

Victor held up a hand to his son. "What took you so long?" he asked.

"Sorry, mayor. I was fishing a couple of bodies out of the water."

"Who were they?" Victor demanded.

"A couple of fishermen who came in on that boat over the weekend." Johnny rubbed his eyes. "When are the state police getting here?"

The mayor hung his head. He set his palms flat against the desk and allowed it to support his full weight.

Johnny looked from him to Brian and then to Darren. "Mayor?" He said the title with the force of a parent disciplining their child. After a moment's pause, he continued. "When do they get here?"

"He hasn't called them yet," Brian said.

Johnny's eyes went wide. His cheeks flushed. "Why the fuck not?" he asked forcefully. Snapping his eyes to Brian, he rose to his full height. "You told him about the bunkhouse?"

Brian nodded. "Yes, sir."

His head whipped toward the mayor. "And about Earnest?"

The mayor started to speak, but Brian cut him off. "He's worried about how it's going to affect his political ambitions."

"You're joking, right?" Johnny stared at Victor, who refused to meet his gaze.

"A man in my position has to make difficult decisions," he protested weakly.

"But this isn't one of them," Johnny said coolly. He pointed toward the door. "Half the damn town has died in just a couple of days. We need help."

The mayor continued staring at the floor.

"Victor!" Johnny shouted, and the mayor's head jerked in his direction. "We need help," Johnny said gently.

Victor sighed and nodded. "You're right," he relented. Pushing himself off of his desk, he dropped into his chair and snatched the phone off the receiver. He pressed it to his ear. After a second, he pulled it away from his ear and stared at the receiver.

"What's wrong?" Brian asked.

"The line's dead," Victor said quietly. He tapped the switch hook several times and returned it to his ear. He shook his head and said, "There's no dial tone." He spun in his chair. "Darren, give me your cell phone."

Darren dug the new IPhone out of his pocket and unlocked it. He started to hand it to his father, then paused. The color drained from his face. "There's, uh, there's ..."

"Spit it out, boy!" Victor bellowed.

"There's no service," Darren said.

Johnny and Brian shared a glance, and each pulled their cellphones out. Johnny unlocked his phone, his eyes flicking to the upper right-hand corner. No Service took up that part of the screen. He shook his head, looking back up to Brian, hopeful. The look on Brian's face told him all he needed to know. He slid the phone back into his pocket and immediately pointed at the mayor's computer.

"Email the governor right now," Johnny said.

The mayor looked both concerned and confused. He slowly turned back to the desk and powered up the computer. When Victor double-clicked the Windows Chrome icon, a white screen popped up. An error message read No internet. What little color remained in Victor's nervous face drained as he turned the screen toward Johnny.

"What's going on, sheriff?" Brain asked in a voice barely above a whisper.

Johnny shook his head. "I'm not sure, but this can't be good." Johnny rubbed his chin. "There's a fiber optic cable the state had installed last year. Maybe it's damaged?" he suggested.

Darren shook his head. "I was here when they laid out the plans. That cable is like fifteen feet underground. There's no way to get to it."

"Nobody is coming to help us," Johnny whispered to himself. "What do you want to do, mayor?" he asked.

The mayor lowered his head again, running his fingers through his hair. It might have been his imagination, but he thought it was thinner than it had been earlier. He tried to weigh out his options. With that many dead workers in his bunkhouse, there was no way he could keep it a secret. He might lose his entire business over this. The idea of a coverup had crossed his mind more than once. He shook it off. There was no way his straight-laced cops would go for it, no matter how much cash he threw at them. Not to mention, a cover up would look bad if it came out during his bid for governor.

"Victor?" Johnny asked more sternly, snapping the mayor from his daze. "We need to send for help," he said softly. "We need the state police, or maybe the National Guard. I don't know. If I leave now, I can be in Frozen Bay by sun up." Johnny took a step toward the mayor's desk, resting his knuckles on the fine wood. Leaning forward, he continued. "I'll take the AR15 and one of the snowmobiles. It'll be a little longer, but it's easier to go around the south side of the mountain."

The mayor shook his head. "No," he said resolutely.

Johnny recoiled. "What do you mean, no?"

"I mean, no, you're not going." Victor lifted his head to meet the sheriff's eyes. "We need you here," he insisted. Victor brought his finger down on his desk for emphasis. "You think the town is going to listen to the fruity black deputy? No!" he spat. "They're going to panic!" Victor slammed his fist down on the desk. "He and Darren will go. You will stay here and keep me safe, goddamn it!"

Johnny extended to his full height. "You're a real piece of shit, Victor. You know that?" Johnny glanced at Victor's Marine Corps memorabilia behind his desk. It made his blood boil. He took a step to round the desk to confront the man, but a hand on his arm stopped him.

Brian was squeezing his bicep and shaking his head. "It's fine," Brian said. "I'll follow your plan. On the south side of the mountain, get to Frozen Bay and hopefully call for help, right?"

Slowly, Johnny nodded. The tension drained from his muscles. "And Darren is going with you," Johnny ordered, pointing at the young man. "Darren, Brian is in charge. You do what he says."

"Absolutely not!" Darren spat. "My dad's the mayor—" he began before Johnny bolted across the room and grabbed him by his shirt collar.

Balling it up in his fists, Johnny slammed him against the wall. "Listen here, you spoiled little fuck." Johnny inched closer to his face. "People are dead. You will do what we say, or I will fuck you up."

"That's enough!" Victor shouted.

Johnny shoved Darren into the wall one more time. "I don't give a fuck if your daddy is over there crying." He threw a thumb in Brian's direction. "Brian's in charge. Say you understand."

Darren's eyes glistened with tears. "I understand," he muttered.

Johnny released him.

Victor was on his feet. "That's no way to handle this situation!" he shouted. The tubby man was moving from behind his desk.

Johnny smirked. "It worked in Afghanistan. But you wouldn't understand that, would you?" he asked as he nodded toward the Marine Corps flag on the wall. He swatted Brian on the shoulder. "Come on." As he exited the office, he shouted back to Darren. "Be at the station in one hour!"

Victor rushed forward. "And you will never put your hands on my son again!" he shouted.

Johnny halted and spun on his heels. He marched back into the room, stopping only inches from the mayor. "And if you ever call one of my deputies fruity again, I'll beat the piss out of you," he whispered into Victor's ear. Pulling away from his boss, Johnny patted the mayor on the shoulder. "Let's get this done," he exclaimed, a phony smile on his face.

Brian stifled a laugh as he closed the door. He could hear Darren muttering about kicking Johnny's ass. They all knew there wasn't a snowball's chance in hell of that happening. Darren continued to argue loudly with his father, and Brian could hear nearly every word as he followed Johnny toward the building's exit. The last word he heard from Darren before the door closed behind him was "faggot."

Brian jogged to catch up with Johnny, who was already walking across the street. "Lost your cool for a minute, boss?"

Johnny shook his head. "Nope. I was cool the whole time. It was just for effect." He smiled at Brian. "Needed them to understand who was really in charge."

Brian laughed and clapped the sheriff on the back.

"I'm just sick of the marine wannabe," Johnny continued.

"Wait. Was he not really a marine?" Brian asked.

"Nope. Dropped out of basic at Pendleton. Something about a toe injury." Johnny held the station door open for his deputy. "The way I heard it, the docs cleared him to roll back to another class, but he declined." Johnny shook his head. "Guess he needed his excuse to get out without looking too bad."

Brian laughed again. "I fucking hate those guys."

Chapter 17

The sun was sinking low behind the trees on the outskirts of town by the time Johnny and Brian finished packing up the snowmobiles. Johnny walked around the machine, taking a quick inventory.

Spare rations? Check.

Extra, full gas canisters? Check.

A gallon of water? Check.

Johnny nodded, satisfied with their overly elaborate preparations for what should be a short trip to the next town over. He tossed the clipboard to Brian, who set it on the bench outside the police station. "I think we got everything," Johnny said. "We just need to grab the rifles before you leave."

Brian nodded, picking up the black Nike duffel bag at his feet. He set it on the back of the snowmobile and unzipped it. Pulling out a balaclava, he said, "It's getting really cold. Can't hurt, right?" Brian pulled it over his face.

It reminded Johnny of playing cops and robbers when he was a kid, except it looked like Brian was trying to be both.

"That's actually a good idea," Johnny said. He was about to say something else when Brian cut him off by clearing his throat. He motioned with his head. Behind him, Darren approached.

He was clad in heavy winter gear. His face shifted from angry to a look of utter disgust when he saw Brian.

Ignoring the disdain in Darren's eyes, Brian crossed his arms and smirked. "Are you ready to go, kid?" Brian asked.

Johnny turned away to hide his smile. Brian was only a couple years older than Darren, and he knew how much being called a kid would infuriate the slightly younger man.

Darren's face turned bright red. "My dad said I have to listen to you, but don't call me that." He pointed a finger at Brian.

"Shut the fuck up, Darren," Johnny snapped. "Do you have everything you need?"

Darren spun, shifting his finger from Brian to Johnny. For a second, he considered cussing out the sheriff. The look in Johnny's eyes changed his mind. "Yeah," Darren said, setting his own duffel bag on the back of the other snowmobile. "Ready whenever you are." He shifted his gaze to Brian. "Boss," he spat with as much hatred as he could muster.

Down the street, a furious-looking Amy marched toward them. The clatter of her boots echoed off the walls of the surrounding buildings and rolled through the empty streets.

"Uh-oh," Brian teased. He quickly turned around and dropped to a knee. He pretended to inspect the treads on the snowmobile.

Johnny rubbed his forehead. He muttered, "Fuck," under his breath, kicking himself for forgetting to tell his wife he wasn't coming home. He turned to face her.

"What the fuck is going on, Johnny? I expected you home hours ago!" Amy said.

"Sorry, babe," he said, taking her hands in his. He quickly leaned forward and kissed her on the forehead. "I'll tell you everything in just a minute," he whispered. "Let me just see them off first."

Her face contorted from one of anger to concern. "See them off?" she asked.

"Babe, I promise." Johnny pulled his hands away from her. "Five minutes, OK?" Johnny asked while holding up five fingers.

"I'll wait inside," she said. Without another word, she turned away from him. She knew he was busy and whatever was going on needed his attention, but she felt dejected. Her husband always kept her informed. Through his years in law enforcement, he always found time to reach out to her and let her know he was safe.

Once inside the station, she moved in front of the heater. She watched through the windows as Johnny, Brian, and, to her surprise, Darren Henry checked the straps holding down an abundance of supplies. She sighed. If Johnny was cooperating with the Henrys, it must be serious. Her eyes felt heavier with each passing moment. Johnny hadn't given her any details yet, but for the last few days, she could sense something was off. Each day, fewer and fewer kids came to class.

Johnny entered the station a few minutes later and walked right past her. "Almost done, babe," he muttered absentmindedly over his shoulder. He quickly made his way into the back rooms and disappeared from sight.

Amy heard him rummaging around deeper in the station before emerging from the hallway carrying a sleek black AR15 in one hand. She wasn't a gun expert, but she recalled every detail of that rifle because Johnny spent every waking moment for a month telling her about it. It sported a forward grip, upgraded sights, and an adjustable stock. Attached to the stock was a pouch for holding a spare magazine. In his other hand was his personal hunting rifle—Amy recognized the bolt action rifle as the same one Johnny taught her to shoot on. Johnny had explained to her that it was essentially the civilian equivalent of the sniper rifle used in the Marine Corps.

He walked briskly past her, using his butt to push open the door. Outside, he handed the AR15 to Brian. "It's less powerful than this one," he said, holding the bolt action slightly higher. "But it's got two thirty-round magazines. You can lay down a lot of hate with it."

Brian looked the weapon over, and a pit formed in Johnny's stomach. "Do you know how to use it?"

Brian whipped the rifle around, dropped the magazine, and made sure there were rounds in it. Reseating it, he yanked the charging handle and chambered a round. He flipped the selector switch from safe to fire then back again. Flashing Johnny a smile, he nodded. "My dad was a gun nut."

Johnny chuckled and handed the other rifle to Darren. "And you?" he asked.

Darren fumbled the rifle, catching it on the second try.

"Uh, yeah. I hunted with my dad." Fear stretched over his face when he gazed down at the rifle. "Once," he mumbled.

Johnny groaned in frustration. "OK. This is the safety. Click it off when you're ready to fire." He explained as he pointed to each part of the weapon. "Once you fire, you need to slide the bolt back to chamber another round. OK?"

Darren ran his fingers over the bolt. "Got it." Both men slung the rifles over their backs, then mounted their snowmobiles and fired them up. The roar of the engines and the light from the station were the only signs of life in the town.

"Listen. You get around the south side of the mountain, you call for help," Johnny said, leaning close to Brian so he could be heard over the snowmobile's engine.

Brian adjusted his balaclava. "I got it, boss. We'll be back in no time." He gassed the snowmobile, revving the motor. He motioned to Darren, and the two men sped off down the street.

Johnny stood there watching them until they disappeared from view. He couldn't help but feel fear for his deputy and friend, and also for the little pissant. A sinking feeling in his gut told him he may never see either of them again.

With one issue down, he pivoted on his heels and entered the police station to address his waiting wife. She wasn't waiting for him in the lobby when he entered. He heard her shuffling around deeper in the station, probably in his office. "Amy!" he called.

"In your office!"

He quickly made his way to the back of the station. Opening his door, he couldn't help but smile. She was reclined in his chair, her tiny feet bootless and resting on his desk. Two steaming cups of coffee sat next to her, filling the room with an amazing aroma.

"Thought you could use a coffee," she said with a smile.

Making his way across the room, he snatched up the coffee and held it with both hands. The warmth felt good against his frozen fingers. He hovered the cup next to his nose and inhaled deeply before taking a sip. "Best wife ever," he said in a state of bliss. "I needed coffee more than I knew."

"More than you needed me?" she asked sheepishly.

"Never that, babe." He leaned across the desk and kissed her. "So, I guess you want to know why I didn't come home?"

"I sure do." She held up a hand. "And if it has to do with another woman, just know, my husband taught me how to shoot," she teased through a smile.

He chuckled. "I'd never dream of it."

Johnny spent the next few minutes recapping the day's events. He skimmed over most of the topics, sparing her from the gruesome details of the state he found Earnest's corpse in, the massacre at the bunkhouse, and the fishermen in the water. Instead, he just told her that they were all dead, and she was aware enough not to ask for details.

When he got to the part of the meeting in the mayor's office, he decided to give her more details.

She laughed when he told her about intimidating the mayor and slamming Darren into the wall. "Good. Someone needed to put that little shit in his place," she said.

"The mayor or his son?" he asked with a wink.

The two talked for hours, Johnny only periodically peeking out the window or checking the battery in the radios. It was the first conversation they had in days. He choked up when they talked about Earnest. Johnny couldn't help but think about his friend's body sitting in the town's makeshift morgue and wished desperately that he could bury him.

He refilled his mug with the last of the coffee, downing it quickly and looked his wife in the eyes. "You remember when I finally told you about that ambush in Afghanistan?" he asked.

She nodded. "I only pleaded with you for a year to let me in. How could I forget?"

He sighed. "I told you how scared I was? How I felt deep in my core that none of us were getting out alive?" She made a noise indicating she remembered. "Well," he took a deep breath, "I have that same feeling now. Something isn't right. I knew it as we drove down that road in Helmand Province, and I know it now. More people are going to die before this is all over." A few tears rolled down his face at the memory of his friends being blown apart in an IED blast. Their humvee had gone up in flames within seconds. Gunfire erupted in his ears, drowning out his squad's cries for help. He shook off the thought.

Johnny peeked out the window again, just as he had done every few minutes, hoping he would see Hanta. With all the excitement, he had nearly forgotten he hired the man to go after whatever was killing people. Regret stabbed at his heart. Hanta had gone into the belly of the beast, and there was no way to call him off.

Amy must have noticed his distraction, because she stood up and crossed the room. She pulled the blinds shut and wrapped her arms around his waist. Slowly running one of her hands up his chest, her fingers played at the buttons on his shirt.

"Hanta's still out there hunting whatever it is," he protested.

"There's nothing more you can do for any of them tonight," she whispered. He started to pull away, but she squeezed tighter. "But you can let your wife comfort you."

He sank into her embrace, a boyish smile across his face. Slowly turning to face her, their locked eyes. They leaned into one another and shared a long, slow kiss.

"Go lock my door," Amy whispered.

Chapter 18

Brian squeezed the throttle a little tighter. There was a slight stutter as the snowmobile picked up speed. Besides that, it glided effortlessly over the frozen road connecting Port Luck to Frozen Bay. Snow started falling as soon as he and Darren left the police station. It started off as a light flurry but was coming down much harder. Walls of snow blew past his face in vicious gusts. He was grateful for the goggles Johnny had given him before they left.

Glancing down at the fuel gauge, he saw it was half full. It was approximately one hundred miles to the next town, which, under ideal situations, would be the absolute extreme limit of his machine. With the deteriorating conditions, they would have to stop at least once to refuel. He looked to the left to keep a close eye on Darren.

Darren seemed to be struggling to keep up. The scrawny man's butt left his seat with several jarring bumps, and the handlebars swayed awkwardly any time he hit a thicker patch of snow.

Brian was concerned Darren wouldn't be able to maintain the breakneck pace. Shaking his head, he wished the mayor wouldn't have sent his son. The guy was only going to slow him down. Sighing, he held out his hand. Waving it in a downward motion, he let off the accelerator, hoping Darren would match his movement. To his surprise, Darren blew past him. The little shit flipped Brian the bird as he passed.

"Motherfucker," Brian whispered to himself.

Darren continued accelerating, pulling farther away from Brian with every second. Around him, the storm continued to worsen. The wall of snow ahead of them thickened, decreasing Brian's visibility even further. Darren managed to pull so far ahead that the only thing visible was the dim red glow of his taillights.

Brian yelled for his companion to wait up only for his voice to be drowned out by the roar of the snowmobile's engine and the howl of the wind. Darren gave no indication of hearing him. Brian tried to yell for him to slow down one more time before grunting his frustration. He squeezed the accelerator harder, hoping to gain a little ground on the childish man ahead of him.

Something moved to his right. He only saw it for a fraction of a second, dancing in his peripheral vision. It was such a fleeting sight that he couldn't be sure he really saw anything. It could have been his snowmobile's headlights playing tricks with the shadows. He turned his head that direction and strained his eyes against the darkness around him. Something moved again. Deep within the trees, it looked like a shadow only somehow darker than the darkness around it. Whatever it was bolted forward, disappearing into a large cluster of trees.

Brian loosened his grip on the accelerator. He no longer cared if Darren pulled ahead of him. His eyes stayed transfixed on the spot where he last saw the shadow. Carefully, he reached back with his left hand and grabbed the barrel of the AR15. He gently pulled it around until it rested across his chest instead of his back. Nausea rolled in the pit of his stomach. He could feel a pair of unseen eyes on him, sending fear-induced daggers of ice through his body.

"What ... doing?" he heard a familiar voice call. Snapping his head around, he saw Darren had come to a complete stop around a hundred yards in front of him. Darren yelled again, but the storm completely washed away his words.

Brian returned his hand to the accelerator and started to depress it when something exploded from the tree line.

He watched helplessly as a creature ran on all fours toward Darren. It was twice the size of the largest bear he had ever seen. Its movement reminded him more of a cheetah than anything he had seen in Alaska. Enormous legs propelled it forward, covering the hundred yards in the blink of an eye.

The beast reached Darren and, instead of stopping, crashed right through him. With a quick upward thrust, it launched Darren and his snowmobile high into the air. Brian watched in slow motion as Darren flew end over end, his legs and arms flailing wildly as he plummeted back to earth. He crashed into the icy ground with an ear-shattering crack that could be heard above the raging storm. The snowmobile crashed down beside him and rolled twice before settling upside down and pinning Darren's ruined legs beneath its weight.

Darren's high-pitched screams filled the air. His arms flew to the snowmobile, and he pushed against it only to immediately release his grip. He collapsed back into the snow, screaming in pain.

The beast stretched to its full height, towering over the injured Darren, who whimpered as he attempted to shimmy his legs free from the snowmobile in a panicked bid to flee from the creature.

The beast howled, sending Brian's mind immediately through every werewolf movie he had ever seen. Its howl stretched on, ringing above the wind and filling the air. When it finished its victorious cry, it laughed—not the animalistic cackles of a hyena, but a deep, throaty, humanesque laugh. Massive, jagged teeth stood out prominently in the headlight of the ruined snowmobile. The monster took a step forward. It grabbed the back of the snowmobile, burying the long claws of its hand-like paw into the metal. They pierced the machine, digging deep into the metal. With one swift motion, the creature lifted the thing above its head and slammed it down on Darren's legs.

Darren's head snapped back as he screamed out. The sickening crack of his femurs snapped Brian out of his fear-induced stupor. Gassing his snowmobile, he allowed adrenaline to propel him forward.

The monster placed a foot on the snowmobile. It slowly applied more pressure, driving it farther down on Darren's injured legs. Relishing the pain it was causing Darren, it leaned forward, brandishing its fangs.

Darren screamed in pain, begging the monster not to kill him. "Stop! Stop!" he pleaded with the beast. Its yellow eyes bore down on him, and Darren could see the joy in its expression. Burying his hands in deep mountains of snow, he attempted to pull away with all his might. The beast's weight on the snowmobile increased. He flipped back over to see something white protruding from one of his legs. The jagged edges of the object were coated in blood and managed to rip through his pants. The realization of what it was hit him. His femur was sticking out of his skin. His eyes stretched wide.

His mouth opened to scream, but the beast's face took his breath away. It inched closer to his own, a long snout sniffing the air around him. Its paw drifted to his shattered femur. Pain ripped through his body as the beast slowly pulled at the bone. The pain was too much. His head lolled back; he managed to see the subtle smile at the corners of the creature's mouth before blackness set in and he passed out.

Brian came up behind the beast as fast as he could as it leaned over Darren with its back facing Brian. He dove off the snowmobile, allowing it to carry on for a few more feet. Dropping to one knee, he brought the rifle to his shoulder and took a deep breath. Every bit of training and instinct told him not to fire. He couldn't tell where Darren was, and one of his rounds could go through the beast. Another voice in the back of his mind urged him on, knowing he would likely lose any chance to survive if he hesitated. He exhaled, steadied himself, and squeezed the trigger.

The muzzle of the rifle flashed, and he felt a slight kick to his shoulder. The explosion of the shot screamed out above the howl of the storm, echoing off of the trees and disappearing into the distance.

Brian hesitated for a moment after that first shot. He squinted his eyes against the dark backdrop to see if he hit his target. The beast continued to hunch over Darren. For a second, Brian thought he might have killed it. The thought caused his heart to do a little stutter step of relief. He started to stand up, but before he made it to his feet, the monster jerked its head in his direction.

Brian dropped back to his knee and raised the barrel simultaneously. He squeezed the trigger again and again, the stock repeatedly kicking against his shoulder as the ear-bursting explosions rang through the night.

The beast turned, shielding its face with a massive arm. It made a noise that mimicked a scream but came out deeper than any noise Brian had ever heard.

He continued pulling the trigger. Round after round struck the beast as it stumbled backward until its feet hit the snowmobile. Brian fired again only to be met with a click. In his adrenaline-fueled rage, the reason for the clicking didn't register right away. Absentmindedly, he pulled the trigger two more times. Nothing happened.

The monster lowered its arms and smiled, then took a step forward.

Brian could see wounds all over the creature's body, but to his surprise, they appeared superficial. Thin lines of blood dribbled from small tears in its flesh and ran down its muscles before getting lost in thick tufts of hair.

He watched the creature take another step before his training kicked in again. Smashing the release, the magazine ejected and fell to the snow. He yanked the spare magazine Johnny had given him from the pouch on the stock of the rifle. Quickly slamming it into place, he charged the rifle. He jerked his head up in time to see the beast sprint to his right. He attempted to track the beast with the muzzle, but it moved too quickly. He squeezed off two shots, missing horribly.

Before he could register what was happening, the monster reached his snowmobile and shredded it. The creature ripped one of the treads in half then flipped the vehicle over.

He tracked the monster over the sights as it brutalized the snowmobile. He fired a single shot, which grazed the creature's back. It glanced back at him, and Brian was sure he could see a smirk on its face. It jumped over the vehicle and sprinted into the woods.

Brian remained on a knee as he watched the beast disappear deep into the woods. He continued staring into that patch of darkness with the rifle up until it weighed down his arms, causing them to shake. It became too heavy to continue holding, and his arms gave out. It plummeted down, the barrel burying itself in the snow. He exhaled dramatically, then began sucking in quick breaths. His chest burned from holding his breath. Adrenaline flushed from his body, leaving him weak and nauseous. Tears flowed from his eyes, absorbing into the fabric of his balaclava.

"Brian? Brian, are you there?" Darren cried out. "Brian, please, help me!"

Brian slumped onto all fours. He took a deep breath, trying to summon the strength he would need to stand, let alone help Darren.

"Please?" Darren's pleas were growing more desperate. His moans grew more agonized.

Brian could hear the snowmobile moving around as Darren fought to free his leg. "I'm coming!" Brian cried as he clambered to his feet. He pulled the goggles from his head and peeled the balaclava up. The snow made it difficult to stand in his disoriented state. He tripped and slid several times while making his way to Darren. Between tripping, his rifle dangling from his shoulder, and constantly looking around for any sign of the monster, it took him way longer than it should have to reach the injured man.

The snowmobile rested directly on top of Darren's left leg. A bloody shard of femur protruded to the sky at a near ninety-degree angle. Nausea rose in Brian's throat. He couldn't tell if it was from the adrenaline and stress or the sight of Darren's disfigured leg, but he leaned over and vomited into the snow.

"Alright. Hang on, Darren," Brian said as he wiped the puke from his chin. He scanned the tree line again, straining his eyes against the storm and the darkness. When he was confident the beast wasn't about to lunge out of the woods, he returned to the task at hand. "OK, man. I'm gonna radio for help. Just hang tight."

"Easy for you to say," Darren replied through squinted eyes and clenched teeth. "I'm really fucking hurting here."

Brian dug the walkie-talkie out from under his multiple layers of clothes. He patted Darren on his good leg. "Be quiet so I can hear."

"Suck my ass," Darren muttered.

He pressed the button on the side of the radio. "Johnny, can you hear me? This is Brian. We need help. Over." Brian held the radio up to his ear, waited a second, then repeated his message. He slid the radio back into his pocket and turned to face Darren, who was growing paler by the minute; blood continued to weep from his open wound. Brian sighed.

"Alright, Darren. I have to roll this thing off of you," he said while pulling off his gloves. "It's going to hurt like a motherfucker. But first, I need to stop the bleeding in your leg."

A monstrous roar echoed through the trees somewhere in the distance, causing both men to jerk their heads in that direction. Brian pulled his rifle to his shoulder and swept the tree line with it.

"Whatever, man. Just hurry up!" Darren cried.

Brian swung the gun over his shoulder. Reaching down, Brian lifted Darren's shirt. He began unclasping his belt. Darren swatted at his hands. "I'm not fucking gay, dude!" he shouted.

Brian shook his head. "Quit being a fucking bigot. I'm trying to save your life." Then, under his breath, he muttered, "You fucking asshole." He finished unclamping the belt and wiggled it free from Darren's pants. Retrieving the knife in his boot, Brian made a rough guess of the size of Darren's leg. He punctured a new hole into the belt and stuck the knife in the snow. "OK. Here we go," Brian encouraged. He reached under Darren's leg and passed part of the belt through.

Darren sucked a painful breath through his teeth.

"On the count of three," Brian said. He fed the belt through the buckle. "One." Brian pulled it through until the buckle was flush with Darren's leg. "Two." Before Darren could brace himself, Brian yanked hard on the belt, sliding the buckle into place.

Darren screamed at the top of his lungs and thrashed about wildly. He tried to push Brian off of him, but he couldn't muster enough strength. After a few seconds of excruciating pain, Darren slumped back against the snow, once again on the verge of passing out.

Moving quickly, Brian propelled himself forward. He grabbed hold of the snowmobile and lifted it. It took him two tries to get it rolled over in the snow, but once he did, the full scope of Darren's injuries came into view. The leg was completely mangled from the knee down. It looked nearly flat. If Brian had to guess, he would assume the bones were completely shattered. The foot was turned in the wrong direction. It was clear Darren would lose the leg if they made it back to town. Brian fought back another urge to vomit.

"How bad is it?" Darren asked in a low whisper.

Brian shook his head. "It's not good." He looked around at their destroyed snowmobiles. Neither one of them was drivable, and he had no clue how he would get the injured man back to Port Luck.

"Any ideas on how I can carry you out of here?" Brian asked.

Darren nodded and pointed at his ruined snowmobile. "The seat detaches. I can sit on it, and you can drag me."

Brian walked over to the machine and detached the seat. It had a handle on the back, making it easy to pull. He carried it over to Darren. "You know your leg will be dragged behind this, right?"

Darren nodded. "You got any better ideas?"

Brian shook his head. "Nope. Just don't want to hear you complaining the whole time."

"I'll do my best," Darren said.

Brian positioned the seat behind Darren then grabbed him under the arms. "Ready?"

Darren sucked in a couple of sharp breaths. "Just do it."

Chapter 19

Johnny climbed off his desk, drenched in sweat. His chest inflated as he sucked in air, trying to catch his breath. He gazed at his nude wife, trying to stifle a boyish smile.

Amy rolled off the desk to the opposite side, a wide grin across her face. "Well, sheriff," she said as she pulled on her underwear. "You may not be twenty anymore, but you still got it."

Johnny barked out a loud laugh. He pulled his shirt over his head. "You hold your own, old lady." He gave her a wink and finished getting dressed.

Amy patted the desktop. She opened one of the drawers and retrieved a stack of napkins. "You know, I put these napkins in your desk a year ago." Dropping them onto the desk, she wiped a streak of sweat from the wood. "I don't think you've used a single one."

"Honestly, I forgot they were in there." He picked a folder up off the ground. "But that's why I keep spare uniforms in the closet," he said, nodding toward a door at the back of his office.

She joined him and began picking up the various items they had knocked over in their lustful recklessness. She picked up a few sheets stapled together and looked them over. It was a printout of a newspaper; the headline read "Portlock Abandoned." Holding it out for Johnny to see, she asked, "What's this about?"

He glanced up as he finished getting dressed. "Oh, it's nothing. I got a little curious, so I started digging."

"And?" Amy asked while motioning for him to continue.

"And I found nothing useful in there. Just a lot of speculation and rumors." He took the paper from her hand and tossed it on the desk. "You know how the town was abandoned in nineteen forty-three? Well, mostly abandoned."

"Yes?"

"I still can't believe everyone left except for the postmaster." Squatting down, he grabbed his wife by her butt and lifted her onto the desk. "Crazy fucker lived out here for a whole year by himself." He brushed his lips against her ear. "Can you imagine?" His lips drifted to her neck.

She pushed him away. "Stay focused, sheriff. What else did it say?"

Sighing, he continued. "It says that people left because it was too difficult to live here."

Amy snorted a laugh. "They got that part right." She leaned in and kissed his cheek.

"Yeah. I should have listened to you and stayed in Cali after I got out of the corps."

She caressed his cheek. "No. Your dad needed you."

He forced a smile. "Well, I needed him when I was fifteen and he didn't exactly come running."

Looking him dead in the eye, she said, "That's how I know you're a better man."

He smiled and allowed her to kiss his cheek again. "Anyway," he continued, "the rest of that article ..." He tapped the paper on the desk. "It's all wild conspiracy theories. People are talking about werewolves, aliens, and yetis." He grabbed the paper and folded it in half before tossing it in his desk drawer. "It's useless."

"They don't seem so wild right about now." Amy leaned in for another kiss, but a squawk from Johnny's radio caused him to jerk his head. Her kiss fell on empty air. The radio squawked again.

Johnny pulled away from his wife and snatched up the radio. He stared at it, waiting for Brian to say something.

When it didn't make any noise, Amy leaned forward. "Maybe he sat on the button?" she offered.

He shook his head and held up his hand, quieting her. He tapped the button on the side of the radio. It was immediately filled with static. Letting it go, he glanced at Amy. "Damn storm is messing with the signal." Johnny depressed the button and tried again. "Brian, come in. Over."

There was no immediate response. The pair waited with bated breath as they stared at the little handheld set. Johnny shrugged. He stepped forward and nearly set it down on the counter when it erupted to life.

"Johnny ..." Ear-piercing static screamed from the speaker. "This ... help. Over." The static continued screaming between the few words he could hear.

Johnny pulled the radio back to his lips and spoke slowly into it. "Brian, can you hear me? Over." He waited a few seconds for a response, then tried again. "Brian? Are you OK?" Static screamed from the radio.

He looked at his wife. "That sounded like Brian, right?" She nodded, eyes wide with fear. "And he said he needed help?" Another wide-eyed nod. "Fuck." He ran a shaky hand through his hair. "OK, grab your shit." He clipped the radio to his duty belt and pulled on his jacket. Hustling through the station, Johnny punched the code into the gun safe and retrieved a twelve-gauge. There was only one box of shells. Holding it near his ear, he shook the box. It was nearly empty. He cursed himself for not stocking up sooner. Flipping the shotgun over, he rocked the slide back and inserted his last three shells. He tossed the empty box onto the floor and racked the shotgun.

Johnny draped it over his shoulder and retrieved his spare Glock from the safe. He held it out, butt first, to Amy. She had been watching from the doorway and didn't immediately react.

"Take it." He shook the pistol slightly, encouraging her to grab it.

Timidly, she reached out and touched the grip on the pistol. Her trembling fingers danced along the length of the grips before she finally closed her hand around it and pulled the gun away. Lifting her shirt, she tucked the pistol into her belt at the small of her back.

"I told you I needed more practice with a gun," she said with a wink.

He motioned toward the door with his head. "Come on, I need to grab some more shotgun shells." The pair moved through the station and out the front door. Johnny pointed across the street to the building that doubled as the mayor's office and home. "Go wake up Victor and meet me at Jackson's."

Amy looked toward the office across the street but hesitated. Her head flipped back toward her husband, but he was already jogging down the street, shotgun still draped over his shoulder. A knot formed in the pit of her stomach as she watched him go. It was the same uneasy feeling she had felt when he deployed to Afghanistan. Burying her fear, she turned and sprinted across the street.

Johnny ran the couple hundred yards to Jackson's General Store as quickly as he could. The high winds ripping down the street fought him the entire way. The store was pitch black. The Jacksons were pretty flexible with their hours but usually closed up by nine—it was well past that. Johnny regretted having to wake the older couple up, but he had no choice.

When he reached the store, he leaped onto the porch, bypassing the three wooden steps, and furiously beat on the door. His frozen knuckles stung as he rapped them against the glass panes in the door. He yelled for the Jacksons to open up.

"Jeremiah! Anita!" he shouted as loudly as he could. The worsening storm seemed to carry his shouts away. "Open up! It's Sheriff Myers!" Johnny cringed at the use of his official title. He rarely used it, but he thought it might help the Jacksons to not be as alarmed.

A few more knocks on the door and a light flipped on from deep within the store. He could make out the staircase at the back of the building. It led up to the second floor, which the couple used as their home. Jeremiah Jackson appeared on the staircase, wearing pajama pants and a white shirt, moving as fast as his old knees would allow. He fumbled with a few more switches and the entire store came to life. He quickly made his way to the front door. Clicking the locks, he tossed the door open. The bell dangling from the top of the door rattled as he did. Jeremiah beckoned Johnny inside.

Johnny brushed as much of the snow from his uniform as he could then stepped through the threshold.

"Johnny, what on earth are you doing?" Jeremiah cried.

"I'm so ..." he said before he was cut off.

"Jeremiah, who is it?" Anita Jackson called from the stairs.

Johnny glanced over Jeremiah's shoulder to see Anita and Miss Grover standing on the stairs.

"It's fine, honey. Just the sheriff."

Johnny waved at Anita, hoping to put her more at ease. "Like I said," Johnny continued, "I'm really sorry to wake you up, but I need shotgun shells."

A severe expression fell over Jeremiah's face. "Well, of course." He moved around behind the counter. "It must be an emergency if you woke us up in the middle of the night." He tilted his head to the side, taking in Johnny's shotgun. "And carrying a shotgun."

Johnny sighed. "Unfortunately, it is. I need a couple boxes of shells."

Jeremiah bent over and retrieved two boxes and tossed them onto the counter.

"How much I owe you?" Johnny asked.

Jeremiah waved his hand. "Just an explanation. We can settle this up some other time."

The bell above the door clanged again, drawing Johnny's attention away from the older man. Amy entered first, followed closely by Victor and his wife, Martha. Victor rudely pushed past Amy and approached the other men.

"Where the hell is my son?" he spat.

Johnny considered lashing out at him for the lack of respect he showed Amy, but just shook his head. "I'm not sure. I got a radio call from Brian." Johnny emptied one box of shells into his pocket. He unslung the shotgun and opened the action. Pulling open the second box, Johnny fed shells into the shotgun until it was fully loaded. "They need help, and I'm going to find them." He cocked the shotgun and threw it over his shoulder.

"And just what do you expect me to do?" Victor shrieked. He threw up his chubby arms in an exasperated motion.

Johnny patted him on the shoulder. "I expect you to come with me," he said with a wry smile. Johnny pushed past the mayor and walked toward his wife. He could read the distraught look on her face and braced himself for the conversation that was about to come.

"I don't want you to go," she begged with tears rolling down her cheeks.

Taking her face in his hands, he wiped the tears away. "Do you remember what I said when the Marines sent me to Afghanistan?"

She smiled through the river of tears. "If not me, then who?"

"And what did you say?" he asked tenderly.

She let out a little laugh. "That's why I love you."

He pulled away from her and turned back toward the mayor. "You coming?" he asked.

Victor stuttered for a few seconds before sighing. "Of course," he said, sounding dejected.

"If you give me one minute, I'll go with you," Jeremiah said. He walked around the counter and toward the stairs.

"I don't mean any offense, Mr. Jackson, but you would probably slow us down."

Jeremiah nodded slowly. "Maybe. But I'm the best shot in town," he said definitively, while pointing at a series of news articles prominently displayed on the wall behind the counter. Each one showed a younger Jeremiah holding a rifle next to various slain animals. "And I wasn't asking."

The man disappeared upstairs, his wife chasing behind him.

"We'll be outside!" Johnny shouted.

After waiting for Jeremiah to finish getting dressed and retrieving Victor's hunting rifle, the three men walked out of town. They had contemplated taking the two remaining snowmobiles the town owned, but with the visibility decreasing rapidly, Johnny shot down the idea. They would be just as likely to crash as find their way to the missing men.

They trudged through the snow. The wind ripped around them, making each step even more difficult. Frigid chunks of snow smacked them from all over, stinging through their layers of clothing.

Johnny continued to try the radio every few minutes as he walked but couldn't hear anything above the storm, even if Brian was replying.

After a few hours of walking, Johnny's muscles burned. His chest ached from breathing in the frozen air, which pierced his body like icy daggers. Numbness took over his fingers and toes almost completely. He was colder than he had ever experienced.

Victor was the first one to give voice to the suffering. "I don't think we can keep going!" he yelled, battling to be heard over the storm.

Johnny shook his head, grabbing Victor's shoulders and leaning in close. "They're still out there!"

"I think he's right!" Jeremiah shouted. "We need to find cover!"

"You guys go back! I'll keep looking!" Johnny protested.

It was Victor's turn to shake his head. He pointed out in front of them. "You can't find them in this!"

Johnny looked in the direction they had been walking. It was completely dark except for his flashlight, which was no good in the storm. He couldn't see more than a few feet ahead. "Fuck!" he shouted.

Jeremiah pointed to his right. "I think there are some trees over there! Let's get out of this wind!" Without waiting for an answer from the others, he walked in that direction.

Victor moved past Johnny, intentionally bumping into his shoulder as he did. Johnny watched him walk, fury at Victor's complete lack of fortitude fueling him with hatred. Johnny couldn't believe how easily Victor had given up on finding his son. Brian wasn't even related to Johnny and he was prepared to freeze to death while looking for his deputy.

Hanging his head, Johnny followed the other two men into a thicket of trees. The men huddled together, trying to shield themselves from the cold air. The darkness of the frozen forest swallowed them entirely.

In the distance, a tree branch cracked.

Chapter 20

Brian's legs screamed with every step. The burning sensation of lactic acid ripped through the muscles. He blocked the pain from his mind, lifted his foot out of the snow, and forced himself to take another step forward. His hands ached from dragging Brian on the seat of the snowmobile.

Darren sucked in a deep breath with each step Brian took. Frozen tears clung to his chin, forming little icicles. His ruined leg dangled uselessly behind him. Every few steps, Brian would falter or they would hit a bump, causing the exposed bone of his leg to dip into the snow. Each time, a shot of pain so intense he passed out twice soared through his body. Darren could do nothing but continue hugging the makeshift sled as Brian pulled him along.

The two men trudged through the snow at a snail's pace. Brian wasn't entirely sure how far away they were from town or even if they were heading in the right direction. The storm was bad enough to cause them to lose all sense of direction. They had argued for a few minutes before Brian started walking in the direction he thought was correct; it wasn't like Darren could stop him.

Brian thought about his parents during the long, isolated walk through the wilderness. They were both back in Anchorage. In their late fifties, his parents were more traditional. In fact, Hank Williams, his father, was downright bigoted. The old man had grown up in the heart of Mississippi before moving to Alaska for his wife. Being a Southern Baptist, his parents weren't exactly tolerant of the LGBTQ community. Brian had kept his sexuality a secret from them for as long as he could. When they did find out, it was in the worst way possible, walking into his apartment unannounced to find him on the couch with another man. That was the last time he spoke to his father. His mother wasn't much better, but she at least talked to him occasionally. Brian decided that if he survived, he would get back in touch with his father. Maybe there was time for them to salvage their relationship, even if his father didn't respect his so called life choices.

Brian had been so lost in thought that he hadn't noticed the storm dying down around them. It was still snowing, but the snow was falling softly to the ground. The wind was no longer howling in his ears and slapping his body with pellets of ice. He could even see a little better.

Glancing over his shoulder, he could make out the faint outline of the mountain against the dark sky. Brian smiled to himself; he had picked the right direction.

The expanse of trees to his left was incredibly thick but familiar. He paused and looked around.

"Why're we stopping?" Darren asked. His voice was sluggish. It reminded Brian of the drunks at the bar when he and Johnny broke up their fights.

"Just getting my bearings," he said. Using his head to indicate the open terrain to his right, he said, "I think one of the old mines is up that way. If I'm right, it's a straight shot back to town." Brian started walking again. It sent a wave of pain through his fingers as they pulled against the seat handle and dragged Darren along. Darren grunted in pain with the first step before falling back into his normal hisses and gasping with each step. The sound annoyed Brian, but he couldn't exactly blame the guy for his pain.

He reached the end of the clearing and had no choice but to push through some trees. "This is going to suck," he said over his shoulder. Brian plunged into the trees, yanking Darren along before he had a chance to protest. The branches snagged at his clothes, tearing small holes in his jacket. With his hands firmly on the seat, he had nothing to shield himself with. He plowed ahead with his eyes closed. The branches smacked him in the face and clawed at his eyes. He couldn't be sure, but he thought he felt the warm sensation of blood running down his cheek as one of the branches caught him above the eyebrow.

He reached the edge of the tree line. Brian summoned a burst of strength and pulled the seat through the shrubs. The makeshift sled caught on some leafless bushes, yanking it from Brian's hands. Brian's momentum sent him tumbling forward. He plummeted downward, burying his face in the snow.

Behind him, the snowmobile seat crashed to the earth. Darren screamed out in pain and surprise. Instinctually, his hand flew to his injured leg. His fingers collided with the protruding bone. He yelped and yanked his hands away.

"You motherfucker!" Darren yelled. "You fucking dropped me!"

Brian rolled onto his back. For the first time since they began their ordeal, he could feel the exhaustion taking hold of his body. His chest heaved up and down.

"Don't just fucking lay there! Get up and help me!"

Brian shook his head. The balaclava covered his disgust. "Should have left your ass back there," he muttered.

"Seriously, Brian! Quit fucking around!" Darren's voice was frantic.

Brian wondered if the injured man could still see him. "One fucking second!" he shouted back. Rolling onto his side, he shook his head. "Impatient son of a bitch," he muttered. Brian sat up and brushed the snow from his arms and face.

A smile stretched across his face. He could see Port Luck. It was still a long way off, but he could see the outline of buildings and smokestacks rising from chimneys.

"I can see the town!" he cried. A new rush of adrenaline filled his body, allowing Brian to push himself to his knees. The muscles in his legs cramped from the overexertion, but he forced himself to stand up. Once he was fully upright, he took in the rest of his surroundings, looking for the easiest way to town. Thick forest and rough terrain stretched out in every direction. That sudden rush of energy Brian felt waned. He looked to his left one more time, scanning the area in front of him.

There was something black protruding from the snow. From that distance, he couldn't be sure, but he thought it looked like the back of a snowmobile. He took a subconscious step forward, determined to investigate, then remembered Darren was lying helpless in the bushes. Brian sighed and walked back into the tree line.

He found Darren exactly where he expected. The injured man was no longer holding on to the snowmobile seat, electing to cradle his injured leg instead. Darren hissed as he worked to untangle it from all the branches.

"Here, let me help," Brian offered.

"Fucking finally," Darren barked. "The fuck took you so long? You see Fruity Frank out there or something?"

Brian put his hands on his hips. "I could just leave your crippled ass here if you want to be an asshole." Brian turned and took a step away from Darren.

"No! Wait!" Darren yelled with panic in his voice.

Brian turned to see him reaching out. A smile threatened at the corners of Brian's mouth. He never had any intention of leaving a man to die, but it was fun watching the bigot squirm for a second. Fighting off the smile, he turned and stared at Darren.

"I'm sorry. I'm just in a lot of pain," Darren pleaded.

Brian dropped to a knee next to him and began untangling the injured leg from the branches. Darren hissed and threw his head back every time Brian did anything, but within about thirty seconds, the foot was free. Brian grabbed the back of Darren's jacket and unceremoniously dragged him through the remaining shrubbery and into the clearing. Once that was done, he retrieved the snowmobile's broken seat and dropped it to the ground next to Darren.

"Climb on," he said.

Darren hung his head and reluctantly climbed onto the seat.

Brian watched him grip the handle and sighed. "You don't always have to be a huge asshole," Brian said.

Darren refused to meet his gaze. "I don't try to be."

"Could have fooled me." Brian moved forward, dragging Darren toward the object he saw earlier. "Seriously, though, why are you such a dick to everyone?"

Darren remained silent as Brian dragged him. When Darren realized they were walking parallel to the town, he decided to use it to change the subject. "Why aren't we walking toward the town?"

Brian shook his head at the obvious evasion. "I saw something up here. Wanted to check it out first."

They fought their way through the thick snow to the overturned snowmobile. "I'm going to set you down while I look at this," Brian said. He lowered Darren as gently as he could, cringing as Darren yelped in pain when his femur bone touched the icy snow.

The rear track of a snowmobile protruded from the snow. Dropping to a knee, Brian shoveled some of the snow away from the machine. He gasped at the deep lacerations in the metal along its side. The track was broken in half, hanging loosely from one side. Claw marks marred the seat. Brian shook his head and chuckled softly. Whatever this thing was, it really hated snowmobiles.

"What is it?" Darren asked. He had propped himself up on his elbow but couldn't get a clear view with Brian in the way.

"A snowmobile," he said. "A very fucked-up snowmobile."

"Do you think your radio might work now that the storm has died down?" Darren asked.

The question caught Brian by surprise. How could he forget the radio? Yanking it from his belt, he pressed the button to speak and held it to his mouth.

"This is Deputy Brian Williams ..." Brian started to ask for help, but a sudden realization stopped him. The radio hadn't beeped when he pressed the button. Pulling it away from his face, he could see the awful truth. The radio was dead.

"Fucking thing is dead," he said.

"You didn't turn it off!" Darren shouted. "How could you be so fucking stupid?"

Brian spun around. "I'm sorry! I was a little busy keeping your bitch ass alive." He turned back to the damaged snowmobile. "Ungrateful son of a bitch," he said loud enough for Darren to hear. Then he walked back to Darren and grabbed hold of the seat. He yanked it up much less gently than before, causing Darren to cry out in pain. He didn't even bother to make sure Darren had a good grip on the seat before he began pulling again. Brian quickly dragged him around the destroyed machine and started down the hill toward town.

They made it about thirty yards when Brian's foot caught on something in the snow, sending him tumbling forward. He fell again, dropping Darren in the process. He immediately jumped up and yelled in frustration. "God-damn it!" he yelled as he kicked at the snow.

"What the fuck?" Darren groaned. "Quit fucking drop-ping me!"

"Fucking tripped on something," he replied. Brian dropped to his knees to investigate the thing that tripped him, and his blood ran cold. It was a boot. His eyes trekked up the foot to a leg and, eventually, the outline of a body buried beneath a mound of snow. "It's a body," he whis-pered. Slowly, he reached out to where he assumed the face would be and brushed the top layer of snow away to reveal chunks of ice stained red with blood. He sank his already numb fingers into the snow and peeled the ice away.

"What? What is it?" Darren asked.

Brian looked down at the mangled corpse. The skull was flattened. The dead man's eyes bulged from their sockets. Frozen brain matter clung to shredded flesh. Brian's eyes drifted to the necklace that lay against the corpse's frozen chest. It was a small metal symbol, a spiral that he recognized. He had seen it on Hanta on the few occasions he had actually laid eyes on the man. Regret gripped Brian's chest, making it difficult to breathe. They shouldn't have sent him out there alone.

For some reason, he felt the need to bring a piece of the dead man back to town with him. He grasped the necklace and twirled it in his fingers before pulling it off of the body. Brian deposited it into his pocket. He patted Hanta on the chest and lowered his head. "I'm sorry," he whispered.

Darren's scream cut off the sentimental moment.

Brian spun around to see the enormous beast, clearly revealed in the daylight, dragging Darren by his uninjured leg toward the trees, the monster's paw-like hand wrapped firmly around the ankle. Darren's broken leg bent horribly as he was dragged away. Brian locked eyes with Darren; Darren's eyes were wide and desperate.

Brian swung the rifle from his back and, like before, raised it to his shoulder. He aimed it at the beast, but before he could fire, it lifted Darren into the air, dangling the injured man between them. Brian's mouth fell open—it was using Darren as a human shield. Brian lowered the rifle slightly, searching for any sign of a clear shot.

Peeking out from behind the suspended Darren, the creature looked at Brian with its dark-yellow eyes. Brian was sure of it this time. The beast was smiling.

It grabbed Darren's left arm with its free hand. The beast's claws dug deep into his flesh, sending streaks of blood gushing across his body. It released its grip on Darren's leg and grabbed the other arm. The strength of the monster was incredible. It held Darren up like a child with a doll, shaking him violently. Once it had a good grip on each of his arms, it held him up for Brian to see. Darren's arms were held straight out at his side, a mockery of Christ on the cross.

Brian watched the scene play out in slow motion. He saw the beast's muscles tense. Darren's face contorted with excruciating pain. The monster pulled, and Darren's arms separated from his body. His armless body crashed to the ground with a sickening crunch. Blood spurted from the open wounds in his shoulders, bathing the creature in crimson. It tossed one of Darren's arms into the air, allowing droplets of blood to rain down on them.

Brian raised the rifle again; his finger drifted to the trigger. Before he could fire the first shot, the beast cocked back and launched the other severed arm at Brian.

Brian flinched and tried to duck, but the flying limb caught him square in the chest, knocking him to the ground, expelling the air from his lungs. He gasped for air, causing a sharp jolt of pain to explode in his side. He immediately knew at least one, likely several, of his ribs was broken.

Forcing himself to sit up through the pain, his hands scoured the snow in search of his rifle. His fingers wrapped around the hard metal of the barrel and yanked it off the ground. Pulling it to his shoulder, he returned his attention to the last spot he had seen the beast.

It wasn't there.

His eyes danced wildly around, scanning for any sign of danger. Wherever the monster had gone, he couldn't see it. Cautiously, Brian climbed to his knees, gritting through the pain radiating from his side. He sucked in as deep a breath as he could before standing, rifle at the ready.

He crept forward. Darren's armless body convulsed violently in the snow. The blood gushing from his wounds saturated the area. The red liquid settled in grotesque pools at his side.

Brian looked down at his disfigured companion and allowed the tears to flow.

Darren was still alive. His skin was quickly turning pale from the extensive blood loss, and his eyes stretched impossibly wide as he gasped for breath. "Kill ..." Darren struggled to say. "Please." He gasped. "Kill." Another sharp intake of breath as he fought against the shock. "Me," he begged.

Brian sobbed. He hated Darren; the man was a bigot and overall asshole. But nobody deserved this. Brian wasn't sure of the legality of what he was about to do, but he knew he couldn't watch Darren bleed to death in the snow. He shouldered the rifle and aimed it at Darren's forehead.

"Do it," Darren encouraged. He lifted his head from the snow, pressing his forehead into the muzzle.

Squeezing his eyes shut, Brian pulled the trigger.

A hole opened in Darren's forehead, snapping his head back. His body stopped convulsing. His cold, lifeless eyes stared up at Brian.

Brian knew that if he survived, those eyes would haunt him for the rest of his life. Tearing his eyes away from the corpse, he swung the rifle over his shoulder and turned away.

"I'm sorry," he whispered, then started his solo march back to town.

Chapter 21

Johnny shivered violently against a barren tree. He sat with his back to it, legs crossed. Beside him, Victor and Jeremiah leaned against him for warmth. The three men had ridden out the storm huddled up, using the trees to break the skin-blistering wind.

He was reasonably certain the other two were still asleep. Their chests rose and fell in slow, steady rhythms. Glancing down, he could see their pale skin and bluish lips from under their masks. The three of them were no doubt on the edge of hypothermia.

Johnny thought of Afghanistan and chuckled to himself. The place was a shit hole and regularly got over one hundred degrees. No matter how many months he stayed there, he couldn't get used to it. Now, huddled up with two grown men, shivering uncontrollably, he wished he was back in the desert. Hell, he would have settled for his

M4 rifle. There was never a problem he hadn't been able to solve with a few magazines and fully automatic gunfire.

Rays of sunlight broke through the trees, signaling sunrise. Judging by its height, it was somewhere between nine and ten in the morning. The brutally long night in the snow was finally coming to an end. They needed to get up and make a decision. The group could push on in search of Brian and Darren or turn back. As badly as Johnny wanted to push on and find the boys, he knew the three of them were useless in their near-hypothermic state. It would be better for them to return to town, warm up, and organize themselves into a proper search party. He kicked himself for reacting in such a panicked and hasty fashion.

A rustling noise snapped Johnny from his thoughts. His frozen brain responded sluggishly at first, acutely aware of a threat but not reacting. The rustling grew closer, followed by a loud snap as a branch was stepped on. The snapping noise finally kicked Johnny into action. He pushed himself up from the tree. The two men leaning on him fell off his shoulder, collapsing to the ground. They mumbled and cursed as they fought grogginess.

Slowly, he slipped the glove off his right hand and drew his pistol, pointing it in the direction of the noise. His hot breath swirled around him like smoke as his hands trembled from a combination of fatigue and cold. His fingers had gone completely numb during the night, the tips burned from the early onset of frostbite. Unsure of where his fingers actually were, Johnny stole a glance at the trigger to make sure his finger was in the correct spot.

A human-like shape emerged from behind the tree branches in front of him. It was still too dark to make out its features, but Johnny could tell it was incredibly tall.

"Shoot it," Victor whispered.

Johnny ignored him, keeping his barrel trained on the approaching shadow.

"What're you waiting for? Fucking shoot it," Victor hissed.

"Would you shut ..." Johnny's retort was cut off by an exhausted-looking Brian pushing through the branches and collapsing to the ground in front of them. He stayed face down in the snow, sucking in deep, labored breaths.

Johnny quickly holstered his pistol and scrambled to his deputy's side. "Brian? Brian, can you hear me?" he repeated. "Help me turn him over!" he shouted to nobody in particular. Jeremiah appeared at his side, and together, they managed to roll Brian onto his back. Johnny's Marine Corps training kicked in immediately. His fingers danced along the younger man, searching for any sign of trauma. When Johnny's hands brushed against his side, Brian cried out.

"Ahhh! Fuck!" Brian shouted.

Relief washed over Johnny. "Don't be a baby," he teased with a smile. Johnny slumped back onto his butt and patted Brian on the chest. "It's good to see you, buddy."

"You too," Brian said through a cough. "Any chance you got water?"

Johnny shook his head. "Nah, it froze up solid last night. But we can get you all the water you want back in town."

Victor must have finally realized Brian was alone because he sprinted over and fell to his knees beside the others. "Where's my boy? Where's Darren?" he shouted. Tears swelled in his eyes. Victor's expression told Johnny he already knew what Brian was about to say.

Brian shook his head. "He didn't make it," he squeaked out through cracked lips. "Fucking monster got him."

"Monster?" Jeremiah asked.

Johnny squeezed the man's shoulder. "He's obviously hypothermic. Probably delusional," he reassured the others.

Brian started to address the allegation but was cut off by Victor.

"Where's his body? I need to get it," he shouted through loud sobs. Victor pushed past Johnny and grabbed Brian's arm. "Where?" The final word came out as a mournful wail.

Johnny held his hand out like a crossing guard stopping cars. "Whoa. I don't think that's a good idea. We need to get back to town and regroup."

"Fuck you!" Victor shouted. His eyes became blood-shot and the tears flowed freely. "I'm getting my son." He jumped to his feet and snatched his backpack from the snow.

Johnny jumped up and stepped in front of the mayor. "That's a bad idea. You don't know where his body is, and this animal or whatever is still out there." He placed a hand on Victor's chest to slow him down.

Victor slapped his hand away. "I don't give a damn! I'm finding my son."

Johnny was surprised at the passion in the man's voice. He would have done the same for his own kids if he had any. Hell, he marched blindly into a storm last night for Brian. But it felt out of character for the mayor. Victor always came across as a self-absorbed asshole. Johnny assumed the news of his son's death struck something primal in the man. Sighing, he stepped aside and watched Victor push through the trees and disappear into the Alaskan wilderness.

"Should we go with him?" Jeremiah asked.

Johnny shook his head. "No. We need to get Brian back to town." He leaned down and took Brian under one arm.

"Come on, kid." Grunting from the effort, he pulled on Brian.

With Johnny's help, Brian managed to stand. His legs felt wobbly under his weight, but he was able to keep from falling.

"Why don't you get Brian back to town, and I'll go after the mayor?" Jeremiah suggested. He pointed in the direction Victor went. "It's not safe for him out there alone, and he'll need help with the body."

Johnny thought about it for a minute before nodding. He retrieved the radio from his belt and held it out to Jeremiah. "It's only about half charged. Keep it off unless you need something. I'll grab one of the spare ones from the station."

Jeremiah clipped the radio onto his belt. There was a look of sadness in the old man's eyes as he held out a hand toward Johnny, who shook it. "If I don't make it back, you tell my wife I love her," he said, regret filling his voice.

Johnny wanted to protest. It seemed stupid to run out in the snow for a dead body, especially with some sort of wild animal on the loose. He started to ask Jeremiah to come back with them, but he knew it was pointless. He had known Jeremiah for a long time, and the man was nothing if not bull-headed. Johnny just nodded. Without another word, Jeremiah disappeared into the wilderness in search of Victor.

Brian clapped Johnny on the chest. "Come on, boss. I'm freezing my ass off out here." He started walking toward town.

Johnny watched the spot where Victor and Jeremiah disappeared for a few more moments before reluctantly following Brian.

"What're we going to do?" Brian asked.

Johnny thought about it. They had no internet. The phones were dead. They had tried sending someone for help and it only resulted in another fatality. There would be no help coming, and people were dying. To Johnny, there were only two valid options. Option one, they hunkered down and waited for whatever was killing people to move on. Or option two, they made a run for it.

"Did you shoot that thing?" Johnny asked.

Brian nodded. "Emptied an entire magazine." He held up his hands to mimic firing the rifle. "I hit it almost every time."

Johnny jerked his head toward Brian. "And it didn't go down?" he asked incredulously.

Brian shook his head. "Bullets didn't even seem to *slow* it down. It trashed my machine and disappeared into the woods after," he paused, emphasizing the word, "I *shot* it." He cracked his neck. "Didn't see it again until ..." His sentence trailed off.

"Until it got Darren," Johnny finished.

Brian gulped. "Yeah." The word came out as a defeated whisper.

The two walked for a few more minutes in silence before Brian spoke again. "There's more." He rubbed his eyes. He couldn't remember the last time he slept. The mix of excitement, fear, and sadness fatigued him even more than the physical trek through the Alaskan wilderness. "I found Hanta."

Johnny stopped walking and stared at Brian, impatiently waiting for Brian to give him the news he knew was coming.

"He's dead," Brian huffed out.

Johnny shook his head. He kicked at the snow and nearly lost his balance. "Fuck!" He kicked the snow again. "Goddamn it!"

Brian gave his boss a wide berth, giving him plenty of room to vent his frustration. When Johnny started walking again, Brian rushed to catch up.

They continued walking in silence until they were almost to town. Johnny hadn't realized how close they actually were. That meant they had barely left town before giving up the night before. A flood of shame washed over him. He was the sheriff, and he was failing. Failing to protect his town.

"Once we warm up, we're going to gather everyone in the church."

Brian shot him an inquisitive glance.

"It'll be easier to defend for the night. Tomorrow, we're leaving. All of us."

Brian smiled. "Sounds good to me, boss."

Jeremiah pushed a branch out of his way to reveal an open stretch of snow-covered terrain leading up a steep hill. Deep tracks marred the otherwise pristine snow. Victor was moving too fast for Jeremiah to catch him. He was jogging as fast as his old, arthritic knees would allow. He had always prided himself on his physical fitness, but as his wife often reminded him, you can't beat time. He sucked in a deep breath, pulled the strap of his rifle tighter to prevent it from swinging, and pushed ahead.

The trek up the hill was long, but near the top, he found Victor on his knees. The man was sobbing hysterically. His body convulsed with each deep wail. Covering his face, his hands muffled his cries.

Jeremiah could do nothing but watch as Victor punched the snow surrounding his son's body. Darren's skin was a pale blue. There was a massive hole in the boy's stomach. Leaning over Victor, he could see straight into the empty cavern of the body. Glancing around, he noticed chunks of eviscerated organs scattered across the ground. The realization made Jeremiah sick, and he forced back a gag. His eyes drifted over the armless corpse to the hole in his head. It was obviously a gunshot wound. By his best guess, it would either be a .223 or 5.56 round. Jeremiah remembered seeing Brian with the AR15 and realized the haunting truth. The gunshot was a mercy kill to put Darren out of his misery.

Victor stopped thrashing and kissed the boy on the cheek, then pulled his son's eyelids down. They stuck a little at first, frozen in place. Victor slipped a hand under Darren's neck and the other under his legs. He grunted as he lifted the body out of the snow and onto his lap.

Jeremiah watched Victor cradling his deceased son. Rigor mortis had set in, probably worsened by the extreme cold. It caused Victor to teeter awkwardly under the uneven weight and stiff position of the body.

Jeremiah waited a few minutes before putting a hand on the mayor's shoulder. "I think we should head back to town."

Victor nodded. "I need to bring him with me, for his mother." He tried to stand, releasing a grunt before lowering the body back to the ground. "He's too heavy," Victor said. Choking back a sob, he slid out from under the corpse. Standing up, he grabbed the back of his deceased son's jacket. With another grunt, he heaved backward, dragging the body several feet through the snow.

Jeremiah watched on helplessly. There was no way the two of them could drag a body several miles through the snow. It would take them all day, and that was if they didn't succumb to hypothermia first. He considered trying to help the man despite his reservations. Before he could take a step, something in the distance caught his eye.

He saw something running out there. Squatting down, he squinted at it. The creature ran on all fours like a dog or wolf. Jeremiah unslung his rifle and pulled it to his shoulder. He quickly judged the distance to be around a thousand yards. Turning the knob on top of his scope, he accounted for the distance. Taking aim, he placed the crosshairs on the front shoulder of the beast.

It was a wolf, one of the largest Jeremiah had ever seen. A smile crept across his lips.

I hope I still got it.

He shifted his weight and led the wolf by a few steps. Exhaling slowly, he pulled the trigger. The rifle kicked his shoulder. His skin bruised much easier than it used to, and he released a soft curse at the pain. Looking through the scope, he watched the wolf take three staggering steps before dropping into the snow.

"I got it!" Jeremiah cheered. "I shot the bastard!" Beaming with pride, he lowered the rifle. "Victor! I shot the son of a bitch!" He looked to the spot where Victor had been trying to drag his dead son.

Victor was nowhere to be seen. Darren's armless corpse lay abandoned in the snow.

"Victor?" Jeremiah said while slowly standing up. "Victor? Where are you?" He spun around, scanning the area around him. There was some disturbed snow that tracked from the woods to approximately where Victor had been standing. He took a few cautious steps toward Darren's body with his gun raised. As he approached, he noticed something buried in the snow behind Darren's head. Bright-red blood stained the area.

Jeremiah moved around the body and plunged his hand into the snow. His finger wrapped around something soft and wet. With a grunt, he yanked the object out of the snow. It was a severed leg, the foot still in the boot.

Instinctually, he dropped the disembodied leg and stumbled backward. Jeremiah quickly lost his balance and fell into the snow. His subconscious mind registered something as he lay there, frozen with fear.

It was Victor's boot.

A scream escaped his lips, and without any further hesitation, he lunged back to his feet and sprinted toward town. Behind him, something laughed.

Chapter 22

Johnny and Brian huddled together in front of a roaring fire, the flames dancing and crackling. They shivered as they waited for the heat to penetrate their bodies and thaw their frozen bones.

Amy came down the stairs of Jackson's General Store carrying two cups of steaming-hot coffee. The aroma wafted through the room, causing Johnny to smile. He and Brian eagerly took their mugs and sipped, and Brian grimaced at the bitter taste.

Johnny smiled. "What's the matter? Not enough creamer for you?" he said in a teasing tone.

"Not at all, but somehow, it's still the best coffee I've ever had." Brian laughed.

Amy moved behind Johnny and rubbed his shoulders. She leaned down and kissed him on top of his head. "I'm glad you're OK," she whispered in his ear.

He patted her arm quickly before stretching it out toward the fire. "I'm not sure if any of us are OK."

Brian shook his head. "Not at all, boss."

Anita Jackson stepped into the room. "I'm sorry. Y'all must be so tired, and I don't want to pressure you, sheriff. I know you're trying to warm up, but I have to know."

Johnny raised his head to look at the frail, old woman.

"Is my husband safe?" she half asked, half pleaded.

Johnny gave her a solemn look. He slowly shook his head. "I'm honestly not sure, ma'am. He agreed to go with Mayor Henry to look for Darren's body."

Anita recoiled. Shock spread across her face. "Darren Henry is dead?"

Amy's grip tightened on Johnny's shoulder.

A creak from the staircase drew everyone's attention to Miss Grover as she crept down the stairs. As soon as everyone's eyes fell on her, she panicked and sprinted back up the stairs, disappearing into her room.

"Yeah," Brian said, drawing their attention back to the issue. "I saw it happen." He pressed the mug to his lips and took a long drink from the coffee. The scalding liquid hurt as it went down. He swallowed hard and looked at Johnny. "It was a monster, boss. I know it sounds insane, but ..." Brian paused. He took another swig of the coffee, forcing himself to quell the panic rising in his chest. "I saw it with my own eyes. It's huge." His voice quavered with the memory. "It ripped Darren's arms off."

"Oh my god." Anita gasped, and her hand flew to her mouth. She took a staggered step back, and Amy rushed to her side and grabbed hold of Anita's arm to steady her. "My Jeremiah is still out there," she said. Nausea bubbled in her stomach as fear overtook her.

"I know. They should be back any ..." Johnny said before being cut off by the chime of the bell above the door. All four of them turned to see who entered the General Store. Jeremiah collapsed through the doorway, falling to his hands and knees. He inhaled deep, ragged gasps of air as he fought to catch his breath. His wind-chapped skin appeared unnaturally pink.

Anita ran across the room and fell to her husband's side. Tears streamed down her face while she pulled him into a hug. Then, without warning, she pulled away and smacked him on the shoulder. "You old fool!" she scolded. "You can't go running out into storms at your age!"

He pushed himself upright, sitting on his heels. Jeremiah pulled his wife in for a kiss and whispered something in her ear. Anita's deep frown turned into a smile.

The bell above the door chimed again, and Martha Henry burst through the door wearing a nightgown, sandals, and one of her husband's bulky jackets. Deep blue bags covered the lower part her eyes, giving her the appearance of a crazy person under her unkempt head of hair. She glanced down at Jeremiah, who was still sitting on the floor, then quickly stepped around him. Striding across the room to where Johnny sat, she put her hands on her hips. "Where are my husband and son?" she demanded.

Johnny set his coffee down and stood up.

Brian opened his mouth to speak, but Johnny shot him a look. The deputy closed his mouth and took his boss's lead, setting down his coffee and standing up.

"Mrs. Henry, I'm afraid I've got some bad news," Johnny said in the most professional tone he could manage.

The woman threw up a hand. "To hell with your bad news, Johnny Myers!" she screamed, taking a step forward. "Where is my family?" Her tone was demanding but quivered slightly.

Something snapped inside of Johnny. He thought about the first time one of his marines died in Afghanistan. The marine assigned to inform him of his friend's death dragged it out. Back then, he wished the guy had just come out with it, ripped the bandage off. He decided that would be the best approach in this situation. "Darren is dead, Martha," Johnny said flatly.

Martha blinked rapidly a few times. She stammered and took a half-step back.

Johnny reached out to grab her arm, afraid the woman would keel over. Just as his fingertips brushed the jacket, she smacked him in the face. The hit didn't hurt, it only stung a little. He forced himself not to react.

She cocked her hand back to slap him again, and Johnny didn't move. He was determined to let the woman take her frustration out on him.

Luckily, Brian stepped forward and grabbed her arm. "That's not helping, Martha," he said sternly.

She glared at him until he released her wrist. Lowering her head, she asked, "How did he die?" Her question was so quiet Johnny wasn't even sure she had asked it.

Before Johnny could answer, Jeremiah appeared at their side. "Victor's dead too," he said solemnly.

Johnny had expected it when Jeremiah had come into the store alone, but until that moment, he had held out hope he was mistaken.

The words crashed into the newly widowed Martha like a wave. She released a primal scream, slumping to the ground and screaming as loudly as she could. Rocking back and forth, she wailed until a blood vessel burst in her right eye, causing the white part to turn a deep shade of red.

Nobody moved to comfort her; they knew there was nothing they could do. The group stood watching her for a long time, until her cries gradually died down. When her wailing finally reduced to pained sobs, Amy and Anita escorted her upstairs. They laid her on the Jackson's bed, rubbing her back in an attempt to soothe her.

Johnny, Brian, and Jeremiah stood silently in the center of the store for a long time. Johnny finally broke the stalemate by retrieving his cold coffee from the table. Raising the mug to his lips, he downed the remaining bit and set the empty cup back down.

"We need to gather everyone in the church," he said confidently. "I'm not sure what's going on, but there's safety in numbers."

"You still want to make a run for it?" Brian asked.

Johnny nodded. "Yeah. I think it's time we get those old army surplus trucks out of storage."

"Do those old rust buckets even run?" Jeremiah asked incredulously.

Johnny shrugged. "Only one way to find out. But first, let's gather everyone up."

Chapter 23

A few hours later, Johnny stood alone on the stage of the church. The old wooden floorboards moaned under his weight as he slowly paced back and forth, waiting for the town's people to find their seats. Typically, Amy would get on to him about his unprofessional habits, but he didn't care about that at that moment.

His eyes drifted to the cross on the wall behind the stage. It was the same worn-out piece of wood that had been there since he was a kid. A strange feeling washed over him. Standing at the head of a church congregation felt like a lie—he and God hadn't exactly been on speaking terms since his trip through the desert.

He gazed out over the faces of the remaining towns-folk while he waited for Brian and Jeremiah to usher the last few people inside. Once they were in, Brian slammed the door shut before turning to Johnny and giving him a thumbs up.

Doing a quick head count, he estimated there were still about twenty-five adults, along with nearly as many kids, still remaining. An icy bolt of panic shot threw him. That was less than half the town. They had seen a lot of dead bodies over the last few days, but he was just now realizing how many people were missing. Whatever the monstrosity was, it had managed to kill more than half the town in only two days, and it had done most of that without being seen or leaving evidence. Pausing his pacing, he reflected on the previous week. Kill wasn't a strong enough word. This creature had massacred the people of his town. It was worse than anything he had seen during his tours in the desert.

The pastor stood and gingerly climbed onto the stage. He reached under the podium, retrieved a Bible, and flipped it open. Setting it down, he waited a moment for the murmurs to die down. "I've known Sheriff Myers since he was a boy," the pastor said. He gave Johnny a weak smile. "He has been an excellent sheepdog to this flock for the last few years. His father protected us before him. I'm sure he has gathered us here for a good reason, and I ask that you give him the full attention and respect befitting his position." Holding up a finger, he paused. "But before he goes into that reason, I'd like to say a quick prayer." He looked back over to Johnny. "With your permission, of course."

Johnny and his wife were one of the only couples who didn't regularly attend church. They didn't pray. Hell, Johnny was an atheist. But he bowed his head out of respect.

The pastor led the congregation in a quick prayer about trusting the Lord to deliver them from these trying times, then stepped off the little stage, returning to his seat in the front row.

Taking a deep breath, Johnny moved to the center of the stage. "I'm afraid I've got some terrible news."

"Is this about the cannery workers?" someone in the back shouted. Johnny looked out to see one of the fishermen he had met that day glaring at him.

"Are they really dead?" a woman asked.

"Where is everyone else?" someone shouted.

Johnny held up his hands in a placating gesture. "People, if I may?"

A man that Johnny recognized as Kevin Beauchamp jumped to his feet. The man was a heavy drinker, and from the way he wobbled, Johnny suspected he was a fifth of whiskey deep.

"Why isn't the mayor giving us this bad news?" he yelled, spittle flying from his mouth. The slur in his words confirmed Johnny's suspicions. The man teetered slight-ly, then threw up his hands. "That rich fuck ain't even here!" he shouted above the growing noise of the impatient crowd. "I bet that lousy bastard is drinking scotch in his fancy office right now!"

Fury bubbled up in Johnny. "He's not here because he's dead!" Johnny snapped back. "Now sit down and let me speak."

That seemed to grab everyone's attention. The townspeople fell silent, a sea of eyes firmly fixated on his every movement. "Now," Johnny continued, "like I said, Mayor Henry and his son Darren are ..." He paused to look at his wife, who was consoling Martha near the back of the church. "They're dead," he said softly. "So are Hanta, Dr. Earnest, and all of the cannery workers. Judging by how few people I see here, there are probably a few others I don't know about yet."

There was a momentary silence that left Johnny's words lingering in the air, then all at once, people erupted into a cacophonous roar. They shouted, demanding to know what happened, what they were going to do, and why Johnny couldn't protect them.

Johnny raised his hands, giving them a quiet-down motion, but the people continued shouting. A few of the more bullish men flew to their feet. They yelled out above the crowd and clenched their fists, acting out of hot-headedness.

"Hey! Quiet down!" Johnny commanded.

The clamor of the terrified townsfolk grew louder as they ignored him.

Brian stepped away from the door and shoved his way into the riotous crowd. He slung the rifle over his shoulder, the butt smacking him in the small of his already sore back. Sticking his fingers into his mouth, he whistled as loudly as he could. The sharp report silenced the crowd, bringing all of their eyes to him. "I know you're scared, but let us do our job!" he shouted. The crowd continued their murmuring, but at a much lower volume A little quieter, he continued. "There's something out there." He pointed toward the door of the church. The heads of the group snapped in that direction, following his hand. "And it's killing people." He pointed back toward Johnny, stifling a smile as they snapped their heads back. They hung on to his every word. "He has a plan," Brian said as sternly as he could. That seemed to settle down the crowd and restore some of the confidence they had in their police force.

"Thank you, Brian," Johnny said, a sense of pride ballooning in his chest. Hopping off the stage, he approached the group. "Listen, I know you're scared, but we have to be smart about this." He rested a hand on Kevin Beauchamp's shoulder. The man slowly nodded.

"Sorry, Johnny," he muttered.

"It's ok, man. We have to stick together." He took a few steps back so he could see the entire group. "The phones and internet are dead, and we don't know why." Johnny rubbed at his forehead, feeling the beginning of a headache coming on. Trying to remember the last time he slept, he grimaced. It must have been at least twenty-four hours. "We tried to call the state police and National Guard but couldn't get through to anyone." He pointed to Brian. "When that failed, Brian and Darren tried to ride out of here last night to get help." His eyes fell. With a half whisper, he admitted, "It didn't go well." His eyes unconsciously flicked over to where Amy sat. She had an arm draped over a zombie-eyed Martha. Ignoring the knot of regret in his stomach, Johnny continued. "Whatever that thing is," he motioned toward the door with his head, "it has only attacked during the nighttime. I'm proposing we take the old army surplus truck from storage and make a run for it."

Several people gasped. A sea of shocked and scared expressions stared back at him.

Kevin Beauchamp stepped closer. The man's impressive size lingered over Johnny.

Brian slowly pushed through a few more people, closing the distance between his boss and the town drunk.

Johnny shifted his weight onto his back foot and braced himself for another confrontation.

"Is it really that bad?" the big man asked.

Brian answered before Johnny could. "I shot it several times and it just kept moving." The revelation that bullets hadn't stopped the thing caused another stir of commotion. After a second, it died down. Brian sighed. "I think it's a were ..."

Johnny jumped in to cut him off. "It's probably some sort of bear or wolf." He shot Brian a death glare. If they mentioned the word werewolf, there could only be two outcomes. Either the townspeople would laugh off the threat and stop listening to Johnny, or they would panic. Neither option was appealing. Besides, they didn't know what they were dealing with. Johnny had seen no evidence the creature was a werewolf, at least not in the traditional movie sense. All they knew for sure was it was wolf-like and seemed impervious to bullets. Hanta's words about an Amarok echoed in his head. The hunter seemed so certain it was a myth, but at that moment, Johnny wasn't sure.

"Either way," Johnny continued, "it's dangerous." He looked across the sea of terrified faces. They were all looking to him for leadership. "So we're going to stay here," he pointed to the floor, "in the church tonight. There is safety in numbers. Then we make a run for it first thing in the morning."

There was a chorus of hushed whispers, but nobody protested. Johnny's eyes drifted over the crowd until he met Kevin Beauchamp's gaze. If anyone would give them pushback, it would be him.

With only a slight alcohol-induced droop to his eyelids, Kevin nodded. The large man looked as scared as the rest of them.

Johnny clapped his hands. "It's settled, then. Everyone get some sleep wherever you can get comfortable. Brian and I will take turns keeping watch over everyone until morning."

Chapter 24

Johnny awoke to the sounds of panicked shouting. The wooden church pew he was sleeping on was uncomfortable, but as a marine, he could sleep on anything. His back cracked when he sat up. The church was almost completely dark except for a few candles adorning the wall. Shadows from the candles danced on the ceiling.

He scanned the pews, groggily searching for the source of the shouting. Curious heads popped up like meerkats, matching his confused look. Then he heard Brian's voice cut through the confusion.

"Martha! Get back in here!"

Johnny's eyes snapped to the open door and his blood ran cold. Gusts of snow swirled into the room. Brian and Jeremiah were leaning through the doorway, shouting into the darkness. Johnny swam through the sea of blankets covering him. The rickety old pew moaned under his weight when he pushed himself off. His hand flew to his revolver and yanked it out of the holster. Still groggy, he was hesitant to raise the pistol with people all around him, electing instead to keep it pointed toward the floor.

People began gravitating to the walkway between the pews, sleepily investigating the disturbance, their bodies blocking his path.

"Move!" he commanded, squeezing between two men.

"Martha! It's coming!" Brian shouted from the front door.

Panic filled the room. Everyone was on their feet then. Shouts and screams filled the church. The crowd rushed toward the stage, intuitively moving away from the door.

Dread swelled inside of Johnny's chest. He surged through them, pushing several bystanders to the ground. Climbing over them, he clambered to Brian's side and raised his pistol toward the door.

Martha Henry stood fifty yards from the church in the almost knee-deep snow, shivering uncontrollably in her thin nightgown. It was the same one she had been wearing when she found out her husband and son were dead, except she wasn't wearing the jacket now. Snow pelted her pale skin with icy blasts. Even from a distance, Johnny could see her lips were turning blue.

Silver moonlight illuminated the streets, reflecting off the snow. Farther down the road, Johnny could make out an enormous black spot in the shadows that seemed darker than the shade surrounding it. He watched as the enormous shadow moved slowly toward Martha. Then the massive creature stepped into the moonlight, and Johnny finally saw it for himself.

It raised to its full height, standing on its back legs. Muscles rippled under scarred, black flesh coated in a mangy coat of fur. Long, sharp claws extended from human-like fingers. For a brief second, he locked eyes with the monster, its yellow eyes piercing his soul. The monstrosity smiled, revealing massive pointed teeth. Strings of saliva clung to them like streaks of a spider web as it opened its mouth and released an ear-shattering roar that rolled up the street.

Johnny only had a brief moment to register the sound before the beast dropped to all fours and sprinted toward Martha. It ran like a cheetah, coiling and exploding in rapid succession, closing the distance faster than Johnny imagined possible.

The woman turned to face the beast, with tears flowing down her face. She screamed a scared, painful shout as it approached, but she didn't try to run.

Johnny stepped through the open door and down the steps but froze when his boots hit the snow. The creature was closing in too fast. He waved his hands at Martha, desperately trying to get her attention. "Martha! Come back inside! You don't have to do this!" he shouted. His voice carried across the empty streets.

She turned her head to look at him. Emotional torment blazed in her tearful eyes. "They're gone. They're both gone!" she shrieked.

The report of a rifle exploded a few feet behind Johnny's, snapping him out of the daze. He involuntarily ducked away from the sound, cupping his ears. The noise of the outside world was temporarily replaced with tinnitus. Looking over his shoulder, he saw Jeremiah Jackson with his rifle raised.

Demonstrating his many years of skilled practice, he yanked the bolt back and chambered another round. He exhaled and pulled the trigger. The muzzle flash lit the area around them, followed by another gunshot.

Johnny turned his head in time to see the creature stumble a bit, but it never stopped moving.

Brian followed Jeremiah's lead, raising his AR15 to his shoulder and firing three shots in rapid succession. Again, the creature recoiled but continued its determined sprint down the road. Brian jumped down the three steps to Johnny's side and fired two more shots as the beast closed in.

The men could do nothing but watch as it reached Martha.

It lunged through the air, smacking into her with bone-shattering force. Its mouth wrapped around her face, the jaws clamping down with tremendous force. Johnny watched as in seemingly slow motion the beast's fangs penetrated the woman's flesh, sinking deep into her skull. With a little more force, her head caved in. Bits of blood and gray brain matter spurted out and coated the snow in sickly gore.

Brian was the first to act. He resumed shooting, firing round after round. His bullets struck the beast several more times, but it didn't seem to notice.

It reared back and plunged one of its enormous hands into Martha's abdomen. When it yanked its hand out again, it was full of blood-soaked tissue. The creature ignored the gunshots ringing out from Brian's and Jeremiah's rifles as it continued to massacre the carcass under it. Blood gushed from Martha's tattered body, intermingling with a mess of other bodily fluids into a morbid soup in the snow. With a tug, it ripped off an arm and flung it toward the men. They ducked in unison as it slammed into the exterior wall of the church with a squelch. It fell lazily to the snow, leaving streaks of blood down the wall.

"Get your asses in here!" Jeremiah yelled from the doorway. He worked the action on his rifle, firing two more shots in rapid succession.

Johnny felt a tug on the back of his jacket. He stole a final glimpse of Martha's ruined body before allowing Brian to pull him back up the stairs. The two reached the door and stood next to Jeremiah, eyeing the creature.

It stopped shredding Martha long enough to look over to them. Blood dripped from its jaws and coated its fur. The beast slowly stood up and took a single menacing step forward. A bit of Martha's innards still dangled limply from its hands. The creature slowly moved its hand to its mouth, tilted its head back, and dropped the ruined organ in. It chewed slowly, savoring the flavor and mocking the men.

Johnny slammed the door shut and clicked the lock. They stood in the near-total darkness of the church, listening as whatever that thing was devoured their late mayor's wife. The smacking sounds of the beast's mouth and the squishing of raw flesh tearing caused Johnny's stomach to flip. Sucking in deep breaths through his nose, he fought the urge to vomit.

The beast's growl reverberated off the walls of the church, stabbing icy knives of fear into their hearts.

Chapter 25

Johnny checked his watch for what must have been the hundredth time. It was difficult to read in the low light, and he had to position it at an awkward angle to catch the candlelight. Squinting to read it, he determined it was a little after seven thirty in the morning. His head lolled back against the door of the church. Sucking in a deep breath, he patted Brian on the leg.

Brian startled awake, hand immediately going to the grip of the AR15 resting across his lap. When he realized it was just Johnny, his grip loosened. Rubbing his eyes, he let out a pitiful groan. "What time is it?"

"It's nearly eight," Johnny said. "We should load up the truck and get it over here."

Brian raised his arms above his head to stretch, then jumped to his feet. He slung the rifle over his shoulder and stuck out a hand to help Johnny up. "Come on, old man," he said with a smile.

Johnny shook his head and took the hand. He grunted as Brian hoisted him up. Twisting at the waist to crack his back, Johnny said, "A few days ago, I might have taken offense to that."

"And now?" Brian asked.

"And now I'm too old for this shit."

Brian burst out laughing. Johnny quickly shushed him to avoid waking up any more of the townspeople. Looking over the pews, he saw a few heads pop up, but most lay back down when they realized nothing was happening.

Johnny motioned for Jeremiah to join them. The old man pushed himself off the wall, walking toward them with a slight limp Johnny hadn't noticed before. He nodded toward the man's leg. "Something wrong?"

Jeremiah shook his head. "Nah. Just old. Damn bum knee is sore." Patting Johnny on the shoulder, he gave the sheriff a reassuring smile. "I haven't seen this much action since Vietnam."

Johnny cocked an eyebrow. "You were in Vietnam?"

The man smiled. "Yes, sir. Marines."

Johnny looked at him incredulously. "How did I not know that?"

The old man chuckled. "Well, unlike you pretty boys, we didn't go around bragging about it during my day."

Johnny smiled. "That explains the shooting then." He leaned in closer. "Brian and I are going to get the truck. You think you can hold things down here?" he asked in a hushed whisper.

Jeremiah looked around the room at the people. At that point, it was primarily the people who lived in the main part of town, including some children. Nodding, he turned back to Johnny. "Yeah, I suppose I could do that."

Johnny squeezed his shoulder and drew his pistol out of the holster. "If we don't come back," he glanced at Amy, who was asleep against the far wall, "just hole up here as long as you can." He sighed. "And, uh ..." He paused, trying to form the words. "Keep an eye on Amy for me?"

Jeremiah nodded.

Johnny turned the dead bolt on the door, then set his hand on the knob and prepared to turn it. "Ready?" he asked Brian. After a moment without a response, Johnny looked back at his deputy.

Brian wasn't looking at the door or Johnny. He was staring back into the church. Johnny followed his eyes and landed on Frank.

Frank was sitting on the stage with tears in his eyes, staring directly back at Brian.

"Make it quick," Johnny whispered.

Without a moment's hesitation, Brian marched across the church. He approached Frank and leaned down.

Johnny watched as Brian whispered something in Frank's ear. A smile stretched across Frank's face, and a few of the tears that had been building up fell. They rolled down his cheeks until Brian pulled away. He rubbed his fingers against Frank's cheeks, wiping away the tears, then pulled him into a deep kiss. The two embraced each other until Brian tore himself away. Frank's hand held onto Brian's for as long as they could. With a smile on his face, Brian jogged back to where Johnny was waiting without looking back.

Johnny was grinning ear to ear.

Brian pointed a finger at him. "Not a word," he said with a smile.

Johnny held his hands up in surrender. "I wasn't going to say anything." He laughed.

Johnny nodded to Jeremiah then yanked the door open. He stepped cautiously onto the front porch, carefully tiptoeing over Martha's severed arm. His eyes scanned the street for any sign of movement. When he didn't see anything, he waved for Brian to follow him.

Brian stepped outside, gun raised.

"Good luck," Jeremiah said. He slammed the door shut, and Johnny could hear the clink of the dead bolt sliding into place.

Johnny sucked in a deep breath to steel his nerves and rapidly descended the steps. The snow crunched under his boots. The air around him felt oppressive; there was no movement or sound except for the occasional gust of wind.

Martha's desecrated body littered the street. The snow was stained red all around the pieces of her. If Johnny didn't know better, he wouldn't have been able to tell it was a human corpse. Tattered skin and organs lay shredded and strewn about. Her crushed skull gave no hint as to the person she was before.

Johnny forced himself to tear his eyes from the gruesome display and scanned for the monster again. He kept his pistol at the ready and took slow, deliberate steps until he reached the street. He turned back to Brian. "The truck is behind the mayor's office. Stay behind me and keep your head on a swivel." He didn't wait for Brian to respond. He turned away and stalked down the street. With every step, his eyes swept back and forth, but he saw nothing. The street was utterly devoid of life. There wasn't as much as the occasional bird call he had come to expect from living in the Alaskan wilderness. Goosebumps radiated up his arms as he strained his ears in search of any disturbance.

They made their way across the street to the mayor's office. Brian continued following Johnny with the rifle at the ready as they went around the side of the building. He carefully kept the barrel pointed down so as not to risk friendly fire.

The front of the truck came into view as they reached the back of the building. Its forest-green paint stuck out like a sore thumb against the snowy backdrop. A blue tarp covered the bed and part of the cab.

Johnny remembered the briefing the Alaskan National Guard had given him when they turned it over. It was a M939. They were preparing to retire the old trucks and ship them off to the scrap yard when Victor Henry pulled a few strings to have one of the trucks donated to the city. Victor was adamant about having it "in case of an emergency." At the time, Johnny thought the purchase was idiotic. For once, Johnny was relieved to have been so wrong.

They reached the truck without issue and wordlessly went to work prepping it. Johnny moved around to the driver's side, removed the bungee cord holding the tarp in place, and tossed it into the snow. Together, he and Brian peeled the tarp back to reveal the rest of the truck.

Johnny eyed the bed. It would be a tight fit, but he was pretty sure everyone in the church would fit if they lapped up and used every inch of available space.

Holstering his pistol, he pulled open the driver's door and climbed into the seat. Fishing his key ring out of his pocket, he thumbed through the dozen keys to find the right one. He squeezed his eyes shut, begged for the truck to start, slid the key into the ignition, and turned. The truck grumbled as it roared to life. Black smoke billowed from the exhaust, and the vehicle vibrated with the power of its motor. Johnny smacked the steering wheel and cheered.

Brian threw a fist up in triumph before climbing into the bed. He rushed to the front of the truck and smacked the roof before falling to a knee. Raising the rifle up, Brian scanned for any sign of movement in the woods.

The gears ground together as Johnny fought to put the old truck in first gear. It lurched forward, shaking off the bits of snow clinging to its surfaces. Johnny turned the wheel, easing it around the side of the mayor's office. He gassed it as soon as they cleared the building. The sound of the truck roaring down the road echoed through the valley. They approached the church at a high rate of speed.

Brian slammed on the roof. "Hey, hey, slow down!"

Johnny blew past the church, careful to avoid hitting any of Martha's remains.

"Where are you going?" Brian yelled.

Johnny could just make out the words over the whine of the motor but didn't bother answering. He stomped on the brakes, stopping the truck in front of the police station before killing the motor.

"What're we doing here?" Brian asked when Johnny exited the truck.

"There's some spare gas cans in the storage room at the back of the station. I figured we'd grab them, just in case."

Brian nodded his agreement, passing the rifle to Johnny as he jumped down from the bed. Johnny quickly handed the rifle back as soon as Brian righted himself and turned toward the station. "Let's go. We're burning daylight."

They rushed into the station and to the back storage room. Johnny threw open the closet to reveal two plastic gas cans. A thought hit Johnny at that moment. It had been foolish to store gas canisters inside the station. He would have to find a better place to store them when they came back. Johnny grabbed the cans and motioned for Brian to head back out of the building. He tossed the gas cans into the bed of the truck.

"One more thing," Johnny said, turning to face Brian. Removing the key ring from his pocket, he fumbled with one of the keys until it separated from the others. "This is the key to my snowmobile," Johnny said, extending it toward Brian. "I want you to grab it and follow along beside the truck. You'll be in a better position to react if anything happens."

Brian took the key. "It'll be hard to shoot and drive."

Johnny thought about that for a moment while rubbing his chin. "Jeremiah can ride with you. It would still be tough, but between the two of you, I'm sure you'll figure it out." He patted Brian on the shoulder. "We're going to get through this."

Brian nodded, tossing the key into the air and catching it. "Let's go, then," Brian said.

Johnny pointed to where the snowmobile was parked on the side of the station. Brian turned and jogged over to it.

Johnny waited for his deputy to start the machine and gave him a thumbs-up before climbing into the driver's seat of the massive army surplus truck.

Johnny fired it up and drove to the church.

Chapter 26

"Line up!" Johnny shouted from his position by the door. He cupped his hands around his mouth to be heard above the movement within the church.

"Single file! Kids in front of their parents!" Brian shouted. He walked along the line with his rifle slung, waiting for everyone to take their positions.

A woman bent down near the center of the line. She was frantically trying to comfort a boy Johnny imagined was about six years old.

He took a step forward, but Brian threw up his hand. "I got it, boss!"

The little boy looked up at Brian with tears in his eyes as he approached.

Dropping to a knee, Brian rested one of his large hands on the kid's shoulders. "Are you scared, buddy?"

The little kid nodded and wiped the tears from his cheeks.

Brian reached into his jacket and withdrew his deputy badge. Holding it up for the boy to see, he unclasped the pin on the back. "Do you know what this is?"

The little boy nodded with renewed enthusiasm. "It's a police badge!"

Brian shook his head. "Even better. It's a deputy's badge. This means I work directly for the sheriff." Slowly, he pinned the badge to the boy's shirt. "You want to know something about this badge?" Brian paused to allow the boy to admire his new shiny hardware. "It makes you brave," he whispered. "Can you be brave for us now?"

The little boy caressed the badge and nodded.

Brian tussled the kid's hair and stood up.

The boy's mother gave Brian a smile and mouthed the words, "Thank you," placing her hands on his shoulders.

Brian gave the mother a half-smile and turned back to the church. His claps filled the room. "Come on, people! Keep it moving! Single file line and listen to Sheriff Myers!"

It didn't take long for the people in the church to form an acceptable line. Brian walked back toward Johnny while taking a head count. When he reached Johnny, he leaned in and whispered, "forty-nine total, including us."

Johnny nodded. "Alright! We're going to march outside in a single-file line and load up into the back of the truck. It's going to be a tight fit, so if you're the first ones in, scoot all the way to the front. Leave no space between you. If you have a small child, please place them in your lap!" He grabbed the doorknob and prepared to turn it.

Brian grabbed his arm. "What about Martha's body?" he asked, nodding his head toward the young child he had given his badge to.

Johnny rubbed his eyes. "Fuck." Brian noticed he sounded defeated. "I forgot about that." He turned back to the townsfolk. "Parents, there is some scary stuff outside! Please cover your children's eyes!" He watched as the mothers and fathers moved their hands to shield their kids' faces. Looking over the group, a sense of dread settled in. It was mostly middle-aged men, but there were quite a few women and children. There was even an elderly couple struggling to stand at the back of the line. Frank and Amy were bringing up the rear of the column with matching looks of worry.

Johnny sucked in a deep breath, then pushed the door open and stepped outside. The sun was resting in the east, just above the mayor's building. It bathed the surrounding streets in bright light. He swept the street with his pistol, searching for any sign of the beast. When he saw no sign of the creature, he lowered his pistol.

A loud smack reverberated off the church, and he jumped and swung around with his pistol raised. The wooden door of the church had slammed shut behind him. He shook his head and exhaled slowly to settle his nerves. His heart slammed against his chest. He smiled a little, grateful none of the townsfolk saw him get scared of a door.

Yanking the truck's back gate open, he poked his head inside. "Alright! Single file line, let's go." Johnny held the door as people filed past him in a surprisingly organized fashion.

Gasps erupted from the adults as they emerged from the building and saw Martha's massacred body. One of the only teenagers in the town, Bryce King, gagged as he stared at the scene. The boy froze in place when he reached the porch. All the color drained from his face, and Johnny was afraid the kid would pass out. The boy's sudden halt created a bottleneck at the door, causing people to bump into each other. The line quickly began losing cohesion as people tried to push past him.

Johnny cursed to himself. He was about to release the door and rush to the boy's side when Brian emerged from within the church. He pushed past the line of people and grabbed Bryce by the shoulders, then guided the kid down the stairs and to the back of the truck.

Several of the mothers were already sitting down with their children firmly pressed on their laps. The kid slowly climbed into the bed of the truck and wobbled to a position near the cab before collapsing.

Johnny shook his head. He was pretty confident the kid would be blowing chunks before it was all over. His mind drifted back to a few days earlier when he found Earnest's body in the tree. He thought he had thrown up then but couldn't really remember. The whole thing seemed so long ago. Reflecting on the week, it all ran together.

Someone squeezed his arm, bringing him back to the present.

Amy's beautiful eyes gazed up at him. "You doing ok?" she asked.

Johnny forced a grin. "Yeah. I'm good."

"Brian has really stepped up through all of this," she said, watching him help people climb into the back of the truck.

Johnny shifted his gaze to watch as well. Brian lifted a kid out of the snow, passing him to his mother in the truck. "He really has. The guy is too good for this town," he said solemnly.

She nodded and started to walk away when Johnny called out to her.

"Amy."

She turned to look at him.

"I need you to ride in the cab with me."

She gave him a curious glance. "Why?"

"I need you to be my navigator."

With a subtle smile, she nodded and bounded down the steps.

Jeremiah Jackson and Pastor Brown were the last two to emerge from the church.

"Is that everyone?" Johnny asked.

"Yes, sir," Pastor Brown said. "Just did a final walk-through together to make sure."

"Thanks, pastor. Do me a favor and sit in the back of the truck with everyone? They're pretty scared, and I think having you back there will do them some good."

The pastor smiled. "I think you might be right," he said before bounding down the steps and climbing into the bed of the truck.

Johnny released the door, allowing it to slam shut.

"Where do you want me?" Jeremiah asked.

Johnny patted him on the shoulder. "I want you riding on the snowmobile with Brian. He might need some help if that thing comes back."

"Can do," Jeremiah said confidently. He unslung his rifle before making his way to the back of the truck, pausing to quickly kiss his wife. The older man pulled away from her and gave Johnny a thumbs up as he climbed onto the back of the snowmobile.

Johnny tugged on the church door to make sure it was closed all the way. He considered asking Pastor Brown to lock it but realized there was no point. Everyone still in the town was leaving.

Johnny bounded down the steps to the back of the truck. Using the metal foot holds on the back of the truck, he pulled himself up. Seeing half a town piled into one truck reminded Johnny of the cannery. They filled every available space, lapping up, sitting on the ground, or standing uncomfortably. Nearly fifty pairs of eyes stared back at him, each glazed over with fear. Forcing a smile, he gave them a thumbs-up.

"Everyone situated?" Nobody spoke, but several of the adults nodded their heads. "OK." He patted the tailgate. "This thing is loud and not very comfortable, but it'll get us out of here." He released his grip on the edge of the truck and fell back to the ground, slipping a little. The snow squelched under his weight. It was beginning to melt, creating a murky soup. He glanced at the back tires—they were subtly sinking into the mud. Johnny grimaced and prayed to a God he didn't believe in that the truck wouldn't get stuck.

He shook his head as he climbed into the driver's seat and fired up the truck. Once again, the engine came to life with a deafening roar.

Amy squeezed his arm and smiled reassuringly.

He winked at her and threw the truck into gear.

Through his window, he watched Brian start the snow-mobile. His deputy and only friend left alive tossed him a half-salute. Johnny returned the gesture and unclipped the walkie-talkie from his belt. Holding down the "talk" button, he spoke into it.

"Brian, comm check."

Amy giggled, and he gave her a curious glance. "Your marine is showing," she said through a laugh.

He shook his head and pressed the button again. "Brian, are we good?"

The radio crackled and Brian's voice broke through it. "Sorry, boss. Damn thing got stuck to my belt."

Johnny looked through the window and saw Brian securing the radio to his jacket. "Alright. Keep it where you can reach it," he ordered.

Brian gave him a thumbs-up.

Johnny checked the shifter to ensure the truck was in first gear and looked over at Amy. "Here we go," he said solemnly. A feeling of dread settled in his stomach. For some inexplicable reason, he was certain more people would die before it was all over.

Chapter 27

Johnny squeezed the steering wheel, his knuckles turning white under the pressure. The deep snow and uneven terrain jerked the wheel every few feet, threatening to overturn the truck. Every time it did, a chorus of screams and shouts erupted from the people in the back. He considered slowing down and taking it easy on the retired military vehicle but felt exposed in the open. The creature hadn't attacked in the daytime, but he was acutely aware of the fact that just because it hadn't didn't mean it couldn't or wouldn't.

They were driving through a large clearing lined with trees. Snow coated the land in all directions, obscuring the ground. They could do nothing but hope they didn't smash into a downed tree or large boulder. It would be a long walk to Frozen Bay if the truck got stuck out there.

Ahead of them, the clearing narrowed between two rows of trees. It was hard to tell for sure, but it looked plenty big enough to get the truck through. Normally a dirt road ran between Port Luck and Frozen Bay. It was difficult to navigate under normal circumstances, but during heavy snow storms like the one they had the day before, the road became impossible to follow.

Squinting in the midday sun, Johnny picked up the radio from its place on the seat beside him.

"Brian, can you see that narrow area up ahead?" he asked as he glanced in the truck's mirror.

Brian and Jeremiah were trailing the truck, flanking it on the left side. They managed to pace themselves to keep about fifty feet between them and the rear of the truck. The distance would allow them to avoid a collision if the truck stopped abruptly as well as give them a better field of view to observe for threats.

Johnny felt a swelling sense of pride for his deputy. It took over a year of training, but he didn't even have to remind the kid.

Brian navigated his snowmobile to the left, swinging it wide of the truck, allowing him to get a clear view of their path. "Affirmative," Brian said into the radio. The front of the snowmobile pitched upward as they hit a large pile of snow. It slammed down aggressively, sending Jeremiah tumbling into Brian's back. The impact looked painful, but Brian accelerated through it.

"I want you to pull ahead and check it out for us," Johnny ordered.

Johnny could see in the mirror that the snowmobile was gaining on them. Within a few seconds, it pulled along next to the truck. Brian gave Johnny a sarcastic salute, then accelerated past them, and Johnny eased off the gas, allowing the snowmobile to gain even more distance.

Ahead of them, snow blasted outward as Brian and Jeremiah pushed the snowmobile to its absolute limits. "You see anything?" Brian shouted, trying to be heard above the roar of the engine and howl of the wind.

Jeremiah shook his head. "No!" He tightened his grip on Brian's waist, fighting to remain on the snowmobile.

Brian squeezed the accelerator harder, urging the snowmobile to go faster. Despite his glasses, he squinted against the wind. His eyes darted back and forth across the tree line. There was nothing there except dead trees and bushes. His hand drifted to his radio, ready to give the all-clear, when he caught movement out of the corner of his eye. He snapped his head in that direction, but whatever it was had already disappeared into the trees.

Brian eased off the gas as they approached the narrow choke point between the trees. He held the radio close to his mouth. "I thought I saw something." He yelled to be heard above the whine of the motor. He could hear Johnny's voice coming from the radio but couldn't make out the words. His grip loosened on the accelerator. Looking over his shoulder, the truck was catching up with them. "Say again, Johnny."

"I asked what it was?"

Brian glanced back at Jeremiah. "Did you see it?" he asked.

Jeremiah just shook his head.

"I'm not sure. Didn't get a good look at it." He slowed the snowmobile to a stop and looked around. All he could see in every direction was endless rows of trees covered in snow.

The truck eased alongside them and came to a stop. Johnny grabbed the crank on the door and rolled down the window. "We good?" he asked.

Brian shrugged. "I thought I saw something over there!" He pointed toward the trees. "But I don't see anything now."

Johnny looked off in the distance and rubbed his chin. "OK. We'll go first, and you follow," Johnny ordered. Without waiting for a response, he rolled up the window and gassed the truck. Brian paused for a moment to allow the truck to gain some distance before accelerating to match their pace.

"It's not much farther now!" Jeremiah yelled into Brian's ear. Brian opened his mouth to speak, but a flash of movement from his right silenced him.

The beast exploded out of the trees, sending snow flying around it. The creature launched itself at them, and before Brian could react, it was on them.

The beast's enormous claws crashed into Jeremiah, ripping him from the back of the snowmobile. The monster brought him to eye level before tossing him aside like discarded trash, and Jeremiah flew through the air. Brian watched in horror as Jeremiah smacked into a nearby tree. The impact crumpled the old man like an accordion. He slid down the tree, staining its bark red with fresh blood. Brian could see shattered bones protruding from Jeremiah's back, and he knew without a doubt the man was dead.

Brian jerked the handle of the snowmobile. Swerving to the left, he dove off his ride. He landed flat on his stomach and swam through the snow, coming to a knee. He instinctively reached back for his rifle, but his hand found nothing but warm blood running down his back. Brian's eyes stretched wide as a burning sensation radiated from the center of his back. His fingers danced along his spine until they found the wound. The creature's claws had cut deep into his skin, sending a blinding pain ripping through him.

He looked around for his rifle and saw it lying about twenty yards away, sticking upright, muzzle buried in the snow. He slowly stood up and watched as the beast marched toward Jeremiah's ruined body.

The monster reached the older man, standing over his corpse for a moment. Its nose twitched as if it was reveling in the scent of fear and death. Bending low, the beast gripped Jeremiah's face and crushed it. The crack of his companion's skull rang through Brian's ears.

The two stood frozen in time, Brian staring at the beast and the beast savoring its most recent kill.

Johnny's voice broke the stalemate as it came through the radio. "Brian! Brian! Are you guys OK? I'm coming back to get you."

Brian stole a quick glance over his shoulder and saw the truck reversing toward him. When he looked back, he saw the beast staring at the truck too. Ignoring Brian, it took a step toward the truck. Brian grabbed his radio and yelled into it. "No! Just go!"

The monster snapped its head in his direction and smiled.

Brian dropped the radio and sprinted with all his might for the AR15. He reached it before the beast could pounce on him. Without raising the rifle to his shoulder, he fired three rounds toward the monster, then turned away and sprinted into the woods.

Johnny stood on the running board of the idling truck and watched helplessly as his friend disappeared into the trees, the monster on his heels.

Mrs. Jackson's mournful cries rose above the screams of frightened children and the loud motor.

Johnny dropped back into the driver's seat. Throwing the truck into gear, he cranked the wheel all the way to the left, determined to save Brian.

Amy placed a hand on his arm. "You can't," she said softly.

His head snapped in her direction, eyes glaring at her. "I'm not leaving him! We don't leave our people to die."

She shook her head. "Your responsibility is to these peo-ple. There are kids back there!" She was shouting, raising her voice to match his own.

Johnny's face turned a bright shade of red. He raised his fist up and slammed it down on the steering wheel. "Fuck! Fuck! You fucking fuck!" He punched it several more times, screaming in frustration with every hit. After a moment, he threw his head back and inhaled deeply.

Amy rubbed his shoulder. "We have to go. Now."

Reluctantly, Johnny straightened the wheel and pulled away from Brian and Jeremiah.

Chapter 28

A tear rolled down Johnny's face. The seed of regret that planted itself in his chest when he left Brian had grown to epic proportions. Hatred and self-loathing seethed beneath the surface. Hatred for the thing that attacked them. Hatred for his father for bringing him to this godforsaken town. Hatred at himself for leaving a man behind.

Losing Brian brought a flood of suppressed emotions rushing to the surface, and images of pulling dead marines out of a ruined Humvee flashed through his mind. The emotions threatened to spill over into an uncontrollable fit. Trying to breathe through the mounting panic attack, Johnny reminded himself that there would be time to grieve the loss of his friend later. For the time being, he had a truck full of people to save.

His foot kept the pedal firmly against the floorboard, watching as the speedometer crept up. It was pushing fifty, causing the truck to shake violently on the uneven ground.

He squeezed the wheel tighter, willing the truck to move even faster. All care for safety flew out the window when Brian and Jeremiah were attacked. His only goal was to get to Frozen Bay. Once the people were safe, he knew he would return for Brian. It wasn't in him to leave his deputy's body to freeze in the wilderness.

Amy's fingers danced through the hair on the back of his head, the soft tips of her fingers caressing his neck. Her touch threatened to drain all of the fight from his system. The pain in his chest begged him to lean into her, to accept her warmth and kindness. She had nursed him back from the brink after his tours overseas, and he knew she could do it again.

"I'm sorry about Brian," she whispered into his ear.

Another tear rolled down Johnny's face. It made its way through the rough grooves of his skin and disappeared into his unkempt facial hair. He brushed his cheek against his shoulder, wiping away the moisture. "We don't know that he's dead," Johnny said defiantly.

"No, we don't," Amy said with a warm smile. Amy had heard stories about her husband from his time in the Middle East. Johnny rarely ever talked about it, but there were rumors. The marines he served with had affectionately nicknamed him Stonewall after the legendary Civil War soldier. For the first time in their marriage, she found herself wishing for that marine to show himself. She wanted him to pack his emotions away just until they got to safety. But she worried if he did, he would never unpack them again.

"Johnny," she said, leaning forward to see his face. "I ..."

The screams of the people in the back of the truck cut her off. Johnny's eyes flicked to the driver's side mirror. When he saw nothing there, he jerked his head to look out the passenger side window, but it was too late to react.

The monster launched itself at the truck, impacting it between the cab and bed on the passenger side. It rocked hard to the left, forcing the truck onto two wheels.

Amy slid across the bench seat and crashed into Johnny. He gritted his teeth, desperately trying to block out the pain and hold the steering wheel steady. The truck slammed back down onto all four tires, and pain blossomed from the small of his back, sending a jarring impact through his spine.

A helpless feeling hit him as he saw several people fall out of the truck. They landed in the snow, disappearing in its thick white powder before popping up again. Two of them reacted quickly, sprinting across the clearing, heading for the treeline. The third began chasing the truck, waving desperately for them to stop.

"Goddamn it!" Johnny screamed and smacked the steering wheel. He tore his eyes away from the mirror and looked through the passenger window.

He watched the beast retreat from the truck. The enormous creature was nearly as large as the truck itself and managed to keep pace with them. It ran parallel with the truck for a few seconds before angling itself toward the truck.

Amy screamed as the beast slammed into the cab again.

Johnny held on to the wheel with all his might. The truck rocked onto one side again, and that time, Johnny could feel it going over.

He felt the truck tilt past that point of no return and knew it was a matter of seconds before the truck would land on its side, spilling the remaining townspeople into the snow.

The beast fell back a few steps, and his next impact sent the vehicle completely over.

The glass in his door shattered, cutting his face and hands. Hot blood gushed from his wounds, temporarily blinding him. His head smacked against the door frame and darkness swam in his vision. Frigid snow penetrated the cab as the truck slid to a stop on its side. Johnny tried to lift his head then passed out.

"Johnny, please wake up!" Amy cried desperately.

He could feel the stinging sensation of her hands smacking his cheeks. Warm liquid ran down his face. There were people screaming in the distance. He could hear the cries of children begging for their mothers. His head spun from the concussion and the pandemonium raging outside the cab. Sucking in a deep breath, he opened his eyes.

Amy hovered over him. Blood dripped onto his face from a large cut on her head. It ran from just above her right eyebrow to her hairline. "Johnny, do something!" she pleaded with him. The screams of the townspeople grew louder as he clawed his way back to consciousness.

"Fuck," he mumbled.

"Oh, thank god. I thought you were dead," she said through a relieved smile. "We have to do something."

Johnny glanced around the cabin of the truck. He and Amy were pressed firmly against the driver's door. Through the windshield, he could see smoke rising from the motor. "We gotta get out of here." He grunted. As gently as he could, he shimmied out from under her. Glass crunched under his boots as he climbed to his feet. Grabbing the handle of the passenger door, he pushed it open. It took a surprisingly large amount of his strength to push the door hard enough to stay open.

"Stay here," he said to Amy, climbing through the open doorway.

"Wait, I'm coming with you," Amy protested.

"Please. If you're out here, I'll be too worried about you. I need to focus on helping them."

Slowly, Amy nodded and sat back down, careful to avoid the large shards of broken glass. Johnny could hear the crunch of glass under her weight. She pulled her knees to her chest and hugged them.

"I love you," he whispered, then closed the door.

Looking up, he finally took in the carnage around him. The bodies of two children and a woman lay broken and bent in the snow beside the truck. Their bones protruded in unnatural ways. Another body rested a few more feet away. It was massacred beyond recognition. Blood-coated organs had been torn free from the body and spread over a large area. The skull was caved in above the jaw, leaving the bottom teeth exposed.

Johnny cringed at the sight. He tore his eyes away and searched for survivors. A scream to the right drew his attention.

A young boy, maybe six years old, was running toward the trees. Behind him, the monster used its claws to rip his mother to pieces. It flung her severed arm like a used napkin and dropped the woman. She hit the ground with a thud. It fell onto her, digging its teeth into her stomach and shredding her abdomen. The woman's screams filled the air. The beast rose to its full height, throwing its head back and swallowing the mouthful of tissue.

Even from a distance, Johnny could see the shock on her face. He had seen it so many times before. There was an acknowledgment of death in her eyes. With the last of her strength, she used her good arm to drag herself away from the monster.

It watched her squirm away for a moment before stepping forward. The beast placed one of its massive feet on the woman's back, forcing her deeper into the snow. It stooped down and grabbed the top of her head. She let out an agonized wail as it buried its claws into her skull. With one swift motion, it yanked upward, taking her head off. The creature held the decapitated head at eye level. It stared at the woman's dead face, its lips curled back in the mockery of a smile.

The little boy screamed again, snapping Johnny out of his trance-like state. The little boy had a badge on his shirt. Johnny's heart skipped a beat.

It was Brian's badge.

He leaped from the truck, landing hard in the snow. His hand snapped to his pistol. Ripping it from its holster, he raised it to the spot where the monster had been a moment before.

It was already moving, bounding after the boy.

Johnny grunted. "Fuck."

The monster was too far; he couldn't make the shot. He watched helplessly as the creature rapidly closed the distance. Just before it pounced on the kid, he had an idea. He pointed the barrel of his revolver into the air and pulled the trigger. The eardrum-bursting report of the shot filled the air. He lowered the revolver and trained it on the beast.

The creature stopped chasing the boy and snapped its head toward Johnny. It looked back at the boy for a second, then at Johnny as if trying to determine which prey to go after. After a brief hesitation, the monster turned away from the boy and sprinted toward Johnny.

He began to backpedal. "Fuck. Fuck. Fuck!" he cried. Johnny turned and ran around the back of the overturned truck. His eyes darted around, searching for a place to hide, but there was nothing but open fields all around him. He retreated until his back pressed against the undercarriage of the truck and waited.

The heavy patter of footsteps drifted over the air. They grew louder with each passing second like they were moving around the back side of the truck. Johnny held his revolver in both hands, said a silent goodbye to Amy, and turned to the right.

The creature's head stuck out from behind the truck. Its long snout sniffed the air.

Johnny pulled the trigger. The pistol kicked as it went off. He immediately pulled the trigger again. The monster's head snapped back, and stumbled a few steps before finding its footing. Johnny fired one more shot as he walked backward toward the cabin of the truck.

The beast shook its head like a football player shaking off a brutal hit. It took a step forward. Rising on its hind legs, it towered over Johnny.

Johnny squeezed the trigger several more times. Each time the revolver kicked, the creature stumbled but never fell. It seemed to recover from its wounds at incredible speed, not even a speck of blood dripping into the snow.

The revolver clicked empty.

He closed his eyes and accepted his fate.

Chapter 29

Johnny could sense the creature looming over him, its immense figure casting a shadow that seemed to engulf him. Foul breath permeated the air as it approached.

Johnny knew he was about to die. It wasn't the first time he had been close to shedding his mortality, but it was the first time he was *certain* it would happen. While he was waiting for the beast to maul him, an unexpected feeling hit him. He felt angry. He wanted to keep fighting to save his people, to save his wife. There was no way he could defeat the creature, and he knew it. The helplessness seemed unfair. His only hope was that his death would delay the creature long enough to give any survivors a chance to flee into the woods.

From somewhere in the distance, he could hear the faint whine of a snowmobile. He snapped his eyes open.

The beast's elongated snout was only a foot from his face. Thick scars covered the monster's face, each telling the story of countless fights. Coagulated blood matted its fur and dripped from its lips. Yellow, cat-like eyes drilled holes into his psyche.

The sound of the snowmobile grew louder.

Ignoring the growing sound, the beast closed the remaining distance between them. Its clawed hand reached for Johnny's head. Slowly, the elongated fingers wrapped around the top of his skull, its nails caressing him, the pointed daggers slowly piercing his scalp. They dug into his skin, the nails scraping against his skull.

Johnny cried out in agony but stood defiantly. He stared through the blood gushing down his face as the beast smiled. It was savoring the thrill of the kill.

A gun shot rang out. Then another. The sharp crack of a rifle filled the air. The beast recoiled, dropping Johnny, who crumpled to the snow. Before Johnny could track the sound, several more shots rang out.

The monster spun, searching for the source of the shot. It seemed to locate the shooter at the same time as Johnny because it growled at the same time Johnny laid eyes on them. The growl was deep, and despite being animalistic, Johnny could feel the creature's hatred in his bones.

Blood seeped from the lacerations on his head, making it difficult to see the shooter as another shot rang out.

The beast stumbled backward and fell against the truck. Wiping away the blood, Johnny could now see clearly.

Brian knelt behind his snowmobile, rifle pointed in their direction. Dried blood coated his face and hands. The shredded remnants of his jacket blew in the breeze, revealing deep lacerations across his chest.

The monster threw its head back and howled a furious cry. Brian cut the beast's howl short by firing another shot.

Johnny wiped more blood away from his face as he struggled to see the scene playing out in front of him. His eyes darted from the monster to Brian.

Brian pushed over a canister that had been sitting atop the snowmobile. It fell on its side, dumping a yellowish fluid across the snowmobile and ground. Brian allowed the rifle to fall to the snow. He quickly retrieved a knife from his pants and flipped the latch on the back of the machine. The seat came loose, revealing the gas tank. Brian plunged his knife into the side three times, creating a trio of massive openings. Gasoline gushed from the holes and coated the ground around Brian's feet.

Grabbing the rifle, Brian stood up and fired two more shots in quick succession.

The beast roared. Forgetting about Johnny, it dropped to all fours and sprinted at Brian. Two more shots filled the air, but the monster never slowed.

Johnny watched in horror as the beast approached his friend. He scrambled to his feet, slipping in his own blood. He sprinted toward the two of them with no plan in mind, determined to find a way to save Brian.

Just before the beast reached him, Brian pulled something out of his pocket and twisted it. The road flare burst to life with a blinding red flame, and Brian held it high over his head.

Johnny could see the look of determination in his deputy's eyes.

The monster lunged through the air, launching itself at Brian, and Brian dropped the flare.

The next few seconds came to Johnny in fragmented images.

The flare tumbled end over end toward the gasoline-soaked snow around the snowmobile. It met the ground at the same time the beast landed on Brian. Its claws dug deep into his skin, slicing through muscle and bone with ease. The ground around them burst into a violent flame, sending fire radiating outward in a vicious wave. The monster sank its teeth into Brian's neck, snuffing his life out for good just as the flames erupted in a ball of fire, engulfing everything around it.

Johnny's feet seemed to weigh a thousand pounds. He stood cemented to his spot, watching the monster writhe in pain. The flames clung to its back. The wind carried the acrid smell of burning hair through the air.

Through the smoke, Johnny could make out Brian's corpse lying limply on the ground, blood spilling from the tear in his neck. The flames licked at his flesh, charring his dark skin.

The beast howled and whimpered as it rolled around, furiously searching for a reprieve from the pain. After a minute of violent thrashing, the beast managed to roll out of the fire. Flames still coated its back and legs as it sprinted across the open field, away from Johnny and any potential survivors.

Johnny watched it run until the orange glow of the flames disappeared in the trees. The beast disappeared from view, but its cries filled the air, growing fainter with every passing second.

His eyes flicked back to Brian's roasted body. The fire raged all around him.

Falling to his knees, Johnny screamed. He yelled and punched the ground, shouting every curse he ever heard and some he made up on the spot. His tantrum continued until a comforting hand squeezed his shoulder. Glancing back, he saw Amy, tears streaming down her face. Behind her was the little boy Johnny had saved, the one he saw running into the trees.

"We need to go," Amy said firmly.

Johnny looked back at his dead friend. He wiped the snot from his nose and nodded.

The little boy stepped out from behind Amy. Stretching his fist out to Johnny, he slowly unfurled his fingers. There, in his palm, was Brian's badge. "He said it made you brave," the kid whispered through his own sniffles. "I think you need it now."

Tears poured down Johnny's face as he fought to contain his emotions. Reaching out, he grabbed the kid's hand and closed his fist around the badge. "I've got my own," Johnny said with a smile. He pulled his jacket to the side to reveal the badge pinned to his shirt. "We can be brave together." Tussling the kid's hair, Johnny wiped the snot from his nose and stood up. "Was there anyone else alive?" he asked with a trembling voice.

"It's just us," she whispered.

Johnny shook his head. "I thought I could get them out of this. I really thought this was the right move."

Amy caressed his cheek. "You did everything you could."

Johnny pushed past her and looked over the carnage around him.

A series of hushed cries from the rear of the truck caught his attention. The slightest glimmer of hope sparked in his chest. He scrambled over several corpses and looked into the bed of the truck.

Frank was sitting up, holding his obviously broken leg.

The two locked eyes, and an understanding passed between them.

"Brian's really dead, isn't he?" Frank whispered.

Johnny nodded.

Frank bowed his head. "He was going to move to California with me."

"Let's get you to a hospital," Johnny said.

Working together, Frank managed to stand up and drape an arm over Johnny's shoulder. They took a few steps in the direction of Frozen Bay. "Come on," Johnny instructed. The four of them stepped over massacred bodies and puddles of blood to start the long trek through the wilderness to safety.

Chapter 30

Johnny leaned against the back of the rigid office chair. Pain radiated throughout his entire body, and no matter what he did, he wasn't able to get comfortable. He shifted his weight again, then gave up on sitting down.

It took a lot of effort to force himself into a standing position. He rested his hands on the large oak desk in front of him and used it to pull himself up. Thousands of needles stabbed his feet as they accepted his full weight. The cold tile felt good against his one exposed toe. He subconsciously tried to wiggle the toes on his right foot despite knowing that most of them had been removed by the surgeon. Johnny couldn't seem to remember which toes were gone. Losing a part of himself was a strange sensation, made even stranger by the fact that he could still feel them there.

His mind drifted to the little boy they rescued, Skylar. Amy, Skylar, Frank, and he were the only ones who made it out of Port Luck alive, a fact that weighed heavily on his mind.

Johnny flexed his right arm. The movement sent a bolt of pain through his shoulder. The weight of carrying Frank for miles in the snow had irreparably damaged the nerves and tendons in his elbow and shoulder. Doctor Willis recommended surgery once he healed from his many other wounds.

His eyes drifted over the plaques and degrees that adorned the office walls. Despite spending nearly every day with the man since his ordeal, he hadn't known that Dr. Willis went to Johns Hopkins, and he couldn't help but wonder what would have enticed the doctor to move to Anchorage.

A solid knock on the door drew his attention away from the awards and degrees.

"Come in," Johnny said in a raised voice, finding it a bit odd that Dr. Willis would knock before entering his own office.

The handle clicked as it turned, and Dr. Willis entered. Wispy white hair stood in stark contrast to his dark skin. Only the top of his signature red tie was visible. The rest was hidden behind a white, button-up medical coat.

There was a brief moment where the doctor's many years were reflected on his face, but the haggard appearance quickly faded. "Johnny," Dr. Willis said with a huge smile. "How're you feeling today?"

Johnny shrugged. "I hurt all over and my feet still tingle when I walk, but I'm getting through it."

Dr. Willis nodded. "That's good. That's good." He held the door open for someone Johnny couldn't see. "Uh, Johnny," he said.

Johnny couldn't help but notice the hesitation in his voice.

"This is Agent Samson with the …" His voice trailed off.

A large man wearing a black suit entered the room. He took his black Oakleys off and tucked them into his coat.

Looking perplexed, Dr. Willis looked back at the mystery man. "My apologies, Agent Samson. Who do you work for again?"

"The Alaska Department of Wildlife," the agent said.

Johnny smirked at the agent's attempt at looking cool. The man had just removed his sunglasses, so either he wore them through the hospital or put them on before entering the room. Either way, the guy was a douchebag.

"Ah, yes. The Department of Wildlife," the doctor repeated. "He's here to talk to you about your experiences over the past few weeks."

The agent stuck out his hand, and Johnny limped forward and took it. He immediately noticed hard calluses.

Glancing down, he saw several long scars stretching across the back of the agent's hand. Catching Johnny's lingering glance, Agent Samson withdrew his hand and slid it into his pocket.

The doctor moved past the two men to take a seat behind his desk, but the agent held out a hand. "Dr. Willis, would you please give us the room?"

Shock stretched across the old man's face. "I don't think that would be appropriate," he said. The tone in his voice had shifted from friendly to defensive. "After all, this is *my* office, and the sheriff is *my* patient."

Agent Samson snapped his head in the doctor's direction. "And *I* am here on behalf of the state to conduct a *criminal* investigation." He poked the doctor in the chest. "An investigation you are currently impeding."

The doctor's face contorted into a look of total outrage. He opened his mouth to speak, his finger flying to the agent's face.

"It's OK, doc," Johnny interrupted before his doctor could get himself thrown in jail. "I'm a cop. I knew this was coming sooner or later."

Doctor Willis stared at him blankly. "Are you sure, Johnny?"

Johnny nodded. "Yeah, I'm sure."

Doctor Willis nodded. He stared down the agent a moment longer, then walked to the door.

Johnny stopped him before he left the room. "Oh, and doc?"

Doctor Willis turned around. "Yes?"

"Can you make sure the nurses have the cafeteria staff bring the kid a vanilla pudding with his lunch? He hates chocolate, but he's too polite to tell anyone."

The doctor smiled then disappeared through the door, closing it behind him.

Johnny limped back to the chair he had been sitting in before and gently lowered himself into it. A pained groan escaped him while he shifted his weight, trying to alleviate the pressure on his injured body.

The agent watched with an expressionless face, silently waiting for Johnny to get comfortable. He reached into his coat, pulled out a cigarette, and put it between his lips. Moving around the desk, he chewed on the end. His eyes drifted over the awards and pictures Johnny had been admiring when the two had entered.

"You're waiting for me to say something," Johnny said flatly.

"First one to speak loses," Agent Samson said without turning around.

Johnny shifted again, still fighting to escape his pain. "Yeah. I took that interrogation course too. Why don't you tell me what you want?" He leaned back in a more relaxed posture.

Agent Samson withdrew a lighter from his pocket and lit the end of the cigarette. He inhaled deeply, the cherry blossoming a fierce red. Exhaling as he turned around, he blew a cloud of smoke in Johnny's direction. Using his leg to nudge the chair away from the desk, he plopped down. The agent smiled while ashing his cigarette onto a stack of papers on the doctor's desk.

"Your story interests the Department of Wildlife."

Johnny shook his head. "See, I find that strange," he said while pointing a finger at the agent. "Because I've heard of the Alaska Department of Fish and Game, but never the Department of Wildlife, and I've lived here a long time."

The agent smiled. He smashed his cigarette into the stack of papers, snuffing it out. "You're a smart guy, sheriff. So I'm not going to bullshit you." He leaned back in the chair. "The Department of Wildlife is real. It's just ..." He trailed off. "Not well known," the agent said with a sly smile. "Would you like a little history lesson?"

Johnny shook his head. "Not really, but I have a feeling you're going to give it to me anyway."

The agent flashed a menacing smile. "You know about Portlock being abandoned in the forties?" He leaned back in his chair. "The official story is that the new interstate made the town economically irrelevant. But," he shifted his weight and waved his hand, "as you unfortunately discovered, that wasn't the whole truth."

"Something did attack the townspeople back in the forties," Johnny said knowingly. For some reason, he had never believed the conspiracy theories, and the events of the past few days turned his beliefs on their head.

"Exactly." Agent Samson leaned forward and rested his elbows on the desk. "Alaska is a big place, and a lot of it hasn't been explored yet." He held up his hands in a shrug.

"Are there more of those things?" Johnny asked as a twinge of fear tore through him. The thought of the beast getting loose in a major city like Anchorage or Juneau sent a shiver down his spine.

The agent looked at him for a moment before nodding. "There are things like it. But I'm not sure if there are more of that particular thing."

A knot formed in Johnny's stomach. Monsters were real. He was about to ask how many different monsters they knew about, but a sudden realization stopped him—there were enough to necessitate an entire government agency.

"Anyway, we can keep talking about this all day, or I can tell you why I'm really here," the agent said. When Johnny didn't protest, the agent continued. "We're going to need to keep this whole thing our little secret. You think you can do that?"

Anger washed over Johnny. He could feel his face flush. "And why would I do that?" he asked through clenched teeth.

"Because it would be in everyone's best interest," Agent Samson said coldly.

Johnny jumped to his feet and slammed his fists down into the desk, ignoring the lightning bolts of pain that tore through his body. "And just how is it in our best interest?" Spit flew from his mouth as he shouted.

The agent confidently leaned forward, coming face to face with Johnny. The two men locked eyes, and Johnny could see the truth. There was no fear in the agent's eyes. There wasn't even a hint of concern. "Because I can make everyone's life a living hell." There was no empathy in his voice. He held Johnny's gaze, daring the sheriff of a newly depopulated town to challenge him.

Johnny stood up and threw his arms out. "You think I give a fuck what happens to me? I already let everyone down." He collapsed back into his chair. "Kill me, send me to jail. I don't fucking care. People need to know what's out there." He pointed toward the door for added emphasis.

The agent's expression never changed. He leaned back in his chair and interlaced his fingers. "Oh, I'm not talking about you," he said. "I know your deputy shot Darren Henry in the head. It would suck if his memory was tainted with a murder accusation." Samson made a *tsk tsk* sound with his mouth. "My agents in the field reported that he acted bravely in the end. I think his parents would want him remembered like that, wouldn't you?"

"I'll kill ..." Johnny said.

The agent raised a hand and cut him off. "Not to mention all of the people that died on your watch. Some would say you were negligent in your duties. Did you know that criminally negligent homicide carries a sentence of ten years in a state prison? Oh, I'm sure we can find something to pin on that pretty wife, as well."

Johnny sank deeper into his chair. He wasn't sure who the agent really was, but the confidence the man exuded told him it wasn't a bluff.

"What I'm saying is there was a rabid pack of wolves that terrorized the town. Brian can still be a hero, and you can take your pretty wife somewhere else to live out the rest of your lives in peace. Do we have an understanding?"

Johnny hadn't noticed the color of the man's eyes were before that moment. With their eyes locked together, they appeared almost gray.

Hesitantly, Johnny nodded his head.

The agent smiled. "I knew you'd see it my way." He slid the chair back and stood up. "Oh, and this goes without saying, but this meeting never happened." The agent took a few steps toward the door.

"I want it known that Brian sacrificed himself trying to save people. I want him given an award," Johnny whispered.

Samson looked over his shoulder. "I'm sure that can be arranged."

"And we're going to adopt Skylar. Do you think you can push that through?"

Nodding, Samson rested his hand on the door. "You stick to the story, or I ruin your life. Got it?" Without waiting for an answer, he threw open the office door and disappeared into the hospital.

Epilogue

Ten years later

Johnny slumped into the chair inside his hotel room. Across from him was a large framed picture. It depicted a scenic view looking over the town from the nearby mountain. Large red letters proclaimed Port Lucky across the bottom. The knot in his stomach twisted, forcing him to fight down a wave of nausea. Cold air permeated the room despite the heater running at full blast. He tried to remember if it had always been that cold or if the warm weather in California had made him soft.

It was a bartender who told him about the new town built over the bones of his fallen friends. The bartender didn't know who he was. He simply mentioned it while pouring a Jack and Coke.

The words made Johnny's blood run cold. He paid his tab, drunkenly drove to the airport, and got on the first flight to Juneau. After a long journey, he found himself in the makeshift hotel in Port Lucky.

Grunting, he leaned forward and laced his boots, cinching them as tight as he could. It was going to be a long walk through the snow, and he didn't want to lose any more toes.

Johnny fished his wallet out of his back pocket and opened the leather trifold to reveal a photo tucked neatly in the center. Amy's beautiful smile stared back at him as she hugged Skylar before his first day of high school. He fought back the tears forming in the corners of his eyes. Leaning forward, he held it to his lips.

"I'm sorry about everything," he whispered, then returned the wallet to his pocket. Johnny stood up. The new boots felt stiff under his feet. "Fuck. I should have broken them in," he muttered before grabbing the backpack and the fifty-caliber rifle from the bed. He set them carefully by the door.

Reaching into his pocket, he withdrew the letter he wrote to Amy. It was folded neatly in a blank envelope. The letter was his last chance to redeem himself in Amy's eyes. He had taken the opportunity to pour all of his emotions and guilt out. For the first time since the events in Port Luck, he told the truth. The letter wouldn't make up for the rampant alcoholism he developed since surviving what had come to be known as the Port Luck Massacre, but it was a start.

The official story was that a pack of starving wolves attacked the townsfolk out of desperation. Against his better judgment, Johnny had gone along with it all those years. Every time there was a news article about a mysterious disappearance near the mountain or a series of vicious animal attacks, he would drink himself into a stupor. Knowing he could have spoken up earlier and prevented even more deaths haunted him. As much as he wanted to, he was never able to overcome the guilt that ravaged his dreams each night.

While writing the letter, he made sure to accept responsibility for their failed marriage. He detailed all the attempts he made to learn what the creature was, from online searches to meeting with experts in Native American folklore. Nobody seemed to have an answer for him. He explained how, as time passed, his search shifted from trying to understand the monster to an obsession with killing it. When he couldn't find a way to do that, a new plan formed in his mind.

He would trap it.

He quickly scribbled her address onto the envelope and returned it to his pocket. Johnny let out a sigh as he picked up the backpack and slung it over his shoulders. Several buckles hung loosely at his sides. He sucked in a breath and fastened each one, securing it to himself as tightly as he could. It was weighed down with camping supplies, rations, and several sticks of dynamite he stole from a local mine. He released a little chuckle. It was the first time he had ever stolen anything. If only Brian could see him now.

He shook his head and picked up the rifle. Depressing the magazine release, he dropped the magazine and verified it was loaded, then rammed it back into place. His fingers wrapped around the cold steel of the bolt. With a powerful pull, he chambered a round. Draping the rifle over his right shoulder, he exited the motel. People gave him curious glances as he crossed the parking lot, but nobody called out or seemed to call the police as he crossed the street toward the post office. It wasn't uncommon to see someone with a hunting rifle in rural Alaska, so he assumed it wouldn't cause too much of a stir.

Johnny had scouted the post office ahead of time and chose it because of the outdoor drop box, figuring it was probably best not to take the rifle to the post office. He slid the letter into the slot and turned to face the mountain.

It loomed large in the distance. Trees coated the base and died out about halfway up its snow-covered peaks. He sighed and started the long trek to the mountain.

The terrain grew steeper as he approached the base. Even without a heavy snowfall, the landscape was treacherous. Loose gravel and rocky outcroppings made the ascent difficult.

He had spent years compiling a list of alleged animal attacks and disappearances in the area. It was pretty apparent once he mapped them all out that they radiated outward from a center point near the mountain's peak. He had gone so far as to interview the friends and family of the kids who went missing on the mountain right before the attacks started in Port Luck. It wasn't a sure thing, but despite that, he knew exactly where he was going.

Night was falling when he reached a large clearing on the side of the mountain. The snowfall had been light but still was deep enough to make crossing the open stretch of field difficult.

As he took a step forward, something caught his eye. He strained his sight against the dying light.

There was a cave.

He immediately dropped to one knee and looked around. The trees around him blocked out most of the little sunlight that was left, making it difficult to see. His heart thudded in his chest. As gently and quietly as he could, he unslung the rifle and rested it against a tree. His fingers quickly danced across the backpack's clips. It made a thud as it fell from his shoulders and landed on the ground. The sound seemed incredibly loud in the near silence of the wilderness.

His eyes darted about, looking for any sign of the creature. He released a slow breath in an attempt to steady his racing heart.

Every fiber of his being screamed at him to turn around and run back down the mountain. The logical part of his brain told him it wasn't his fight anymore. Then images of Brian's charred body on the otherwise pristine-white snow danced in his mind. He could see Earnest's massacred corpse, the bodies of all the town's people he had sworn to protect.

With a renewed sense of determination, he pulled his backpack to his side and opened it up. The four sticks of dynamite were buried deep inside the bag. He had wrapped them in a towel before piling everything on top, just in case a police officer questioned him while he was in town. He dug through the bag until his fingers wrapped around the cloth. Carefully, he slid them out and put two in each of his pockets.

Johnny grabbed the rifle and stepped into the open field. The sun was completely behind the mountain, and light from the full moon above reflected off the pristine snow.

His heart slammed against his chest with each step. The entrance to the cave loomed massive in front of him.

A foul odor wafted from the mouth of the cave. Johnny's eyes watered as it assaulted his nostrils. He immediately recognized the malodor—it was the stench of death. The image of the beast inching toward his face with its snarling snout flashed in his mind. He stifled a gag and pressed forward, rifle at the ready.

He reached the mouth of the cave with no issue. In the bright light of the moon, he could see small bones scattered around the ground. They appeared brittle like they had been there for years. He noticed a strange looking pyramid of bones in the corner.

Johnny stood at the cave's entrance, half expecting the monster to lurch out of the darkness and pounce on him. He kept the rifle ready, hoping to get off at least one shot. The smaller rounds they had used on the beast ten years prior had almost no effect on it. If he was lucky, the massive fifty-caliber rounds in this rifle would at least injure the creature.

He moved to a corner of the cave. Squatting with his back to the wall and the rifle draped across his lap, he quietly dug one of the sticks of dynamite from his pocket and placed it gently on the ground. He unwrapped the plastic that protected the wick and rolled it out. Moving to the opposite wall, he repeated the process.

He pulled out his lighter and flicked it. The lighter sparked immediately, washing his immediate surroundings in an orange hue.

The plan was to place the dynamite at the mouth of the cave, light it, then sit back and watch the cave collapse, trapping the beast inside. But a sudden realization hit him in that moment.

What if the monster wasn't in the cave?

His heart seized in his chest. He cursed himself for not thinking of that sooner. Johnny racked his brain for an idea of what to do next. On one hand, he could blow it and hope the creature was in there. On the other, he risked letting the beast escape and all of it would be for nothing.

Closing the lid of the lighter, he was about to return it to his pocket when he had another idea. He threw the rifle over his shoulder and removed another stick of dynamite from his pocket. Holding the stick out in front of him in one hand, he raised the lighter to it with the other. He gently walked forward, straining his ears for any sign of the monster.

After a few more steps, the light from the moon completely dissipated, and he was plummeted into near-complete darkness. He sparked the lighter again. It cast its warm glow outward a few feet in every direction. The cave was wide enough to drive a truck through, but it narrowed drastically as he walked. Johnny tiptoed over broken bone fragments to a bend in the tunnel in front of him that veered hard to the right.

There was a loud crunching under his feet. He squeezed his eyes together and cursed himself for being careless. Looking down, he saw the dried bones of a small animal, maybe a rabbit, crushed beneath his boots. He lifted his boot as slowly as he could, but the sound of crunching bones reverberated off the walls and echoed through the cave.

His breath caught in his chest. The noise was subtle, almost indistinguishable from the dying echo he had made, but he was sure he heard it. Something was approaching.

A low grumble radiated from beyond the bend in the cave. He watched as the shadowy outline of a snout peeked out from around the bend. The beast sniffed loudly, taking in his scent.

Without hesitation, Johnny dipped the fuse into the flame. The strand of rope ignited immediately. Sparks flew from the fire as it raced its way down the fuse. He stepped forward like a quarterback launching a Hail Mary and threw the explosive as hard as he could. For a moment, he watched the stick fly end over end through the air as the monster came around the corner. It extended to its full height, and in the dim light, he could see the burn marks that scarred the left side of its body.

Johnny turned and ran toward the exit of the cave. The rifle thumped against his back as he ran. The beast bellowed a furious roar and took off after him. Johnny slid to a stop on one knee near the entrance of the cave. He quickly pulled the rifle off his shoulder and, without aiming, fired two rounds. The ear-shattering report of the rifle was drowned out by the even larger explosion from within the cave. Two enormous holes opened up in the monster's chest and spewed black blood onto the cave floor.

The creature stumbled but never stopped its rabid charge. A fireball blew outward from the back of the cave, partially engulfing the monster. It burst through the flames, swiping its massive claws at Johnny.

Pain blossomed from Johnny's right leg before he had time to register the impact. His leg gave out under his weight, and he crashed to the floor.

Around them, the roof began to collapse. The beast pulled back, preparing to deliver the final blow, when an enormous chunk of rock came loose from the ceiling and landed on its leg. The weight of the boulder pushed the beast onto the ground next to Johnny. It threw its head back and yelped in pain.

It wasn't a complete cave-in, only a few massive rocks had come loose, but it was enough to trap the monster temporarily.

Johnny couldn't feel anything below the knee. Panic swelled in his chest as his eyes drifted to his leg. Blood spurted from a stump just below his knee. Shock took over, forcing his brain to search for his severed leg.

It was in the monster's hand.

Johnny stared at the beast that massacred his friends and ruined his life. Rolling to his side, he wormed the rifle out from beneath him. He raised the rifle to his shoulder and shot the creature again. A third large hole opened in its shoulder. The beast howled in pain but continued trying to free its trapped leg from underneath the rock. His vision swam as the effects of blood loss set in. He pulled the trigger again only for it to answer with a click. Looking down the rifle, he saw a partially ejected shell casing had caused the rifle to jam.

Tossing the rifle aside, Johnny fished the fourth and last stick of dynamite out of his pocket. He rolled onto his stomach. Taking a deep breath, he crawled toward the exit, leaving a trail of gore in his wake.

Behind him, the beast thrashed violently. It rolled from side to side, digging its claws into the ground. Its shoulder muscles flexed as it pulled itself forward. It flipped again, its legging coming closer to freedom.

Johnny glanced back at the beast.

It was on its back, pushing against the boulder with all its might. The boulder shifted slightly.

Johnny's eyes stretched wide. He glanced back toward the exit and then to the beast. He wasn't going to make it. Pain, anger, regret, and hatred swirled inside him, forming an amalgamation of feelings that led him to one conclusion. He couldn't let it escape again. Rolling onto his back, he forced himself into a sitting position. "You're going to die in here, you motherfucker," he spat.

Johnny could see the desperation in the monster's eyes. He wondered if the beast knew what was about to happen to it. Ultimately, he didn't care. He would avenge all those people.

He would avenge Brian.

Opening the lighter, he flicked the sparkwheel. The fuse ignited as soon as the lighter's flame touched it.

The beast glanced back, understanding reflected in its eyes. It turned back to the boulder, pushing hard, frantically trying to free its trapped leg.

Johnny tossed the lighter aside and withdrew Brian's police badge from his pocket. Flipping it over in his hand,

Johnny eyed the badge. The top read Township of Port Luck, and on the bottom was his name.

Deputy Brian Williams.

Looking back at the monster with hatred in his eyes, Johnny tossed the badge at it. The badge bounced off the beast's back and ricocheted off the floor. "This is for Brian, you piece of shit."

Johnny moved closer to the beast, crawling through his own blood. Each pull sapped his quickly waning energy. He fought against the darkness forming in the corners of his vision. He could feel his heartbeat slowing in his chest.

The spark was approaching the end of the fuse.

The monster released one final, desperate cry.

Johnny seized the opportunity. He punched his hand forward, jamming the dynamite into the beast's mouth.

Seemingly acting on instinct, the monster clamped its jaws shut, taking the stick of dynamite and half of Johnny's arm into its stomach.

Johnny jerked backward, falling onto his back. His eyes drifted down to the stump that used to be his right arm.

A moment later, an explosion propelled him against the cave wall. His head smashed into the stone, sending burning pain through his neck.

The monster's abdomen erupted outward, coating the walls and ceiling in gore. Its head lulled to the side, mouth open.

Johnny stared into the beast's lifeless eyes with a smile on his face. With the knowledge that he had avenged his town, he gave in to the encroaching darkness.

About the Author

Timothy King is an adult horror author who enjoys delving into the complexities of human nature. When he is not writing spine-chilling tales, he is spending time with his wife and kids in beautiful Tampa, Florida.

You can find him on Facebook, Tiktok or by emailing him at:

Timothykingauthor@gmail.com

If you enjoyed this book, please consider leaving a review on Amazon or Goodreads!

Other Works

Seven Rabbits

Fuck Them Kids

www.ingramcontent.com/pod-product-compliance
Lightning Source LLC
Chambersburg PA
CBHW030135310726
48970CB00005B/1446